S.A.S.S.Y.

S.A.S.S.Y.

Another suspense novel by Martin Keating

"Martin Keating knows how to write a thriller. THE FINAL JIHAD proved that. S.A.S.S.Y., his new declassified briefing, is another nonstop read."

—PEGGY FIELDING,
award-winning author, editor, and speaker

"S.A.S.S.Y. is weapons-grade writing."

—ED WRIGHT,
former U.S. Navy TOPGUN instructor

S.A.S.S.Y., on the heels of his successful THE FINAL JIHAD (still selling since its initial publication in 1996), is Martin Keating's newest thriller-espionage novel. It begins with the discovery of a top-secret U.S. Army plan to capture and "chip" the elusive Big Foot. Not one in twenty Americans has ever believed in the large ape-man, but the Army possessed decades of growing evidence to the contrary, dating back to General MacArthur and the Korean War. If such a creature could be caught and controlled, it would be the perfect killing machine for Pakistan, Afghanistan, and similar "difficult" locales. However, a much larger conspiracy quickly comes into focus. A troika of enemies from China, North Korea, and the Middle East plans to steal and use the crypto-animals as part of a diabolical agenda to exploit an unrecognized vulnerability of the United States. If this monstrous scheme were to succeed, the results would be catastrophic. Every part of America would be threatened, and the flame of liberty would be extinguished. Two thousand years of Western Civilization would be obliterated, and man would return to the cave.

Hideous animal experiments, the seizure of a major U.S. military base by a foreign power, the threat of hundreds of underground "dirty bombs" across the nation, murder, treason, kidnapping, and betrayal. Something for everyone.

U.S. intelligence operatives aren't calling S.A.S.S.Y. fiction. They did so with Keating's THE FINAL JIHAD, to their shock and chagrin.

For the Army,
it was the tale of an ape-man.

For the Navy,
it was the tail of a dragon.

> "I want S.A.S.S.Y. to be a good read, a temporary escape. But I also want possibilities and a repeatable story. Ultimately, something thought-provoking and inspiring."

Martin Keating
January 21, 2015

To Fr. John H. Gaffney, O.S.A. and Peggy Fielding, two of my most important and beloved writing mentors

And for all things Navy, to my late uncle Captain Barney Martin, U.S.N. (Ret.)

S.A.S.S.Y.

Martin Keating

PROLOGUE

Vancouver, British Columbia

TUESDAY, 1 January – 8:10 P.M. PST

Three armed Navy agents delivered the latest "Alpha Tier" classified report personally to four-star Admiral Donald J. Rourke, Chief of Naval Operations. It had been received by Strategic Communications less than 90 seconds earlier. The message was so sensitive that the couriers had orders to defend it with their lives.

This newest and highest "eyes-only" document confirmed that eleven years earlier, and more than a half-century after the precipitating events in North Korea, three men with military haircuts who appeared to be in their mid-thirties had boarded the <u>Canadian</u>, VIA Rail's flagship transcontinental streamliner between Vancouver and Toronto. It was a frigid winter evening. They carried bulky backpacks and wore padded jackets and baseball caps. Several older passengers smiled at their clean-cut looks.

The three found their double bedroom in the Cameron Manor sleeping car. Precisely at 8:30 P.M. Pacific time, the 18-car all-stainless-steel train, dubbed #2 for its eastwardly run, slowly eased from Vancouver's Pacific Central Station. It would take nearly four days to reach its ultimate destination.

Pulled by powerful, twin General Motors F40PH-2 diesel locomotives, Train 2 accelerated and climbed eastward into the night, toward the Rockies. While other passengers drank and laughed and appreciated the view of the fading city and bright stars from the domes of the four Skyline cars, the three clean-cut men remained inside their quarters.

Kamloops, British Columbia

WEDNESDAY, 2 January - 6:00 A.M. PST

At six o'clock the next morning, as Train 2 pulled into Kamloops, 266 miles from Vancouver, the three men assembled in the cold vestibule between the Cameron Manor and Fraser Manor cars. The moment the train stopped, they pulled open the door and jumped off. Two young men waiting outside grabbed the three men's backpacks and ran for an Army-green Humvee parked in a nearby lot. The five were over a mile away less than two minutes after the <u>Canadian</u> arrived at the station.

Lac du Bois Provincial Park, British Columbia

WEDNESDAY, 2 January - 6:03 A.M. PST

"Twenty-three minutes, via the Halston Bridge," a man announced as he glanced at his watch. He pulled the cuff back to cover his wrist and jogged from side to side for warmth. With their binoculars, the others observed the Kamloops train station from a bluff above the city. No one else spoke.

The man raised his arm and made a circling motion. Three black Mercedes behind him purred into readiness.

The Humvee made its way into the park and skidded to a stop on the gravel next to the automobiles. The men who had boarded the <u>Canadian</u> at Vancouver grabbed their backpacks and dashed for the Mercedes, one to each vehicle. The trio of cars pulled away.

"Two sightings over the past week," the lead driver spoke into a boom microphone. RadioConnexx, a UHF skip-system used for ultra-secure operations, transmitted his voice to the other cars. "One here in the park, the second ten miles north."

"Who saw it? Or them?" asked one of the men in the third car.

"Ours. Credible, both," came the reply. "You have the maps and four days. The plane will be at the Kamloops airport for a 0800 departure Saturday. The refrigerated truck's in our hangar. You'd damned well better need it. Washington's about to have our gonads for all the missed opportunities."

Chicago, Illinois

WEDNESDAY, 2 January – 12:00 noon CST

"Some say the southeastern quarter of Oklahoma should be called the Loire Valley of the United States."

Dr. David Summers cleared his throat and began his opening address to the winter conference of the Mid-Continent section of the Geological Survey of America at the Ritz-Carlton in Chicago.

"Not that most Americans or anyone else cares," he added. "Very little fruit of the grape is produced in this neck of the woods, so to speak. However, it offers more than a hundred thousand acres of prime wine-growing soil. Connoisseurs of the world's finest champagnes could hail from there, yet this area has been known mostly for its output of marijuana and methamphetamine."

Summers' speech was covered by local print and television media and excerpted by Reuters and the Associated Press.

David Summers was one of the most-respected anthropologists in the world, having taught the subject for a quarter of a century. He had published dozens of articles in international peer-reviewed journals as well. He also had a doctorate in geology, plus a professional fascination with cryptozoology.

Summers took seriously the tales that accompanied his on-the-ground research. His address to the GSA was titled, "The Oklahoma Triangle: its beauty, history, and mysteries."

"Heavily forested with deep valleys and rich mountains, one of which is even named that, this part of the world is largely overlooked or unknown. As a part of the Ouachita Mountains that rise gently between the Rockies and the Appalachians, it possesses a beauty rivaled only by a half-dozen international competitors. With such a small population per square mile, where one's neighbor could be a dozen or more miles down a rutted road, it's the perfect place to hide."

A Chicago Tribune reporter frowned at Summers' last remark.

"Oklahoma is unique among the fifty states," Summers went on. "It alone encompasses eleven distinct ecological regions, ranging from arid plains to subtropical forests and mountains. It has more geographical diversity per square mile than any other state, by a wide margin.

"Oklahoma is close to the geological center of the 48 contiguous states. With often bitterly cold winters and hundred-degree summers, this state is not only the geographical bull's-eye of America, it possesses much of the nation's unresolved history, including serious tales which no one talks about, or wants to."

Summers reached beneath the podium and retrieved a glass of water. After a moment, he continued.

"Most people don't know how to pronounce Ouachita. It's 'WASH-e-tah,' a Choctaw word meaning 'big hunt,' which, in its broadest sense, describes the flora and fauna of southeastern Oklahoma, a green jewel of nature. A vast array of wildlife abounds in this remote paradise, among and around clear rivers, lakes, and streams, forests of pine, oak, and hickory, and moss-draped cypress trees. Many parts of it have never been explored. For the intrepid hiker, there are large runestones believed to have been carved and brought here by the Vikings. Something for everyone, a timeless treasure."

Summers rearranged his notes and made a few marks in the margins.

"The Choctaws were relocated to southeastern Oklahoma by the Federal government in the 1830s, and they, unlike the Cherokees who were moved to northeastern Oklahoma, were far from disappointed. Their great chief, Pushmataha, reportedly exulted, 'We have acquired from the U.S. the best remaining territory west of the Mississippi.' Pushmataha led the Choctaws in support of the United States against the British during the War of 1812. When he died, he was given full military honors as a brigadier general in the United States Army and buried in the Congressional Cemetery in Washington, the only Native American chief so honored."

Summers wrapped up with some of the curiosities of the area.

"In addition to its natural beauty and unique history, southeastern Oklahoma is also known for its 'lore of gore,' tales of the unimaginable, and strange and unnatural occurrences. UFO abductions are only halfway up the list. There are periodic bus tours to events in the area, celebrating everything normal and the sometimes-weird, but one occasion stands out: The Big Foot Festival and Conference each October in the tiny town of Honobia, right in the middle of the thick forests.

"Directions to Honobia aren't easy," Summers said with a smile, "since it isn't close to anything. Two days of fraternity and frivolity go on there each year for something most people consider to be as real as Santa Claus or the Easter Bunny. However, thousands of true believers and the simply curious fly, drive, and hitchhike from 40 states and twelve foreign countries to this odd little town for what resembles a pilgrimage to a sacred shrine.

"Parents bring laughing children, primed for a weekend of scary tales. There are covered wagon and pony rides and a possible spotting of the Big Foot impersonator, for which they could receive a prize.

"Jane Goodall, Grover Krantz, and Jeffrey Meldrum are three 'big names' who have argued that Big Foot probably exists. Other serious geology and anthropology academics, myself included, attend the conferences in Honobia to discuss the veracity of the stories about the fabled creature, the true significance of the Oklahoma Triangle."

Summers concluded, "According to legend, Big Foot is a large ape-man. For hundreds of years, he has been spotted in most parts of the world, but he's never been captured. In North America, he is also known as Sasquatch. Elsewhere, he's called Yeti. Some societies believe he came from outer space and could control human behavior and emotions. Others argue he was only what we used to be: simple, kindly, and a friend of the earth. Big Foot, to anyone's knowledge, has never harmed an innocent person.

"Over the past century, Big Foot has been sighted at least 4,000 times in dozens of locales around the globe. It's even been reported that his images exist in the military's grainy photographic and black-and-white movie records of the bitter winters of the Korean War.

"In the past four years, Big Foot has been seen by law enforcement, military, and other professional observers some 900 times, 367 sightings in southeastern Oklahoma alone. Many genuinely believe the creature survives among us and that it's only a matter of time before we encounter him face-to-face. I invite you to go to Honobia and search for yourself. If I'm right, you just might be surprised."

Six hundred miles to the south, a man finished reading the online Summers speech and closed his laptop. He looked through the windshield at the vast forest that lay beyond and slowly shook his head. This place wasn't the same as when he was a boy.

1.

-January-

THE DEAD HAND

"It isn't what it is. It is never what it is.
It is what it can be made to look like."

–From the motion picture, Edge of Darkness

CHAPTER 1

Krebs, Oklahoma

WEDNESDAY, 2 January – 11:40 P.M. CST

In the dim moonlight, two beefy Pittsburg County deputies drove to a dilapidated wooden house a mile east of McAlester, just outside the tiny town of Krebs. It had been less than ten minutes since the "911" caller, a neighbor, said she'd heard screams from next door.

Both men fitted on trooper hats and got out of their patrol car into the cold darkness. The creases in their shirts were sharp, almost knife-like. The driver sucked on a toothpick for a second, then flipped it aside. They drew their weapons and crept toward the dark house. It was a ramshackle, weed-infested place that resembled an abandoned dwelling from the Depression-era 1930s. Known as the "Lambert place," and occupied by an eccentric widow, it was given a wide berth by superstitious locals.

The deputies silently reconnoitered the perimeter in opposite directions, pointing their flashlights along their paths. There was nothing obviously out of the ordinary. They returned to the front of the house and stepped onto the porch. Everything remained quiet. They called out; their condensed breaths hovered in the silence. There was no response.

The first man saw that the front door was ajar. He motioned his partner to push it open. The thin door yielded with a creaky sound. Both deputies peered inside. They announced themselves again. There was no answer from the darkness.

The deputies stepped into an old-fashioned living room and immediately noticed a large pool of brown-streaked liquid next to an antique sofa. The stench was intense.

"What the shit is that?" the first man exclaimed as he pointed his flashlight and walked to the edge of the smelly liquid. The odor was that of decaying flesh. The pool was about eight feet in diameter and nearly an inch thick. It looked like dirty Jell-O.

The second man gasped at the foul smell. Then he noticed what appeared to be chunks of white hair, skin, and bones in the liquid. When he saw an eyeball, he dropped the flashlight and put his hand over his mouth.

"Oh, Jesus Christ!" the first man yelled as he stared at the pool. "That's old Mrs. Lambert. Call it in! Call it in!"

As the second deputy fumbled for his shoulder mike, the men heard a series of moans from the adjacent kitchen. The trembling voice seemed to come from an elderly woman.

"Is he gone yet?"

CHAPTER 2

Maritime Patrol, Northern Gulf of Mexico

THURSDAY, 3 January – 12:05 A.M. CST

A line of unidentified minisubmarines had been spotted 175 nautical miles south of Port Arthur, Texas, heading north at 45 knots. They advanced at depths ranging from 125 to 325 feet. At their current speed, they would reach the American coastline in three hours and 53 minutes.

A United States Navy Boeing P-8A Poseidon on patrol from Naval Air Station Jacksonville, dubbed "Snoopy-3" by its crew, had located the flotilla of seven intruders after intercepting a transmission from an oil tanker to the south. A spotter on the ship had seen one of the minisubs rise out of the water at a 30-degree angle, skip erratically across the surface for 100 yards, then submerge again. The Navy figured the excursion was probably the result of a guidance failure.

The P-8A, a next-generation adaptation of Boeing's 737NG, first flew for the Navy in 2009, one of a reported total order of 117. The actual planned, classified number was 174, with options for an additional 33. "Snoopy-3" was the third such aircraft to join the fleet. It possessed both the latest wide-area acoustic search system and high-altitude anti-submarine-warfare weapons capability. According to a Boeing trade journal advertisement, in addition to keeping sea lanes open, the Poseidon was designed to "combat the increasing threat of hostile submarines." Today's mission was tailor-made. The size of the submersibles didn't count.

The P-8A observed electronically that the first minisub was separated from the last by a mile, along an east-west line. This was hardly the first time minisubs had been intercepted in the Gulf of Mexico. Vessels of choice with drug cartels and terrorists, unsophisticated versions had been observed as early as 1995. However, by 2005, seizures were mostly of advanced GPS-guided models that featured double hulls and diving rudders that allowed these undersea craft to cruise as deeply as 400 feet. They could carry ten tons of contraband, drugs, or explosives. It was a huge and disturbing leap in technology. No less troublesome was the discovery of operating manuals in Arabic with Spanish translations. By 2010, minisubs built in Thailand and other countries in Southeast Asia were abandoned on beaches in southern Texas and Louisiana, mostly in wildlife refuges and preserves. Their cargoes of cocaine were gone, except for dustings inside the holds. Whether or not the minisubs carried personnel other than the driver was unknown but suspected.

The Poseidon commander reported his find and coordinates to NAS Jacksonville.

"Return to base, Snoop," came the reply. "Gravely is moving in to intercept. Good job."

CHAPTER 3

Krebs, Oklahoma

THURSDAY, 3 January – 12:25 A.M. CST

Shortly after midnight, hospital medics, Pittsburg county detectives, and attendants from the Blondett Funeral Home arrived at the Lambert house. It was within a half-hour of the deputies' discovery of the mysterious liquid and the elderly woman.

The deputies had laid Mrs. Lambert on her bed. She seemed unhurt and in no immediate physical danger, other than weighing only about 80 pounds. She told them she had heard rustling sounds outside her house just as The Tonight Show was wrapping up. She was afraid to get up to investigate. Suddenly, the front door had burst open. A white furry ape-like creature had dashed inside and made clicking sounds with his mouth. He was at least seven feet tall, and he had flexed his arms, one after the other.

The old woman had screamed, then she ran toward the kitchen. She heard the television set explode. The house went black. She burrowed into the space under the sink and tried to suppress her breathing. She didn't move. She heard a gurgling noise, then silence until the deputies arrived, about ten minutes later.

As the various personnel moved about the house, and the medics tended to Mrs. Lambert, three large white vans roared up outside. There were no identifying marks or numbers on any of them. A dozen men in HAZMAT suits jumped out and raced inside. They knew exactly what they were doing.

"Everybody back!" the leader commanded. "Federal agents."

The locals stopped and stared. The outsiders quickly went about their business, holding their witnesses at bay. It took less than five minutes to collect every molecule of the liquid from the floor with a large, specialized vacuum cleaner. The visitors were gone within eight minutes. Nothing remained of their presence.

"Who the hell were those guys?" yelled a detective as the vans coursed down the rutted driveway and skidded onto the highway, heading toward McAlester.

"Did anyone get a uniform ID? Anything on the vans? Anything? Logos? License plates?"

No one responded.

"Well, geniuses, we just got screwed," another detective exclaimed. "Shit!" He slapped his forehead. "I can see the News-Capital headline: 'Hicks Slicked!'

"Damn it to hell!" He slammed the wall. "Damn, damn, damn!"

The two deputies drove back to the sheriff's office. The second man recapped for his superior.

"Mrs. Lambert is being taken to McAlester General Hospital, that filthy liquid has been removed to God knows where, and the funeral home vehicle returned home, no body. All back to normal, right?"

The first deputy stewed before unleashing his fury. "What the hell just happened? Who engineered this operation, and why? What was that liquid, and where is it now? This was black ops stuff, through and through, and I'm going to find out what it was all about and who's behind it if it's the last thing I do." He paused. "And I know just where to start."

CHAPTER 4

Maritime Patrol, Northern Gulf of Mexico

THURSDAY, 3 January – 3:40 A.M. CST

The USS Gravely was eight nautical miles northwest of the line of seven minisubs when the P-8A Poseidon made contact. Based on the P-8's updates, the ship immediately computed and headed for a rendezvous point to the east-northeast, some six minutes away.

Today's plan, as practiced in simulation numerous times, called for a dozen small depth-charge missiles (nicknamed "M-80s" because of their size and fishermen tales over the years) to be launched for impacts along and ahead of the line of mini-subs. The resulting concussions would disable most, if not all, of the undersea boats.

Eliminating their power and control systems with explosions beneath would force the craft to the surface where Gravely would be waiting. The intention was not to destroy the subs; it was to disable them so that their cargoes could be inspected and the subs themselves brought aboard for a more thorough examination once the destroyer was back in port. Gravely also carried several arrays of 20-, 25-, and 127-mm guns to stop any errant subs on the surface after the depth-charge barrage.

As Gravely coursed through the cold, choppy surface of the Gulf, the position and speed of each of the minisubs was monitored, and targeting was honed by computers onboard the ship.

Deck members of the crew stared into the darkness ahead. The moon had risen at midnight and was two days from its last quarter. It provided little illumination for this evening's mission.

A loud "whoosh" and a deafening roar followed as six missiles were simultaneously fired from the deck. The immediate area around the ship was lighted as bright as noon by their solid-rocket motors. Then, an array of six more missiles blasted into the night. Twenty seconds later, the 12 missiles were mere white dots high above the bow of the ship.

As crewmembers below watched on high-definition monitors, six geysers erupted, vertical columns of tons of water less than a mile ahead.

"Damn nice cannonballs!" Gravely's captain exclaimed as he stared at one of the screens. They reminded him of films of depth-charge explosions during World War II. Only this time, what he saw were green, night-vision images. Then, there were six more geysers.

"An M-80 is the only way to go fishing," his executive officer replied with a chuckle. "Or so my Pa told me, as we lighted and threw them into the lake back home."

Over the next twenty minutes, six large, coffin-shaped objects bobbed to the surface. Gravely fished out four. Two had apparently sunk quickly, and the seventh never appeared.

Shortly before 4:30 A.M., the initial analysis was in: The four internally controlled minisubs were completely empty.

"Nothing," Gravely radioed Norfolk, its home base.

"Say again?" The voice was incredulous.

"Nothing. Not even any evidence of dustings of cocaine or anything else." The destroyer's communications officer clicked off.

Gravely's captain motioned to his intelligence officer.

"Get me a Q-line!" he ordered as he hurried to his quarters.

He picked up the handset.

"You'd better be sitting down for this." His voice was taut. "They weren't bringing anything in. Not a molecule of contraband."

There was a moment of silence.

The man replied. "Your take?"

The <u>Gravely</u> skipper took a deep breath.

"They were coming in to take something out."

CHAPTER 5

McLean, Virginia

FRIDAY, 4 January – 5:15 A.M. EST

Robert Ledane pulled away from the last streamers of his bad dream and welcomed the insistent electronic buzz of the alarm. He reached and tapped the bar atop the clock. The nightmare was still close, its fingers stroking his clearing consciousness, asking for a commitment for the next evening, but he opened his eyes and let it slip away.

Ledane stretched out under the smooth sheets and sensed his wife's presence. He turned toward her in the darkness.

"I'm awake." Her voice was strained. He knew she had been up during the night, maybe most of it, as she had been since the telephone call two days earlier.

"Sheila…," he started.

"Don't, Rob."

Ledane closed his eyes and exhaled audibly. He knew she'd try to sleep today while he was away. It was her new routine. Nights were hers to watch over him and to listen and wait. He sat up and looked in her direction. He could barely make out her soft form under the covers.

"Listen to me…" he began.

She cut him off. "You'll be late for your ride." Her tone was sterile.

Ledane sighed and threw back the blanket and sheet and swung his legs into the chilly room. He positioned his feet over the hardwood floor. He hoped his slippers were nearby. They were. He stood and made his practiced way to the master bath. He closed the door and flipped the switch.

We'll button up this merger in a few hours, he thought as the fluorescent tubes illuminated in sequence across the tiered ceiling. He rubbed warm water over his face. Then, maybe we can back off from some of this security. Ledane looked in the mirror and rubbed at the stubble on his face. He tried to ignore the weariness in his reflection.

And maybe we can get back to normal around here, too.

Justice had had no problem with the merger, he reminded himself as he pushed the plunger on the shaving cream can. The Department of Defense was solidly in support. Had been from Day One. State had long since given its blessing, and the Securities and Exchange Commission had notified their attorneys the previous day, in a delayed but final decision by certified mail, that the tender offer documents were in order for a January 7 effective date.

Ledane considered the dollop of white foam on his fingertips. Monday, if all went according to plan, his Defense Technology Strategies, Inc., more commonly known in the industry as "DTS" and headquartered in Arlington, VA, America's fourth-largest producer of classified computer software and equipment for military and other government applications, would officially become the world's second largest "SimBioChip" company.

"'SimBioChip?'" he muttered then shook his head.

"Another bullshit buzzword." Ledane leaned closer to the mirror. It was a term coined by Aviation Week & Space Technology magazine a year earlier.

Ledane hated the new moniker.

"Thanks to AvWeek, BioData, and their friends and fellow-travelers, we're stuck with it, good or bad, whatever the hell it means or implies. Or hides."

He smoothed the foam across his face and carefully maneuvered the razor down his upper lip.

In a series of acquisitions over eighteen months, DTS had absorbed twenty biotech and communications firms in seven countries. Its merger with giant U.S. BioData Corporation, based in Palo Alto, would top off a growth effort Fortune magazine called "one of the smoothest finesses ever executed in modern international business annals." The periodical praised the 47-year-old Ledane's stewardship of Defense Technology throughout the intricate assembly process and held him out to be "a leader worthy of watching well into the 21st century."

After the merger, Ledane's company would be the surviving entity and would continue to trade on the New York Stock Exchange under "DTS," its current symbol.

Defense Technology Strategies had earlier produced the concept that would have allowed a new killer satellite, code-named Butler, to locate and neutralize hostile reconnaissance satellites in orbit. Titled after its supposedly efficient human counterpart, "Butler" was designed to sweep the skies clean of hostile eyes in time of war. Congress had terminated the project in 2000, during the initial euphoria in the wake of the so-called "death of Communism" after the Soviet Union imploded.

Even after 9/11, no one gave much credence to the saber rattling of China, Iran, North Korea, or the other countries that threatened to launch their own killer satellites. The world was mostly at peace, or so most politicians wanted Americans to believe.

However, once the United States sank into the military, economic, and political mire of Iraq and Afghanistan, especially after Bin Laden was located and killed, and the rogue terrorism card was increasingly being played in the Middle East by violent new groups, diabolical Islamic radicals, Pakistan, and China, the equation changed, almost overnight. DTS was back in business, big time. "Homeland Security" was the defense contractors' ATM. Money was immediately available to anyone who had a track record and answers. Now, with BioData, DTS had a corner on both.

Ledane twisted his razor in the column of water and forced a smile. There were still no better allies in Washington than an alarmed Pentagon and a furious Congress. Having friends in other high places didn't hurt either.

Ledane eyed his wristwatch, dried his face and hands, and walked to the telephone unit on the wall of the bathroom. Ten seconds later, it rang.

"Mr. Ledane?"

"Speaking."

"Our car will pick you up at exactly six o'clock."

Ledane recognized the voice of Curtis Dowling, a decorated former Army Ranger and now DTS's chief of security. The message was incorrect, as planned.

Ledane showered and wondered again who was behind the recent personal threats. The warning really didn't seem to warrant the elaborate precautions his company was taking. It had been the recorded voice of a man with an Oriental accent who'd simply said that certain peoples, plural, weren't happy with his and DTS's plans "for the world" and that they were going to do something about it, "at whatever cost."

Maybe we're overacting, Ledane thought, but, then again, he wasn't sure. He always trusted his gut, and an alarm was sounding.

Over the 48 hours since the cryptic call, DTS's security learned that similar calls had been made to CEOs of other major defense contractors across America. What had seemingly started as a run-of-the-mill corporate espionage curiosity by the silly "Occupy" movements was, in Ledane's mind, developing into a genuine international threat to the United States.

Two days earlier, an Arlington County policeman on patrol in his squad car had chased two men from DTS's front gate. It was just before dawn, and he lost them before he could pursue on foot. Fresh snippings of copper wire were found dusted into the street a few feet from where the suspects had been spotted.

The police surmised that the wire might have been part of a detonation mechanism for a bomb, but, at the time, it was just a guess.

Ledane knew that Curtis Dowling had nearly lost an eye in a terrorist attack against British Petroleum where Curt had worked earlier. Many environmental groups were incensed about BP's Gulf oil spill in 2010 and its commitment to continue drilling. They had threatened retaliation. The nail-filled package that blew up in Dowling's office was just as heinous a device as any of those employed by any other terrorist group. Ledane had learned that Dowling sensed in the current threats the presence of another, larger cadre of committed zealots, this time with far more dependable weapons and opportunities. That fear reminded Ledane to call Fritz Halsey when he got to the office.

Ledane heard the muted gong as the centerpiece clock on the downstairs mantle struck six. He verified the time against his watch in the light from the bathroom and removed his suit coat from its polished wooden hanger in his closet. As he turned off the light, he heard the car approaching. He put on his coat.

"Bye, sweetheart," he whispered into the bedroom. He listened for either a reply or the sounds of his wife's slow breathing. He hoped she'd fallen asleep at last. He heard nothing. Ledane descended the stairs in the darkness and pulled on his overcoat. He waited by the front door.

His driveway from Crest Lane curved inside a ten-foot-high stone wall that formed part of the inner perimeter of the home. DTS security had assured itself that no observer on the ground outside the property could see anyone entering or leaving the front portico, as long as such movement was conducted within the enclosure of the stone wall. Ledane heard the car stop and a door open, then shut. It opened and shut again. Precisely thirty seconds after it arrived, the car departed. He knew the decoy would be given an eleven-minute head start before his actual transportation arrived.

Exactly on time, the second car drove under the alcove. Ledane knew that would be Dowling himself. The car stopped, and Ledane ticked off the seconds. Five...ten... The security chief would be checking to see if anyone had followed him into the driveway. If that had happened, he would drive away immediately. Twenty-five seconds...thirty.

Ledane dashed from the house. The car's front door was pushed open. He got in and pulled it shut. The car accelerated down the driveway without headlights.

"Curt, this is really professional." Ledane looked over at the driver. It was still too dark to recognize his face.

"Indeed, Mr. Ledane," an unfamiliar voice spoke from the back seat. "It certainly will be."

The old man shuffled then stopped and rocked back and forth unsteadily on his ragged cloth-topped sandals. After a pause to catch his breath in the frigid atmosphere, he leaned forward and resumed his wobbly walk. At the closed service gate of DTS's complex of buildings, he aimed for the stability of one of the large garbage bins outside. Once there, he balanced himself against the heavy metal box and cinctured up his rope belt. The first light of the winter sun filtered through the neighborhood trees and illuminated his unshaven face.

The man grinned at the arrival of a new day. Already thirsty, he patted his coat pockets for the half-pint he'd tucked away earlier. Nothing hard resisted his open palm.

"Damn! It <u>had</u> to be there, unless someone <u>stole</u> it." He patted again, and a look of panic took charge of his watery eyes. "Who would steal food from an old man?" he mumbled. He started to cry and looked around for a place to sit.

"Who could be that low?" he blubbered as he moved jerkily toward an inviting roll of carpeting. The old man moved closer and squinted. No, it wasn't a roll of carpeting. Maybe a blanket? He shuffled forward until his toes touched a solid object. He saw the top of a man's head at one end. "Why, it's a fellow gentleman of the street," he observed, "all rolled up and still sleeping.

"Not too many of us left around Arlington anymore," he muttered to himself, with the pride of a member of an endangered species. He pressed his foot against the back of the inert figure. There was no response. He did it a second time. The old man knelt next to his prostrate comrade and tugged at his shoulder.

"You OK, buddy?"

With a slight rocking motion, he tried to roll the other man onto his back. Suddenly, the torso wheeled toward him. Its severed head remained facing the wall. The old man began to retch.

CHAPTER 6

Outside Kabul, Afghanistan

FRIDAY, 11 January - 8:00 A.M. AFT

Army Lieutenant General Robert Thompson, tall, thin, and nervous, paced the small room and chewed on his unlit cigar. He wasn't P.C. He just didn't have a match. Given the chance, he'd cram a flaming cigar down the throat of a tree-hugger. Right now, Thompson was about to meet with the top three Army generals for southern Asia, an area of festering evil falling under the military jurisdiction of USSASIACOM. The new command was carved out of USCENTCOM and USPACOM after the strong resurgence of al-Qaeda, the Taliban, the so-called Islamic State of Iraq and Syria, and related terrorist groups. It encompassed the land of the worst threats to the civilized world. Thompson was the boss of his three "guests."

The last time they met here, he'd pounded the table so hard the heavy Army Team Alpha ceramic mugs bounced.

"Where the <u>hell</u> are those goddamned 'special' troops we've been promised? Years of blowing smoke," he'd yelled. They'd debated various courses of action. The session was another waste of time. This time would be different.

"The bullshit's over," he whispered to himself. "Time to take this directly to Barnes at the Pentagon." He glanced at his watch when he heard the knock on the door.

The four were meeting in one of the two remaining hidden and fortified U.S. military installations on the ground in Afghanistan. Ever since the President had withdrawn most of America's soldiers in an attempt to demonstrate "good will" to the Islamic world, a move Thompson privately denounced as "suicidal," he'd called this base "Outpost Gehenna." The only major presence of the United States in the country today was airborne: Air Force and Navy. However, several special ops boot-centric units continued their deadly clandestine work in remote mountainous areas. Thank God for those guys, Thompson whispered to himself. He said a quick prayer then motioned the men inside. As they took their chairs, Thompson looked around the table.

"Before anyone asks," he announced, "this is the last time we're going to meet to wonder about the so-called 'Super Soldiers.'" He pulled the cigar from his mouth. "We've gotten nowhere following channels and kissing rings and asses over the past year or so. I'm going to put my stars on the line and go straight to the Chief of Staff. It's time, and I want this to be our joint effort." Thompson took his seat at the head of the table.

"After all the withdrawal crap and humiliation, it's still been my job to be Mary Poppins and present a Milk of Magnesia turd to Washington each morning. No more."

Army Brigadier General Albert DeLong interrupted his boss's soliloquy with a raised arm. "I think we're all in agreement, General. God knows we've talked this to death. Bob, may I recap the situation, at least from our perspective?"

Thompson hesitated. DeLong was an optimist. He nodded. "Go ahead." He'd save the big news for last.

DeLong clasped his hands together and looked over his half-moon spectacles.

"Over the past three years alone, so we're told, Congress has appropriated $14 billion for this particular 'off-the-books' mission, and we still have shit to show for it. Nothing tangible, no 'creatures,' just more promises. Constantly slipping specs and delayed delivery dates. One step forward and two back."

DeLong could see that the other brigadiers were nodding their agreement.

"Not even close to what we expected and need, especially now. We've argued for these 'Super Soldiers,' but the Pentagon has pushed back, or not replied at all. At least for a year, that I know of. What the hell does that mean?

"They've said they had," DeLong continued, "or were pursuing, a special cadre of soldiers that could get into some of the caves to root out the bad guys. Specialized, better than scorpions in this terrain and far more deadly. One of these so-called 'Supers' could do the work of a dozen regulars, or so they told me. Despite my inquiries at the command level, I haven't heard anything since a year ago December. How are we supposed to incorporate these new assets into our planning if we can't even be sure they exist, will exist, and will ever be delivered?"

Moving his arm in a wide arc, DeLong added, "The Devil's out there, with thousands of his acolytes. For God's sake, Bob, if we're not going to have the usual contingent of the proverbial 'boots on the ground,' we <u>have</u> to have effective substitutes. The three of us on our side of the table, so to speak, are in full support. We <u>have</u> to break the goddamn logjam and get these "Supers." He sat back and exhaled.

Thompson stood up slowly and walked to the window. He rapped his West Point ring against the three-inch tempered glass but stayed silent. After a few more seconds, he turned, walked back to the table, and remained standing behind his chair.

DeLong resumed, looking at his cohorts but glancing at Thompson out of the corner of his eye.

"You're absolutely right, it's time. It's past time, damn it. We <u>have</u> to take effective, final action. I've had serious doubts about this whole pursuit as it's evolved over the years, but there've always been sufficient facts dribbled from credible sources to sustain believability. Supposedly, after years of failure and billions of dollars, they're now very close to creating a non-human 'Super Soldier.' They say it's actually some sort of 'Bionic Man,' almost a lab creation, but a man-like hominid, trained or controlled and honed. If such a soldier really exists, and works, its deployment could solve most of our immediate problems. Last I was told, possibly ready within six months." He shook his head.

"But six months from when, Al?" General James Robertson demanded.

DeLong took a deep breath. "I was told this last August, five months ago, so that'd be next month."

"Christ, Al, we all know the Pentagon," Robertson continued, "still an edifice of bullshit." He looked at DeLong. "What else?" The three generals had agreed before the meeting that DeLong would speak for all. The others would provide any "color" he missed.

"Enough, gentlemen!" Thompson waved his hand and stopped the banter. "It's <u>this</u> month, and it's any day." He pushed the dead cigar back into his mouth and sat down. The three surprised men stared at him.

"I was going to wait for one more confirmation before telling you this, but it's intel direct from Aberdeen. I'm convinced it's reliable. Been hard to get anything from those über-black spooks, but the first shipments of the 'creatures' are expected at Aberdeen momentarily. From where, I don't know, but my sources are certain about the timing. That's all I have right now. I will contact you the second I get more."

Thompson nodded curtly, stood up, and gave a modified salute, signaling the end to the meeting.

"We're done?" General DeLong asked, a look of surprise on his face.

"We're done," Thompson said, "but I could call you back at any time. Literally, and not necessarily here. You'll probably want to bring a toothbrush and a sleeping bag." He walked toward the door.

"Safe transit to your bases, gentlemen."

CHAPTER 7

Aberdeen Proving Ground, Maryland

FRIDAY, 11 January – 10:10 A.M. EST

One of the Navy's best, most recent intelligence summaries of certain activities at Aberdeen Proving Ground was provided by an operative who had worked at the facility for a year as a special liaison with the Army. He had the ability to fit in easily and work his post without arousing suspicion among the "ground-pounders," even when he strayed into territory that was supposedly off-limits. His writing style was concise, but, more important to his superiors at ONI, his content was usually a dead-on peeling away the curtains of secrecy.

Aberdeen was the U.S. Army's oldest active proving ground, having been established in 1917. It covered 113 square miles northeast of Baltimore in the hilly Maryland countryside just east of the I-95 corridor from Washington to Philadelphia.

According to the public visitor's guide, APG "remains one of the Army's most active and diversified installations in the world." Many military and other travelers have called this a simple and seemingly direct explanation, but it was woefully incomplete as a statement of purpose. Words can hide as well as reveal. APG today is indeed active, but calling it "diversified" was a gross understatement.

Among the national scientific labs for specialized services, on a scale of one to a hundred (with Los Alamos, Sandia, Oak Ridge, Livermore, and Berkeley being in the middle), APG was near the top. There was no simpler comparison than Sprite to Dom Perignon. APG merited its high ranking.

It wasn't always this way.

Before 9/11, Aberdeen carried out its prosaic duties of producing various new ideas and testing garden-variety ordnance for the Army. After the terrorist attacks of 2001, a tight veil of secrecy was pulled over the complex. Everyone who worked there was subjected to intense personal scrutiny. No one was immune. Without explanation, some older, reliable operatives were summarily dismissed, and many were reassigned. It was no longer business as usual. APG became a creative center in the war on terrorism. Millisecond digital video cameras even monitored employees' personal activities in the closed stalls of the restrooms, three cameras per toilet enclosure. All bets were off. This was a new world.

In 2004, according to intelligence gathered by the Navy, APG was ordered to build a complete–and secret–enterprise to clone and control living creatures, especially mammals. This was an "off the books," black ops mission. APG was also tasked to hire the "best of the best" in the scientific community. Cost was no object. Initial staffing and acquisition of the necessary equipment took two years and required $3.2 billion, not a penny of which was ever questioned by Congress. The total was spread throughout and buried in the Defense Department budget over several fiscal years.

APG was now recognized by a few at the top of the DoD as the finest such facility in the world, although, for security purposes, it couldn't brag about its lofty status. The first experiments began in January of 2005.

Starting with non-mammals, APG proceeded through various types and levels of primates. Cloning was the first order of business, but the secondary purpose was controlling the behavior of the cloned mammals. APG tried and failed more than

300 times. Not at control but at cloning. They partially cloned 95 animals. The genetics were wrong, and the oldest lived for seven months. For control, every type of brain scan was used, but establishing an effective and reproducible means of directing the primates' actions proved to be disappointing. One APG physician even proposed the replacement of part of a primate's frontal brain with that of a human donor, someone who already possessed the psychotic qualities they were seeking, such as a killer on death row, but since such neuroscience was in its primitive stage, the idea was abandoned, at least for the present. Others suggested the implantation of a chip controllable from a distance. Since this, too, involved research in its infancy, it also was ruled out for the time being.

The APG team finally concluded that while the combination of "chipping" and control was theoretically possible, the two were probably decades away.

That all changed when MCAAP at McAlester became involved.

CHAPTER 8

Suitland, Maryland

FRIDAY, 11 January - 10:55 A.M. EST

The Office of Naval Intelligence was based just east of Washington, D.C., in a part of the Suitland Federal Center in Prince George's County, Maryland. ONI was at the heart of the National Maritime Intelligence Center, a Navy complex that also included the Naval Information Warfare Activity and the Coast Guard Intelligence Coordination Center.

The Suitland Federal Center resembled a country club but with Wal-Mart-like stores sprinkled around. There were architecturally proud as well as prosaic buildings, vast parking lots, manicured lawns, tulip beds, lakes, and groves of trees. The only thing missing from the landscaped campus was a golf course. More than 7,000 people worked there.

When his iPhone buzzed across his polished desk, Navy Captain Frederick William Halsey had just been informed of Rob Ledane's murder earlier that morning. He was shocked. The past never seemed to loosen its grip.

The phone buzzed again.

Halsey glanced at the screen and picked up. It was Anoli, but not her usual number or ringtone. He frowned.

"Catman," he answered, with his Navy handle.

"Fritz, the carpenters are coming to check the porch again," his wife announced matter-of-factly.

"Really?"

"They think it might be termites."

Halsey shifted upright in his chair.

"Termites? They said that?"

"Yes, but they have to do some underground sampling. Probably tomorrow afternoon."

"OK, sweetie, thanks. Keep me advised. I gotta go. Late for a meeting." He disconnected and sat back.

"Termites" was their rarely-to-be-used code word to mean serious trouble. This was the first time they'd needed it. They would reconnect by an untraceable landline exactly four hours later.

CHAPTER 9

Tulsa, Oklahoma

FRIDAY, 11 January - 9:50 P.M. CST

Sam's Place Comedy Club had been an on-again, off-again oasis of laughter in south Tulsa ever since the late, great screamin' Sam Kinison's days in town. Sacrilegious Sam, a local boy and a preacher's son, transitioned from Scripture to scatology here and had gone on to fame, fortune, and an early death at age 38.

Samuel Burl Kinison was buried with other members of his family in Tulsa's Memorial Park Cemetery. His body lies in the Garden of the Apostles section, and his grave marker reads, "In another time and place he would have been called prophet."

A prophet wannabe took the mike in the mostly empty club and began his quest. The audience had been encouraged to welcome "the funniest guy this side of Loco, Oklahoma." A skinny man stood under red, white, and blue lights and nodded at the two or three who applauded.

"I talked with an old acquaintance the other day. He called to give me his cell number." The comedian paused. "It was 232, at the Tulsa County Jail."

Only the soldier at a stage-side table laughed. Two men in a back booth stared at the soldier.

CHAPTER 10

Tahlequah, Oklahoma

SATURDAY, 12 January – 3:30 P.M. CST

Carl Windemere and his thirteen-year-old grandson Zack had driven 70 miles from Fort Smith, Arkansas. It was their annual "Bud Day." They'd made it a regular twosome event for years. This time, they ventured into Indian Territory.

Once, they'd spent the day at Arkansas' Crater of Diamonds State Park, 135 miles south of Fort Smith, where Zack had uncovered a small sparkling chip that was appraised on the spot for $700. He got to keep it, since that was the park's policy. Another year, the two of them paraglided for hours above Mena, Arkansas. Zack was ecstatic and thought his "Poppy" was the coolest. Carl, to this day, grimaces and grabs his chest with a mock grin at the mention of their aerial adventures.

This time, the Windemere "boys" had come to visit the vast Cherokee Heritage Center. Hamburgers and fries followed, then they carefully stepped up a rocky bluff overlooking the east side of the cold and turbulent Illinois River at Tahlequah to watch for and photograph eagles soaring above the scenic waters under a chilly, breathtaking cobalt-blue sky. They knew that hundreds of magnificent bald eagles had made their way here from Canada to roost and breed. It was a spotter's paradise.

As they looked for a place to sit, their awkward footing chipped pebbles and chunks of dirt sixty feet straight down into the river.

Carl and Zack immediately noticed occasional rafters already in the water, even this early in the year. Regardless of the cold temperature, rafts, canoes, kayaks, and large tubes studded the fast-flowing river every few hours.

Carl and Zack spotted two men in a raft. Another man, in a black wetsuit and in the water, trailed by thirty yards, holding onto a line, grinning and waving. Suddenly, two other men, also wearing black wet suits and masks, rose up in the river behind the raft. They grabbed the man holding the line, snapped his neck with an audible crack, and forced his body underwater for a minute or so. Then, they, too, sank beneath the surface, taking the limp figure with them.

The Windemeres watched in horror.

The two men in the raft didn't seem to notice anything. They never looked back. Carl and his grandson didn't see the lone swimmer or the men in wet suits again. They stared downstream in silence.

Carl grabbed Zack by his jacket.

"Shit, boy, let's get out of here."

CHAPTER 11

Islamabad, Pakistan

SUNDAY, 13 January - 10:00 A.M. PKT

Two men sipped Kenyan tea outside the hilltop Cafe Lazeez. They were seated well away from the other customers. A few people scurried by on the street below.

"Inshallah, we shall succeed," the first man spoke into his raised cup, in Arabic. "The 'creatures' of the American infidels continue to be both our divine lures and diversions. Allahu Akbar."

The second man stared across the boulevard.

"Allah is also patient."

The first man put down his tea and stroked the face of his watch with his index finger.

"There will indeed be many radiant sunrises across their land. Many, and soon."

The second man stirred milk into his cup. He smiled.

"Jazaka Allahu khairan."

CHAPTER 12

Fort Smith, Arkansas

MONDAY, 14 January – 3:30 P.M. CST

"Poppy!"

Zack Windemere ran through the entrance, pulled off his overcoat, and tossed it across a chair in the front hallway. He hadn't needed to ring the bell. Carl Windemere's front door was always unlocked for his grandson who had a habit of dropping by on his way home after school.

"Poppy!" he shouted again.

His grandfather still didn't respond.

"Hey, Poppy! You home? Earth calling Poppy!"

"Zack, get back here!" It was Carl's voice.

"Look at this!"

Zack dashed for his grandfather's study. Carl held up the Fort Smith <u>Times Herald</u>.

"It's a story about that guy we saw drowned at Tahlequah on Saturday."

Zack plopped down on the sofa next to his grandfather and took the paper.

The Associated Press headline read, "Body of Soldier Recovered from Illinois River."

"Omigosh!" Zack exclaimed.

The story reported that a member of the military in artillery training at the McAlester Army Ammunition Plant was the fourth person to drown in the river in a month. The man was "floating with two men he had recently met in training." The soldier "had been swimming behind the raft the group had rented," and his body was found Sunday at about 9:40 A.M.

Zack turned to his grandfather. "But that's not what happened."

"Plus, soldiers don't train for artillery at McAlester," Carl replied. "They train for that at Fort Sill, hundreds of miles away."

"So, what do we do?"

"We call the sheriff in Tahlequah. Something's really squirrely about all of this."

CHAPTER 13

Suitland, Maryland

MONDAY, 14 January - 4:30 P.M. EST

Halsey had camped in his ONI office most of the weekend, collecting facts and preparing. For exactly what, he wasn't sure. It seemed as if a dozen jigsaw puzzles had been mixed together and dumped on his desk. All of them presented dark and confusing pictures. And someone's clock was ticking.

As arranged, he'd called Anoli four hours after their Friday visit. One of their discrete-session protocols was for any especially important call to be made between two public, landline telephones, one in Oklahoma and the other in Virginia or Maryland. Both never-repeated phones had to be more than 25 miles from the location of their most-recent cell call, and that's what they did on Friday. However, after what Anoli told him about the "termites," Halsey concluded they'd have to upgrade their personal communications security. Future such long-distance contact may have to be other than telephonic.

Anoli was not only his wife of five years, for the previous 30 months she, as an Army medical doctor, had headed the medical staff at the McAlester Army Ammunition Plant in Oklahoma. She'd started Friday's second call with, "Something really creepy is going on here." She hurried through a recitation of worries far broader than anything she had told him over the past year.

"More trucks. Specialized, custom-made, the length of 18-wheelers. Like tanker trucks. All stainless steel and unmarked. Never together, but sometimes only hours apart. No escorts, armed or otherwise. I've seen a couple of dozen over the past week, all arriving after dark. None has left, that I know of." She thought for a moment.

"And remember the tractor-trailer trucks I told you about right after I took the post here? Maybe as many as twenty? They all went into that off-limits building that still doesn't have a name. I never saw them leave, but, then, I went home every night, to be with my new husband. More could have arrived."

Halsey looked around the isolated phone booth and closed his eyes. More puzzle pieces, but to what?

"The runway preparations continue east-west on the north side," Anoli went on. "As far as I can tell they're putting in steel matting, probably to allow heavier aircraft to land. Narrow, maybe 40 yards wide and more than a mile long. I can't get out there. Restricted access. No docs allowed."

"Anything from the air?" Halsey asked. He knew his wife had recently taken a round-trip flight from Tulsa to Dallas-Love. Supposedly, she'd told her friends, for shopping at Neiman's. She had sat at the window on the right side of the Southwest 737. The flight route extended south from Tulsa then doglegged to the southwest over McAlester. MCAAP lay below and just to the right. At 22,000 feet, it was the perfect aerial platform for a look at the massive complex, especially for someone who was looking for something.

"No. Their work is being well concealed from the air. They may be using grass mats for ground cover. Looks like some mowing, nothing more."

"Well, I've been fishing in shallow waters up here so far," Halsey replied. "A lot of box canyons, but many of the arrows are pointing your way, sweetie. We're having a big powwow Wednesday. I'm trying to collect everything relevant, but I think I'll need to come home soon. I'll be in touch."

CHAPTER 14

The Pentagon

TUESDAY, 15 January - 4:10 A.M. EST

Six specialists were on duty at the Army's Afghanistan desk when General Thompson's call came through.

One of the men pressed his mute button. "It's General Thompson, sir. We need General King for this." His supervisor nodded.

The man pulled the boom microphone closer to his mouth. "General Thompson, please hold. We're getting General King." He punched in King's private, secure number.

"What is it?" Lieutenant General Terrance King answered sleepily from his home in Alexandria. He peered at his bedside clock.

"Jesus Christ, it's four in the morning!"

"Sorry to disturb you, sir, but General Robert Thompson is calling from Afghanistan. He says it's critical."

King rubbed his face, closed his eyes, and pulled himself up in bed.

"All right, put him through."

"Terry? Bob Thompson. I've told them it's all real, the 'Supers.' Now I need more answers, explanations."

King sat in silence. His expression changed.

"God damn, Bob!" he exploded. "I <u>told</u> you this whole thing is still classified, it's in flux, and we don't have crap to report yet. I <u>told</u> you…"

Thompson broke in. "I told them the shipments were already on their way to Aberdeen."

"Oh, fuck! Why the <u>hell</u> did you do that?"

Before Thompson could respond, King hit him with, "General, I'll cut off your balls if you got into sources."

Thompson didn't take the bait.

"Stuff the threats. I didn't tell them sources because I don't <u>have</u> sources. I'm being torn apart over this endless 'Super Soldier' bullshit. They've reamed me out, and they surprised the hell out of me about how much they already know. The party's over, Terry. I need the latest."

King gritted his teeth.

"Well?" Thompson asked.

"I'll get back with you, damn it!" King snapped. "I need to make a couple of calls, but I <u>will</u> get back with you." Both men slammed down their phones.

King stared at the ceiling.

"Shit!"

He was not looking forward to this next call. King put on his reading glasses and coded in the secure number. Twelve hours earlier, General Benning at MCAAP had attempted to give him an abbreviated but positive version of the January 2 fiasco in Krebs, Oklahoma, but only after King had been shown an article in the <u>National</u> <u>Enquirer</u>. King's patience ran out halfway through Benning's spins and excuses, and he'd slammed down the handset.

This was a nightmare, and not the kind that clears up after forty winks. King had Benning's butt on the grill. Now was the time to add more fuel.

After several clicks, Benning was on the line from his home in McAlester. He immediately tried to engender some empathy.

"Oh, my. Do you know what time it is, General?"

King ignored the feint and resumed where they'd left off.

"And just how the <u>hell</u> can you be sure no one's connected this to us?" he yelled into the telephone. "Are you <u>God</u>, you son-of-a-bitch?"

The secure line carried King's diatribe directly and clearly to Benning's ear, 1,068 miles to the southwest. King went on.

"You let one of the bastards escape, then you sent three unmarked vans speeding through a sleepy town and out to some old biddy's house to clean up, right in front of a dozen professional witnesses. No, no chance anyone thought they were Army. Probably just a bunch of drunken local teenagers in U-Hauls and Halloween costumes. A simple winter's night on the town. Nothing suspicious at all."

"Oh, chill out!" Benning snapped, then he resumed his affected syrupy voice. "I have it under control. No pictures, no media of any kind. Nothing left behind except imaginations. It's over, buried, period. Forget about it."

"It's in the police report, for Chrissake! How do we explain that?"

"We don't. We don't have to. There are a lot of UFO sightings in those police reports, too. The conspiracy theorists will work overtime in our favor, discrediting the report in the eyes of the general public. No, we just sit tight."

"You'd damn well better be right, Einstein, and it'd better not happen again or I'll personally nail your ass to the cross before our mutual court-martial."

"Oh, don't worry. The others are under triple guard until we get the chip control right."

"And just when might that be?"

"A week, ten days. Delivery in two weeks."

"Well, you'd better pray to God that none of the others ever sees the light of day down there, or I'll personally barbeque your nuts on my backyard grill."

Benning clicked off.

• • •

As Benning reached to turn off the light, he told himself not to worry about General King's "threats." After all, they were both in this together. Besides, Benning lived the adage that failure was not an option. He smirked as he contemplated the acronym for Special Army Suicide-Soldier Yeti: S.A.S.S.Y. One for the history books.

CHAPTER 15

Suitland, Maryland

WEDNESDAY, 16 January – 9:30 A.M. EST

Navy Captain Pierre Archambeau stood before Vice Admiral Raymond Collins, director of the Office of Naval Intelligence, and three other senior-grade officers seated at a large table in the secure Annapolis Room of the director's complex. Dimmed lighting shrouded all but Archambeau at the lectern beneath two spotlights. He brushed the microphone with his fingertips.

"Gentlemen, let's begin." He picked up a folder.

"Each of you has been provided with a copy of this, but it's read-only and not to leave the room. It's the chronology and some supporting documentation of what we know about the Army enigma, so far. From Aberdeen to McAlester. They've kept the lid on so tightly we probably have only ten percent of what we usually get from our sources. Quite frankly, from an intelligence perspective, it's scary what we don't have."

For the next 30 minutes, Archambeau highlighted the seven sections of the classified material. He began with the early messages from a Navy informant at Aberdeen that had begun more than five years earlier, and he concluded with a focused bio of "Catman" Halsey. "You must really know the man before you can understand his mission."

He began reading.

"Frederick William Halsey, Navy handle 'Catman,' was born in McAlester, Oklahoma, on May 13, 1963. He was the second child of William and Margaret Halsey. Bill Halsey was a descendant of Navy Fleet Admiral William F. ('Bull') Halsey, the ultimate 'sea dog' and hero of the Second World War who was called 'the face of the Navy.'

"The William Halseys were transferred to McAlester, Oklahoma, in 1960 when Bill, a Lieutenant Commander, was assigned to the McAlester Naval Ammunition Depot, now the McAlester Army Ammunition Plant, or 'Mack-App' as MCAAP is called. Captain Halsey was born three years later.

The ONI director motioned.

"Pete, let's skip the rest of his bio for now. We're familiar with Captain Halsey. He knows the place. Officially, he lives there, has a house, his wife is the MCAAP doc, he's perfect. I'm tasking him to get to the bottom of what the hell the Army is up to. Bring him in."

Archambeau pressed a button on the lectern.

While they waited, two men silently read highlights of the rest of Halsey's bio.

His sister Rebecca was five years older. She died in a school bus accident in Arkansas in December of 1972 when Catman was nine. He rarely talks about it.

Catman's father, William Farragut Halsey, was born in Worcester, Massachusetts, on November 26, 1923. He graduated from the College of the Holy Cross in 1945 as World War II was coming to a close. Bill had enlisted in the NROTC when he entered Holy Cross three months before Pearl Harbor, and he was commissioned an Ensign on May 28, 1945.

Bill Halsey met Margaret Rummerfield at a Holy Cross senior graduation dance in Worcester. They were married five months later while Bill was posted to the Pentagon.

"Good morning, gentlemen." Catman Halsey walked in briskly. He took a chair across from the director. He exuded readiness. Admiral Collins knew he'd selected the right man.

CHAPTER 16

The Pentagon

The Office of the Secretary of Defense and thousands of employees of the Department of Defense have been the major tenants of the Pentagon since 1943. The SecDef oversees, coordinates, and supervises all military elements of the U.S. government relating to the national security of the United States. This includes the three components of the Departments of the Army, Navy, and the Air Force, plus many DoD branches, such as of the Missile Defense Agency, the Defense Advanced Research Projects Agency, the Pentagon Force Protection Agency, the Defense Intelligence Agency, the National Geospatial-Intelligence Agency, and the National Security Agency. The department also operates several joint service schools, including the National War College.

The secret Army briefing was set for 1000 hours in one of the new, high-tech/soundproof MacArthur conference rooms in the Secretary of Defense's E-Ring office complex. The adjacent rooms, of varying sizes, were built after the 9/11 attack. According to the still-secret specifications, their reinforced composite walls were seven-feet thick at the outer perimeter of the building, secure against a repeat of a Boeing 757-200 penetration at an even faster velocity than the American Airlines jet attained in 2001. Today, a 757 aircraft at 490 knots would completely disintegrate within two meters (6.56 feet), substantially less distance that the depth of one ring of the Pentagon, not the three rings as occurred on September 11.

Lieutenant General Terrance King, head of the Army's Special Operations Command, was first to arrive. He feared that this wasn't going to be his finest hour. King was escorted to his seat by his aide. Next came General Richard Barnes, the Army's chief of staff, followed by General Ralph McNerney, vice chief. As McNerney was sitting down, the Army Secretary was announced from the door.

"Gentlemen, Secretary Creekmore." Everyone rose.

Lawrence Creekmore walked in briskly and took his place at the head of the table. He carried a black alligator notecase that he opened. He pulled a Montblanc pen from inside his jacket. He smiled curtly.

"Please be seated, gentlemen. General King?"

King pushed his chair from the table and walked to a large screen at the end of the room facing Secretary Creekmore. He carried a penlight laser pointer. He stepped behind the podium.

"As you know, for years we have actively sought an alternative force to our regular personnel. We narrowed our selection to one particular non-human animal that can be programmed for specific missions."

He tapped a recessed button on the top of the podium. The lighting in the room dimmed, and a grainy black-and-white photograph appeared on the screen. King turned toward the picture.

"Our search had its genesis in December of 1950. This is a Signal Corps photograph taken by an H-13 helicopter, the bubble-top Bell 47 made famous by the television show M.A.S.H. The location is North Korea, ten kilometers south of the Yalu River and the Chinese border. The date is 17 December 1950, a Sunday."

King pointed his laser at the upper-right corner of the photograph.

"Two groups. Note the grove of snow-covered trees, then the men in white camouflage 200 meters to the west. Army Intelligence later determined that the men were Chinese soldiers, members of the People's Liberation Army. Some 15,000 at that location alone. At the time, the United States did not know they were there."

He directed the laser a few inches to the right.

"Now, please look carefully. This second group was not comprised of Chinese soldiers. Chinese, five or so feet tall. This group, seven- and eight-feet tall. Chinese, white padded uniforms, hats, and weapons. Second group, no uniforms, hats, or weapons. Just white body hair, or fur. Twice the bulk and build of the Chinese. These figures, some 75 at that location alone, remained apart from the soldiers in all of our later photos. Whatever their intentions, they shadowed the Chinese, but they did not intermingle or interfere."

King faced his audience.

"Before the Korean armistice in 1954, the U.S. Signal Corps returned with hundreds of photographs and movies of what some, including military analysts, would later term 'science fiction.' The Department of Defense, the Air Force, and the Marines brought back 776 pictures and movies of the same odd scenes. The Navy never made public what it found. A small amount of this is redacted and available to researchers with clearances at the National Archives. Of course, while all of these records predated the Freedom of Information Act, much of what's still classified might be forthcoming because of three pending Supreme Court decisions. In time. Not that it will make much difference now."

General King tucked the laser pointer into his pocket.

"However, what we're discussing at this meeting will never see the light of day. Until it's all cleared and released, of course. It's at the highest-priority level."

"General," Army Chief of Staff Barnes interrupted. "Before you go any further, who else outside this room knows what you're about to disclose? Not including those directly involved with the work, of course."

"No one," King lied.

"Army or other military? Navy, Air Force?"

"No one, sir, inside the military."

"No one inside, General? But what about <u>outside</u> the military?"

"No one, sir."

General King quickly moved on. "They exist. We have these creatures, and we can control them. The first stage has been successful. The debate is over." He didn't acknowledge the surprised expressions.

"We never considered what the Chinese called 'yeti' to be anything more than legend. That is, until we captured them in Canada in 2002. Two dozen in the first two years alone." King didn't stop. "When we discussed the possibilities of employing alternate forces for asymmetrical warfare, we were anticipating the ultimate challenges of Afghanistan and Pakistan. And elsewhere."

He tapped at the control panel. A picture of the topography of Afghanistan appeared on the screen. King pointed out various areas with his mini-laser.

"Three places in particular. Here, here, and here. They're hell for our men, especially now. We can't get in there without suffering major casualties. We lose one for one, or worse, and it hasn't changed. Pakistan is even worse. We need something different, something that can get in, kill, and be gone, with minimal hazard to our troops. Now that we've pulled out of most of those areas, we have to have something to allow us to maintain some semblance of order. Otherwise, chaos. We believe we have the answer."

The only sound in the room was the whisper of heated air through the floor-level registers.

"The yeti is the one creature on earth that has been sought for hundreds of years but never caught, until we succeeded. It's been the stuff of legends and cable channels. It roams at will, it has never intentionally killed a human being, to our knowledge, but it's extremely effective when it chooses to be. It has taken out animals three times its size. It eats voraciously, then disappears. It'd be the perfect soldier."

Secretary Creekmore held up both hands. "General King, This is astounding. You're talking about a 'Big Foot'?"

"Yes, sir. Yeti, Sasquatch, Big Foot. Several varieties but same root species. If we do it right, this will be a high-tech and very effective killer. We have the control procedures well underway, almost finished. If we're correct, for pennies on the dollar, we can wipe out the Islamic radicals and similar enemy combatants in the most difficult battlefield locations in the world, at minimal loss of life. Human life, that is."

"Where are we doing this work?" Creekmore asked.

"Aberdeen in Maryland and MCAAP in Oklahoma. More than $9 billion has already been spent by way of special Army research accounts. We're nearing the end. I have every confidence we'll be successful."

"General, if so, when might you have operative 'creatures' for Army use?"

King rubbed his forehead. "We've been fast-tracking the work at the two sites for the past year. They'll be on their way to Aberdeen momentarily. Four hundred or so of what we're calling 'Super Soldiers.' Deployment possible within three weeks."

Creekmore sat back into his chair and sighed. Then, he smiled.

The translator in Islamabad finished the briefing in Arabic. The robed men nodded their satisfaction.

CHAPTER 17

Northern Virginia

THURSDAY, 17 January – 11:00 A.M. EST

The meeting with the Secretary of the Army lasted precisely 60 minutes. Creekmore stood. His aide motioned toward the door.

"I prebooked a 15-minute open session with the President, figuring I'd have something special to report. This is going to take at least an hour, if I'm lucky. He'll be very pleased with your progress and outlook." Creekmore pointed at General King. "<u>And</u> he'll want regular updates."

The SecArmy briefly shook hands all around.

"These 'Super Soldiers' could be the breakthrough we need as a nation and what he needs to preserve his administration. You'd damned well better pull it off. Everything's on the line. I'll let you know what he has to say." He singled out General King with a concluding nod.

Six members of the Secretary's security detail escorted him to his limousine. They would lead and follow in heavily armed black SUVs. The route to the White House would take them up Washington Boulevard to the Arlington Memorial Bridge then east into the District of Columbia.

The security detail checked and received its clearance to proceed, and the motorcade was underway. Immediately north of the overpass for the George Washington Memorial Parkway was an exit from Washington Boulevard, followed by an entrance.

As the motorcade passed the exit, the chief of the security team called out a potential threat. To his right, he saw a 9,000-gallon gasoline tanker truck speeding toward the entrance.

"Watch that goddamn truck!" he shouted into his headset. The truck began to weave violently as it merged with the Washington Boulevard traffic. The SecArmy's motorcade was some 75 yards behind the tanker truck.

"Condition Red!" the security man screamed. "That's not just a truck out of control. It's a hit on us!"

Too late.

The truck rolled over twice, smashing into cars, and blocking all lanes. Its gasoline cargo exploded. Massive flames boiled into the atmosphere. Seven vehicles drove into the 1,000-degree inferno, including Secretary Creekmore's motorcade. No one survived.

CHAPTER 18

Tulsa, Oklahoma

MONDAY, 21 January - 2:35 P.M. CST

When the seatbelt sign switched off, Halsey rose and retrieved his bulky carry-on from the overhead bin. He'd arrived on his favorite civilian airliner, the Boeing 757. It was American 1690, a through flight from Reagan National to Tulsa via Dallas-Fort Worth. He'd chosen 2-F, a first-class right side window seat, even though he knew the northbound route from DFW would be too far west for him to see his ultimate destinations, McAlester and MCAAP.

Halsey looked more business-casual than military. Polo shirt, slacks, and leather jacket. He knew he was probably already under the gaze of certain people, so it really didn't matter what he wore. However, he'd like to be seen as simply a guy returning home to see his wife. Nothing going on here, folks, just move on, so to speak.

Halsey smiled and put on his aviator glasses and was first off the plane. No checked bags, just direct to his rental van. Someone at the Pentagon had cut an especially good rate for ONI. His black Lincoln Navigator was ready.

The Tulsa airport was 79.1 nautical miles north of the McAlester airport. Halsey knew the precise figure because he had personally flown the route several times alone. That'd be 91 statute miles or about an hour-and-a-half on the road, if he didn't stop on the way. Today, however, he planned one stop.

Halsey maneuvered the SUV through the rental car parking lot and headed south. As he drove, his thoughts came in slivers. First, various pleasant memories of McAlester. He'd been born and raised there, but so much had happened since. He again blocked the thoughts of his sister's tragic death.

He rarely thought about the details of his childhood, but he smiled at the recollection of catching a bobcat when he was a nine-year-old Cub Scout. Well, accidently <u>trapping</u> a baby bobcat on an outing was more accurate. "But Momma Cat could have been right there and done me in good," he mused in Oklahoma-speak. The event earned him the moniker "Cat-man" which had stayed with him all these years. Most people, especially his Navy buddies, thought he'd done something heroic involving a carrier catapult as a naval aviator. Halsey had often tried to correct their misunderstanding, but he gave up after his Dad told him that "Catman" was the perfect Navy handle, a combination of cunning and bravado, especially for a carrier jet jockey. "Roger, that," he'd finally said.

Halsey did a quick mental review of the city and MCAAP.

McAlester, in the heart of southeast Oklahoma's ten-county "Kiamichi Country," was both pretty and prosaic. Like most small towns in "fly-over" America, it held little interest for busy commuters who traveled between the coasts at 39,000 feet. However, similar to many other "invisible communities" across the country, McAlester possessed power and prestige far beyond its size and appearance.

Much of the real business and strength of the United States originated from and was sustained by these uncelebrated pockets of creativity. McAlester was one of them, not only for its political heritage, which was significant, but mostly for its locus of military and other critical national security operations, especially after September 11, 2001.

Around town, more than 300 military businesses were disguised behind innocent-sounding names in undistinguished strip centers. Halsey recognized one of them: Pittsburg Pizza. Owned and operated by the Army since the day it opened in 1999. This was "Pittsburg" country, not Pittsburgh, as in Pennsylvania. High-tech avionics here, but great pizza as well. He smiled.

Eleven miles to the southwest of the city was the McAlester Army Ammunition Plant, the largest and, in Halsey's mind today, the most important defense facility in America, spread over and beneath an area larger than the District of Columbia.

MCAAP was the largest of the Army's four "Tier 1" installations in the United States. It was tasked to deliver ordnance quickly during the first 30 days of any military conflict, giving time for the smaller, mothballed facilities around the country to gear up into the supply chain.

At its inception in 1942, MCAAP was a Navy operation. Its accelerated growth began after it was transferred to the Army in 1977. Other depot operations around the country, Savanna, Red River Munitions Center, California's Sierra, Texas' Lone Star AAP, and the Kansas AAP, were relocated to McAlester. Its workforce expanded by thousands, and its mission broadened to encompass most anything explosive and creative the military wanted. Over the years, without fanfare, technical research and development had eased its way to the top. Although few were aware of it, in the post-2001 world, MCAAP was now the scientific equal of Aberdeen.

Army Brigadier General Thomas Allen Benning commanded the 22,000 military and civilian personnel at the McAlester Army Ammunition Plant, a supposedly descriptive but almost deceptive name for a facility possibly as important to national security of the United States as Los Alamos had been during World War II, if Navy intel were right about the Benning intercepts. MCAAP's work might be greater than the challenges which America had faced in developing the atomic bomb, or so said the general himself in what he thought were secure conversations.

Halsey reflected on what the Navy had learned about the Army's ultimate black-ops experiments supposedly being conducted at MCAAP, now just 55 miles ahead. If the reports were true, and it was his job to find out, never before had mankind attempted anything as ambitious as the chip control of sub-human primates. Never before had scientists reached so far beyond the commonly perceived limitations of their grasp.

He stared at the highway and felt the bumps of the expansion joints in the concrete.

The Army's byzantine multi-layer shroud of secrecy across the entire Defense spectrum for this effort was puzzling. Better yet, Halsey concluded, worrisome.

Halsey knew Tom Benning from the old days. Halsey's father was the last Naval commander of the McAlester base. Today, there should still be a semblance of cooperation and compatibility between Army and Navy, two men, for family reasons, if no other. Halsey was betting on their long acquaintance to work, at least to open a door or two without raising suspicions.

Halsey thought again about the horrific murder of Rob Ledane, his friend since they were boys in McAlester. Rob's dad had been the Army's first commander of MCAAP. He wondered what its current C.O. had done to the place. He'd find out, he hoped, because of the Halsey-Ledane connection.

"So little time," he whispered to himself as he slowed and steered the SUV off U.S. 75 into a McDonald's parking lot at Okmulgee, Oklahoma. He was 49 miles from McAlester. He eased into a parking space near the restaurant's entrance and braked to a stop.

Out of the corner of his eye, Halsey saw the Jeep with the Texas plates.

He pushed open the door of the Navigator with the feigned fatigue of a weary traveler. It was for show, for anyone who might be watching. Just in case. He stepped onto the asphalt pavement, shut and locked the SUV, and sauntered into the restaurant.

Fewer than a third of the tables were occupied. Those, mostly by families. Three singles stood in line at the one open order lane. Halsey took his place behind a large woman and squinted at the menu on the overhead panel. He decided on something other than a burger.

"I'll have the premium bacon ranch salad with grilled chicken, large fries. That's all."

"Something to drink?"

"Nah."

Halsey's salad and bagged fries slid down a greasy metal ramp from the back. The employee who'd taken his order and money plopped them on his tray. He found a table at a window near the side door and sat down.

Chipping, not cloning, he mused. For difficulty with higher primates, an order of the lesser magnitude of a thousand. Easier to "chip," that is, but still unattainable by known science. He remembered the report of the "creature" that broke into the old widow's home. Unless.

Halsey shook his head. There were a myriad of parts to this puzzle. He felt as if he'd been inserted into another time and place. He knew that clock was ticking, but where was he along the continuum? He finished his lunch and checked his watch. He'd been inside McDonald's for 25 minutes.

Halsey stood and collected his trash. He dropped it into a bin as he walked down a short corridor to the men's room. He hadn't seen anyone enter or leave the washroom in the past ten minutes. He pushed open the door. One stall, one urinal, one sink. All well used and mostly clean but not necessarily sanitary. A standard McDonald's facility. He entered the empty stall and quickly removed the spare roll of toilet paper from its metal dispenser. He retrieved a 3x5 slip of paper from inside the cardboard roller and tucked it into his jacket pocket. He stepped to the urinal. As he washed and air-dried his fingers afterwards, he glanced around the small room. No windows or storage closets. He walked back into the restaurant and turned for the side door. As he exited the building, he saw that the Jeep had departed.

He got into the SUV and thumbed open the piece of paper. Two words, in pencil: "Inola, OK." He smiled and started the engine.

Fifty minutes after leaving Okmulgee, Halsey turned off the Indian Nations Turnpike. It was a short drive into McAlester. Officially, the four-lane road from the turnpike was the Carl Albert Parkway, named for Oklahoma's favorite son and the 54th Speaker of the U.S. House of Representatives. Back then, most everyone called Albert the Little Giant from Little Dixie. McAlester was still known as the "Capital of Little Dixie," from its former prominence in old-time Democratic politics.

Halsey was 13 when he met the Speaker at a Navy dinner on the "base" a few months before his Dad handed over the reins to the Army and Albert stepped down as Speaker. The younger Halsey sat next to Albert at the head table. It was a portentous evening. He'd never forget what Albert had told him, "Follow in your father's footsteps, son, and you'll make history." Halsey had come full circle, from McAlester to McAlester. If Carl Albert's advice were correct, this was the place where it all might happen. Or be happening.

Anoli was also born in McAlester, but she came with a different pedigree. Her parents were Choctaws whose ancestors dated back before the "Great Removal" led by their proud chief, Pushmataha. In 1831, the Choctaws were the first to be forced to move from their southeastern U.S. homes to Indian Territory along what would later be called The Trail of Tears, a harsh journey of at least 1,200 miles. The Cherokees were last to migrate.

Halsey remembered the note: "Inola, OK." It was the name of a real Oklahoma town, but it was also an anagram for "Anoli," and it meant he could come home without any subterfuge. It was their "all clear"; no need to meet in secret, at least not this time. They'd be careful with their conversations, but at least they'd have some semblance of normalcy. He shook his head. No guarantees for the future, of course.

Halsey headed for the home surrounded by stately trees that he and Anoli had received from his parents. His body was already anticipating Anoli's embrace. He smiled.

CHAPTER 19

Suitland, Maryland

TUESDAY, 22 January – 12:00 noon EST

The New Hampshire woman's call to the Office of Naval Intelligence was recorded, as were all incoming ONI telephone connections to specific recipients. Outside direct cell calls to ONI numbers were also automatically retained.

More than 90-percent of the calls went directly to their intended recipients, via the appropriate four-digit suffix numbers. The remaining were answered by one of ONI's five telephone receptionists who were trained to separate the wheat from the chaff. What they got was usually chaff.

A receptionist clicked on. She pulled her boom microphone closer to her mouth. "ONI, may I help you?"

"Uh, yes," a woman's voice replied hesitantly. "I hope so."

"Ma'am, please go ahead."

"I am Mrs. Elizabeth Byars, the widow of former Navy Captain Barnard Byars. My late husband was a Korean War veteran and a pilot who went on to a wonderful 20-year career with American Airlines. But the real reason I'm calling is what our family just found at our New Hampshire farm. You know it's so pretty up here, year 'round."

"Yes, ma'am. What did you find?"

"Well, my husband died ten years ago. He was just 70 and in really good health, so, you know, it was a shock to all of us.

Cerebral hemorrhage. The doctor said he didn't suffer, thank heavens."

"Yes, ma'am."

"We never knew about his notes until my children decided I should sell the farm and move closer to them. One of my sons found a safe buried at the north end of the barn as we were clearing out everything before the sale. He was raking, cleaning up the stalls and all, when he scratched across the top of something metallic. As I said, Barney died ten years ago, so the safe just sat there, buried for all that time. We never even suspected."

"Yes, ma'am. So why are you calling us?"

"Oh, I know I must be boring you. My children always say I talk on and on, but my grandchildren say I don't talk enough, at least not to them."

"Ma'am, you called to say you found a safe in a barn?"

"Oh, no," the woman responded. "We found my husband's notes, mostly hand-written or personally typed, about his flight from the USS Valley Forge in late 1950, on General MacArthur's personal orders. Barney took pictures of those creatures in North Korea. He even made drawings. He was a pretty good artist. General MacArthur had my husband's film seized when he got back to the carrier, so Barney never saw the developed film, but we have his notes. At least a thousand detailed pages, plus other materials. I don't know what it all means, so I decided to call you. He was Navy, you know."

The receptionist squinted.

"Creatures?"

"Yes. My husband drew these tall white apes that he saw, at least that's what they look like to me. He has arrows and lines from the top of their heads down to their feet, then he wrote heights next to the lines. My family thinks Grampa was a little creative with some of his stories, but I know he was always so particular and detailed about real events. He didn't exaggerate. A very good pilot for a combined 40 years with the Navy and the airline. When General MacArthur met with my husband in early 1950, he immediately called him by his Navy handle,

'Vampire.' McArthur loved that name. He said my husband was the best stealth 'picture taker' under his command. Anyway, Barney said the shortest creature in his notes was, I think, seven feet tall. The tallest..."

"Ma'am," the receptionist held up her finger and interrupted. "Please hold."

She punched "1000" into her console, the suffix for the ONI director's office.

"Roberta, it's Monica, you <u>have</u> to hear this caller.

"Channels, Monica."

"You don't understand!" Her voice was agitated. "This caller is talking about General MacArthur's 1950 orders to a Navy pilot, this woman's late husband, telling him to take pictures of 'large ape-like creatures' in North Korea. Does that ring any bells? Large ape-like creatures?"

"Give me a second." Roberta's tone was all business. The line went silent for almost a minute.

She clicked back on.

"Monica," she spoke without emotion, "please direct the caller to Captain William Edwards. Extension 1411."

"But shouldn't this be passed to the director immediately? Or higher? It's what..."

"Captain Edwards. 1411," the woman repeated.

Monica disconnected and stared at the wall for a second. She quickly typed a message, then forwarded it. She clicked back on.

"Ma'am, I'm transferring you to Captain Bill Edwards. Please hold." She tapped in "1411."

"Captain Edwards."

"Sir," a woman's hesitant voice replied. "I'm supposed to talk with you about my late husband, Barney?"

Edwards saw Monica's note on the screen about a woman calling from New Hampshire.

"Yes, Mrs. Byars. The receptionist said your husband, Navy Captain Barney Byars, left some notes."

"Yes, sir. We just found them. And they recorded what Barney did on one of his missions during the Korean War in 1950."

"Yes, ma'am."

"He was under orders from General MacArthur himself to take pictures in North Korea. Three sets. It was the third one that got Barney's attention. He thought he was going to be able to review the film when he got back to his carrier, the <u>Valley Forge</u>, but his CAG said the canisters had been removed and sent directly to MacArthur in Seoul, on the general's personal orders. As far as Barney knew, that had never happened before, so he thought the general was looking for something specific."

"And your husband believed he photographed what the general was looking for?"

"Oh, yes. Creatures of some sort, tall, covered with white fur. Just standing there. Most of them were seven or more feet tall. Maybe 75 or 100 of them. He was sure he got good pictures. He was the best at that."

Edwards tried to type as fast as the woman spoke.

"And you...have these notes?"

"Yes, sir, about a thousand pages. Maybe more. Including the drawings, it's probably closer to 1,200. Since Barney was a Navy pilot, and he was never able to find out what happened to his photos, I thought the Navy should know that he recorded more than just pictures. Lots of notes. I have them. It sounds so strange to me. Do <u>you</u> know what happened to his film, Captain?"

"Ma'am, I think we'd better have a Navy courier pick up your husband's materials, then we can talk."

"No, sir," she responded immediately. "Absolutely not. I'll have to give them to someone in authority, personally. Not just anyone. It's what Barney would have wanted."

Edwards paused then thanked the woman.

"Ma'am, we have your number from caller ID. I'll call you back as soon as I can get a date and time for a proper transfer."

Edwards hung up and immediately telephoned his aide, Commander Roscoe Cogen.

"Ross, I want you to get me everything on a Captain Barney Byars. Navy pilot, veteran, Korea. Let's meet in my conference room at 1600 hours."

At 4:00 P.M., Cogen lugged two bulky expanding-wallet file folders into Edwards' soundproof room, one under each arm. He dropped them onto the main table.

"All the relevant printed materials I could find in four hours, but there are references to many other paper documents in storage. A lot of digital files also. I'm surprised we had this much."

Edwards untied and opened the first folder. He slid out its thick contents and picked up the cover summary.

"The basics. Barnard Milam Byars, born August, 1925, enlisted in the Navy as a pilot in December, 1941, right after Pearl Harbor. He served as a F9F-2 Panther pilot assigned to the USS Valley Forge, from 21 October 1950 to 14 June 1953. The mission under scrutiny today was 18 November 1950, when Byars was a full lieutenant."

"How old was Byars when he enlisted?" Cogen asked.

"Uh, sixteen."

"Sixteen? We took him when he was 16? And he was already a pilot?"

Edwards picked up another page.

"Says he learned to fly before he enlisted, got his civilian ticket and instrument rating from his dad, an instructor in Pensacola, former Navy. We took Byars because we needed him. That was right after Pearl, you know."

Cogen nodded. He pointed.

"Lots of classified material markings here, probably most or a lot of it declassified and available to anyone by now."

Edwards thumbed through the contents of the two folders. He was surprised at the number of redactions in Byars' own documents, submitted to the Navy both before and after the November, 1950, flight. He was curious as to why most of what Byars saw and wrote about in what the Navy had compiled from his reports and film was either missing or blacked out. Plus, he guessed, what Byars supposedly recorded in his personal notes was probably five times more than what he debriefed the Navy. Apparently, Byars learned a lot after his flight for MacArthur, especially since the general dropped him into a black hole. He hoped the 1,000 pages from Byars' widow would fill in the blanks. He picked up the handset and punched in the ONI director's private line.

CHAPTER 20

Tahlequah, Oklahoma

WEDNESDAY, 23 January – 10:00 A.M. CST

"There it is, Poppy! Two-thirteen. See, it says 'Sheriff's Office'."

Carl Windemere peered over the top of the steering wheel at the sign in front of a stone building.

"You're a great navigator, Zack."

His eleven-year-old grandson returned a thumbs-up. Carl turned into one of the angled parking spaces and braked. He shut off the engine and remained in thought for a few seconds.

"Ready, Poppy?"

"Uh, yes, right. Let's go tell him what we saw."

They walked to the front door, with Zack ahead. Carl lagged his grandson by a few yards.

Gold letters on the glass of the entrance read, "Cherokee County Sheriff's Office, Joseph Lesser, Sheriff." Zack pulled open the door.

A corpulent uniformed man stood next to a secretary's desk, hands on hips. He turned at the visitors' entry.

"You the Windemeres?"

"Yes, sir," Zack replied. "I'm Zack, and this is my grandfather. His name's Carl. We're here to see Sheriff Lesser." He added, "Sir!"

"Well, you're quite the professional, young man. I could use somebody like you 'round here."

Zack stood tall and beamed.

"I'm Sheriff Lesser," the uniformed man said as he reached out to shake hands. He gestured to an open door. "Why don't y'all come into my office?"

The three sat down in a large, musty room that had probably been someone's office ever since the building was constructed by the Works Progress Administration in 1936. Cracks in the walls were covered with photographs, half in color and half in black-and-white: the sheriff and his deputies, governors, Cherokee Indian chiefs, and other important visitors. Sheriff Lesser was in most of them. He picked up a used toothpick from the top of his desk and got right down to business.

"Now, Mr. Windemere, you say you seen a man killed on the river 'bout ten days ago?" With a beefy hand, he inserted the toothpick into his mouth.

"Yes, sir," Carl replied. "Saturday, the 12th." He recounted the events they'd witnessed, most of which he'd already told the sheriff over the phone.

"I can still hear the crack when they broke his neck."

Sheriff Lesser rested his elbows on his desk and tugged at his ear lobe as he listened. His expression remained impassive throughout Carl's ten-minute narrative. Finally, he exhaled audibly, sat back in his chair, and intertwined his fingers over his ample belly. He looked at the ceiling and rolled his thumbs.

"Well now, Mr. Windemere," he said with deliberation, "I've checked around since you called me. I've checked around a lot. I've spoken with the rescue folks, the Army at McAlester, the Highway Patrol, the rivers commission, and several others who also seen the men in the raft. No one, no one saw anyone come out of the water and tackle a guy holding a line behind the raft, including the soldiers in the raft.

"You talked with the soldiers in the raft?" Carl asked.

The sheriff frowned. "Well, not exactly." He sat up. "I talked with this Army spokesman in McAlester who said the soldiers

MARTIN KEATING

were all tore up at the loss of their buddy. They said he just plumb fell out of the raft and drown-ded before they could do anything. Ya see, they was in a rough patch of water and must have bounced across some rocks. That's what tossed the poor guy into the river."

"The newspaper said the soldier's body was found in a cove the next morning, Sunday," Carl offered.

Lesser nodded. "Yep, he'd been drinkin', and he wasn't wearin' no life jacket. A terrible but..." he paused for effect, "an accident jus' waitin' to happen."

Carl wasn't at all satisfied. "Where'd they take his body? An autopsy would have discovered his broken neck."

The sheriff leaned forward and pointed at Carl. "You know what, Mr. Windemere, I asked that very question, but the Army guy told me the soldier did have a broken neck, but that's what a drunk gets when he falls into turb-lent water with slippery rocks all around. Yessiree, it was all that soldier's fault."

Zack shook his head. "But soldiers don't train at McAlester. I just can't believe..."

The sheriff held up his hand and leaned toward the boy.

"Son, soldiers train wherever the Army wants 'em to train. Besides, they got so many things goin' on at McAlester these days I wouldn't be surprised if they have a lot of training goin' on down there as well."

Carl and Zack glanced at each other. This conversation certainly wasn't what they'd expected.

All of a sudden, Sheriff Lesser placed his hands firmly on his desk and pushed himself up. He put on a wide campaign grin.

"I sure am glad y'all came over today. I hope I've been of help. Sometimes things are just what they appear to be."

"Couldn't have said it better myself," Carl spoke in a low voice as he rose.

"What's that?" Lesser asked as he came around his desk.

"I said, you're right."

Within three minutes, Carl and his grandson were back in their car.

"Now what?" Zack asked.

Carl started the engine. He had a faraway look in his eyes.

"Zack, we saw a man murdered, and we're not going to run away from that. Just can't. Just won't."

CHAPTER 21

Namp'o, North Korea

THURSDAY, 24 January – 7:45 P.M. KST

Barely two hours after sunset, eight Navy SEALs arrived at the south bank of the Taedong River opposite the port city of Namp'o, North Korea. Their objective was to photograph and inspect a nondescript industrial building on a small inlet at the western edge of the government-designated "Special City" of 400,000. Intelligence had confirmed the increased presence of Farsi-speaking nuclear and electrical engineers, along with some of North Korea's best of the same. The place was guarded by an unknown number of armed soldiers within a 100-meter perimeter. The highest estimated number of personnel inside this evening, including security, was 25. Activity seemed to ebb and flow without any discernable pattern. Two automobile-size wooden crates had been shipped from the location by rail a month earlier, but verification of their contents had so far proven fruitless.

Even without night-vision aids, because of an array of four high-intensity pole lights at the corners of the metal facility, the SEALs could see their target area a mile away, due north across the river. Most of the rest of the city was in darkness as was usual every night in the impoverished Democratic People's Republic of Korea.

The SEALs had left a tiny South Korean island forty-eight hours earlier and traveled 80 statute miles overnight at sea in two specially constructed rigid inflatable boats, called RIBs. The new versions, at five-meters-long each, were less than half the size and weight of the some 1,000 regular RIBs in service world-wide with Naval Special Warfare for insertion and extraction. These all-weather craft were powered by silent lithium-battery electric inboard water-jet stern drives instead of diesel engines, and their classified maximum surface speed was in excess of 60 knots, or nearly 70 miles per hour. The improvements also in-cluded a half-dozen secret stealth additions that were especially useful in the ultra-hostile waters of the DPRK.

The eight men had spent the previous night in a nearby un-derground garbage disposal cave located by a North Korean agent who had worked for U.S. forces for a decade. Thanks to the omnipresent goons of the DPRK, most such operatives didn't survive even their first gratuitous act for the Americans.

The plan was to cross the Taedong River between 8:15 P.M. and 9:15 P.M. Ideally, they wanted a full three hours at the site, then a rapid water return to South Korea well before dawn. At 8:03 P.M., however, that plan changed.

A muffled explosion shook a merchant ship in Korea Bay nine miles off the North Korean west coast. The ship was within the territorial waters of the DPRK and on a straight-line latitude with the Taedong River. The sound was loud enough to be heard as far inland as Namp'o. The eight SEALs looked to the west but saw nothing. Within 60 seconds, North Korean sentries activated multiple high-decibel alarms along the river, and, by 8:10 P.M., DPRK patrol boats with powerful search-lights and heavy machine guns roared from hidden sheds and headed for the bay. The SEALs held their concealed position and watched the developing scenario. Having swarms of North Koreans coursing the river wasn't exactly the ideal condition for a crossing.

The SEALs silently gestured alternatives to one another when a series of much larger explosions reverberated from the west. The sky suddenly brightened with lights, including many white pops well above the horizon. The loud reports continued. More DPRK boats joined the flotilla. The SEALs considered waiting until most of the surprises had been sprung, but no one knew when that might be. In any event, their patience might not prove to be prudent. The mission clock was winding down.

At 8:35 P.M., the SEAL team leader made a circular motion with his raised arm: time to go. He extended two fingers and nodded toward the river. Whatever was happening in Korea Bay might be a blessing in disguise, as it was drawing the focus of the local North Korean military. The men gave their leader thumbs-up signals. Within ten seconds, all eight had sprinted from their shore cover and were in the water. A moment later, the surface of the river showed no evidence of their presence. The 4,200-foot crossing would require 50 minutes.

Each man was winter-wet-suited in what resembled an airman's tight G-suit, and each carried a minicam and various close-arms weapons. However, without question, the SEALs most important safety device was contained in arm and leg tubes attached by Velcro strips. Two parts. The first was a fine powder drug-dispersant developed by the Navy under a $340 million contract through the Defense Advanced Research Projects Agency that most everyone knew by its acronym, DARPA. Upon exposure to the oxygen in the air, the dispersant fulminated a thousand times in volume, spread its invisible cargo up to 50 yards, and remained mostly cohesive for 20 to 30 minutes before decaying into the harmless components of the ambient atmosphere. A rocket scientist's analogy might be that the dispersant was the fuel and the atmosphere was the oxidizer. What made the product so effective in this and similar missions was the second ingredient, its pressurized cargo, the active additive it dispersed in a large, stable aerosol oval as it expanded: K.O.STAT®, a unique "designer" derivative of the opioid fentanyl that was 500 times more potent than the original anesthetic drug's chemical structure. It also contained Phenegren®, a Navy-developed additive that held the suspended opioid molecules closer together for a longer time before dissipation. It was the ultimate knockout weapon. Theoretically, the eight SEALs carried enough K.O.STAT® to render every football fan in a packed Dallas Cowboys Stadium unconscious for two hours.

During their river crossing, the men remained submerged, breathing through fitted, removable snorkel tubes that attached to their goggles. Their separation array of 25 feet from one another in the river was not spotted by the North Koreans.

One by one, as planned for the blackness of 9:25 P.M., the SEALs slowly lifted their heads above the surface to just below eye-level. They had arrived at the edge of a concrete seawall along the north bank of the Taedong River. The area was not lighted, and they had escaped detection, so far. In slow motion, seven of the SEALs turned toward their leader. He dipped his face into the water, gradually, a signal for them to inject the last of the K.O.STAT® antidote. The powerful sleeping gas was generally not effective on human subjects who, over a two-week period, had built and maintained a blood concentration of 0.02% of a secret drug, a "back-door blocker" protective developed against the chemical structure of K.O.STAT®. Following this last injection, elimination would follow polyexponential kinetics, with a half-life of approximately 7.6 hours. The majority of the antidote would be eliminated in the SEALs' feces. They would be protected against the gas for their entire remaining stay in North Korea.

The target facility was 1,000 meters ahead on a small north-south river estuary, although it wasn't visible from the SEALs' present position. They had practiced to approach the building from two directions, north and south. The estuary paralleled the east, and a three-track railroad yard formed the western boundary. The apparent main entrance was on the north side, although intelligence reported that a deep tunnel from a tower at a DPRK military base inside the Namp'o city limits had rapid elevator access to the target facility. The elevator capacity was estimated at 20 100-kg riders or their equivalent cargo.

The wind at 9:35 P.M. was light and variable, a good omen. Satellite imagery of the area, available on the SEALs wrist units and viewable only through their polarized night-vision goggle lenses, indicated there were seven guards outside the building, three at the north entrance and four along the southern perimeter. All seven had to be neutralized at virtually the same instant. The building had to be gassed and breached no later than a minute afterwards. That meant the introduction of the K.O.STAT® into the target's air system had to occur almost simultaneously with the removal of the seven "perimeters."

So far, there had been no resistance. The SEAL team leader waved KILO-1 forward. Seconds later, he dispatched, and joined, KILO-2. For an instant, he wondered if they were walking into a trap.

At 10:07 P.M., the two SEAL teams were in position. They didn't wait for a signal. The eight men broke the glass tips of the K.O.STAT® tubes on their right arms and pointed the nozzles. The hypergolic chemical reaction began immediately, and the nearly invisible spray shot forth. The seven North Korean guards wavered and dropped to the ground without a sound. The DPRK was hyper-vigilant about most security procedures. However, they had counted on the perimeter guards to keep immediate intruders at bay. The Navy also knew they were often sloppy about the maintenance and operation of the nine cameras positioned around the building. Today, the cameras were turned off.

The teams quickly opened the building's two air inlet valves and released the contents of eight leg tubes of K.O.STAT®. They could hear the fans humming, drawing in the gas. They had figured on ninety seconds to eliminate most of the threat. "Three minutes to make it a walk in the park," one of the men whispered.

Entry began at a large metal plate on the east side of the building shortly before 10:15 P.M. The SEALs had decided it was the easiest route. Remove the plate and gain access away from the barriers at the usual points of entry.

The SEALs dashed inside a large room with desks and computers. Five North Korean operatives were unconscious. One had fallen to the floor and was bleeding from his forehead. Half of the overhead lighting was flickering. The SEALs ran to the stairwells.

The basement level was two-stories high. There was no human movement there either. Six white-suited men lay awkwardly across the equipment of a sophisticated assembly facility, the highest of high tech. Three narrow production lines, probably equal to what the West could build, but all were empty. The men descended to the "factory" floor and continued their observation and picture-taking. They also collected a stack of what looked like schematics and specifications, and a letter. What they saw everywhere, on the walls, boxes, and even the floor, were yellow and black radioactivity warning signs. And many photographs of the DKRP's work-product.

"Jesus Christ!" the SEAL leader exclaimed. "It's fucking true! They're assembling nuclear weapons here!"

He started to add "suitcase nukes" but was interrupted by an explosion that blew out a section of the wall. A dozen men burst into the room firing automatic weapons. Two of the SEALs died standing. Two more were dead seconds after they crumpled to the floor.

The irregular current from Korea Bay was slow near the inlet on the Taedong River. Polluted water, barely a few degrees above freezing, contained fetid streamers of outbound human waste, but the debris from the destroyed merchant ship continued its inexorable invasion of the DPRK. Thousands of pieces of wood no larger than shoeboxes were all that remained of the vessel. The only sounds in the blackness were the occasional muffled bumpings of pieces of the boat against four plastic scuba tubes.

CHAPTER 22

McAlester, Oklahoma

SATURDAY, 26 January – 11:45 A.M. CST

"Big Mac, Coke, no fries."

Halsey was in his well-patched red Ford pickup at the drive-in speaker at McDonald's.

"That you, Catboy?" a woman's scratchy voice came over the speaker. He recognized Clara's signature sound. That was the only thing about her that hadn't changed from their grade school days.

"One and the same, kiddo," he responded.

"Well, boy, you need two Big Macs, for all that 'man' work you do."

Halsey grinned. "One'll do me for today, Clara. Maybe tomorrow."

The woman laughed. "You know where to come, baby."

When he picked up his order, she added with a wink, "Hey, love to Anoli!"

Halsey headed south, past the McAlester airport. Traffic was light in both directions. He turned left onto a dirt road. Clusters of scrub oak trees were barely in sight of the road.

He pulled underneath a well-shielded area. His hunger was paramount, so he chomped into the Big Mac. With the other hand, he keyed in a code on his encrypted satellite phone. When a voice answered, he said, "Two seven Delta. Dot three. Dot Orion."

"Verify Orion," the voice replied.

"Orion double zero, 2-6-6."

There were clicks, then another voice.

"Tinker, tomorrow, Navy station, departure 1700 hours local, Laconia, New Hampshire, 0900 Monday Byars interview, complete orders on board the C-20."

Halsey took no notes. He had been anticipating this call.

"Righto." He clicked off, inserted the phone into a receptacle in the specially constructed steering column, and finished his Big Mac. He saved the Coke for later.

CHAPTER 23

United States Naval
Special Warfare Command

SUNDAY, 27 January – 10:00 A.M. PST

The Navy SEALs had been garrisoned at the Naval Amphibious Base Coronado in California since the NSWC was commissioned in 1987. Today, the SEALs comprised less than one percent of all Navy personnel worldwide. However, many called them the "tip of the U.S. military spear."

At Coronado, news of the North Korea mission was still incomplete, as communications had been spotty, at least until yesterday. Four dead, four safe in South Korea. The SEALs had returned with the bodies of their comrades.

The initial analysis of the mission was fruitful. Photographic and video evidence from Namp'o was compelling: The North Koreans and the Iranians apparently were assembling small nuclear devices of some sort and may have already shipped some, number and destination yet undetermined, although a port in China was suspected as a transfer point. The Navy had yet to analyze the documents the SEALs had brought back.

Having even one rogue "nuke" unaccounted for in today's unstable world was worrisome. Having an uncounted number available to the world's terror masters was unthinkable.

It looked like South Korea, without coordination with the United States, had blown up a merchant vessel, the <u>Persimmon</u>, close to or within the territorial waters of the Democratic People's Republic of Korea. Their plans probably included a follow-up landing or other attack in the DPRK.

While the action of the South Koreans might have endangered or even thwarted the SEALs' mission, it hadn't. Actually, it probably granted the SEALs protective cover. In the eyes of the North Koreans, it was immensely preferable to blame any such incursions on the hated "servant" South Koreans rather than on their "masters," the fully despised Americans. Having to admit that the U.S. Navy SEALs could come and go almost at will would be a devastating and unacceptable confession of national weakness. It would never happen.

So, officially, the SEALs were never there. And that's the way Coronado liked it.

CHAPTER 24

Laconia, New Hampshire

MONDAY, 28 January – 9:00 A.M. EST

Halsey arrived from Tinker Air Force Base in Oklahoma the previous evening as the sole passenger on an unmarked Gulfstream C-20D, the Navy variant of the Gulfstream III. He rented a car and stayed at a motel under the name Brad Williams, for which the Navy had given him a New Hampshire driver's license. Among the several other items in his briefing pack were a credit card in the fictitious name, $5,000 in cash, and transcriptions of various meetings at which Barney Byars was discussed. After three hours' review, Halsey felt comfortable with the information. At least he would be able to carry on an educated conversation with Mrs. Byars. He was expected back at the Laconia airport by 8:00 P.M. that evening.

The drive to the Byars' home on Lake Winnipesaukee took 20 minutes. He arrived right on time for his appointment.

The house was set 50 yards from the lake on ten acres of tree-, moss-, and fern-covered property that included walking trails and even a small landing strip.

"Wow, what a jewel!" Halsey exclaimed as he looked around. Anoli and I could really get used to a place like this, he thought.

He stopped his car on the driveway close to the front porch. He had a tape recorder in his padded jacket, but he didn't know if he'd need it. Well, depending on what the notes contained. He stepped out of the car.

"Good morning, young man," a cheery voice greeted him. Halsey looked over the top of the car and saw an older lady smiling at him from the large front porch.

"Mrs. Byars?"

"And you're Captain Halsey. I suppose I should add, 'I presume.'"

Halsey grinned. He walked up the steps and planned to shake the older woman's hand gently. However, her grip was tight, and she pumped his hand vigorously. From her voice and handshake, Halsey would have thought she was 20 years younger than the 75 his briefing papers indicated.

"Please come in," she said as she patted him on the shoulder. "Barney always said this was his home port, so the Navy's always welcome."

Mrs. Byars gestured toward an expansive living room.

"I can't pretend it's modest. Four bedrooms, three baths, 200 feet of shoreline with a sugar-sand beach. Big place. That's why I'm selling it. Pretty empty now. My children just don't come home as they used to. All grown up, with my grandchildren. Plus, they want me to be nearer. I suppose they're right. Please, let's sit here."

Halsey sat where she indicated, a wide, curved sofa with a magnificent view of the lake. She joined him.

"I've fallen in love with your home, Mrs. Byars."

"Want to make me an offer?" she said with a twinkle in her eye. "I can cut you a nice deal." They both laughed.

"Was that an airstrip I saw on the drive in?"

"Yes, Barney had a plane that he flew until a year before he died. A Piper twin with all the electronic gizmos. Loved to take people up and show them the area. Everyone always called him 'Captain,' both from his Navy days and his American Airlines career."

Halsey could have visited all day with this charming woman, but he had serious business to discuss. Mrs. Byars seemed to sense it was time. She pointed to a large box next to the sofa.

"Barney's papers that we found hidden in the barn. Buried, actually. I suspected that there was such a treasure. He was always writing about things he'd encountered over the years, especially the 'secrets' he occasionally talked about. He treated his accounts with reverence, but he never seemed to have a big collection in his office. That's why I suspected that he'd hidden most of it."

"What do you mean by 'secrets,' Mrs. Byars?"

The woman stared out the window.

"Whatever he saw in Korea made a big impact on him, worried him even. He figured that he took pictures of something so special that General MacArthur classified it, made it a military secret. No one ever acknowledged what he'd found, and that bothered him. He <u>knew</u> what he'd seen. Since they wouldn't talk with him, he started to investigate on his own. Barney wasn't a conspiracy type, but he was concerned that the Army was pursuing something very important to national security because of his efforts, and he wanted to know what it was. I don't think he found out during his Navy service, but he kept asking questions, digging for information, and making notes. Kept it up when he started flying for the airline. Just never gave up. About a month before he died, he told me he'd finally solved the puzzle. He was so excited. It was like a heavy weight had been lifted from his shoulders. He was a different man, Captain Halsey. He seemed to relax, really relax. This may sound strange to you, but I think Barney felt his work was done and he could now die in peace. Sadly for me, he did just that."

"Did he tell you what that puzzle was?"

"No, and that's what's strange."

"Ma'am?"

"He wrote down most everything he was curious about, especially the really important things. This solution was the <u>most</u> important, yet it was not in the materials we found. I knew he was convinced that what he saw in North Korea was the beginning of some sort of threat against the United States, and not just by some 'creatures,' but he never told me what exactly he'd concluded. All we've found is what's in that box. Some of the material he edited and retyped, some he just left in his notebook."

She lifted a scuffed spiral notebook from the box and handed it over. "Here, you probably should start with this. It's all handwritten...or hand-printed, actually. That was Barney. A lot of the rest of his notes he typed on his old Underwood."

As Halsey lifted the cover of the notebook, his mind was trying to catch up with the implications of what Mrs. Byars had just told him. The printing was in pencil, light but legible.

"May I look over some of this now?" he inquired.

"Please do, but I've made copies for you, so you don't have to take notes."

"Really?" Halsey smiled. "How nice of you."

"Yes, I copied all of it, and you're welcome. Anything to help complete Barney's mission."

"'Vampire,'? That was his Navy 'handle'?"

The elderly woman giggled.

"Good gracious, yes, from his Pensacola days. His buddies said he hunted best at night and always found his target. Had a nose for the kill, just like a bat. Sounds kind of silly now, doesn't it?"

Halsey reached over and squeezed her hand. "No, Mrs. Byars. It's insightful. I really wish I had known your husband."

He started reading from Captain Byars' notebook.

Dates of Military Service: 1945-1965

Date of Invasion by North Korea: 25 June 1950

Date of Truman/MacArthur Wake Island Meeting: 15 October 1950

Four days before the Chinese crossed the Yalu River on a secret initial mission, President Harry Truman asked General Douglas MacArthur at their Wake Island meeting, "What are the chances for Chinese or Soviet interference?" MacArthur replied, "Very little. Had they interfered in the first or second months, it would have been decisive. We are no longer fearful of their intervention. We no longer stand hat in hand. The Chinese have 300,000 men in Manchuria. Of these, probably not more than 100,000-125,000 are distributed along the Yalu River. Only 50,000-60,000 could be gotten across the Yalu River. They have no air force. Now that we have bases for our Air Force in Korea, if the Chinese tried to get down to Pyongyang there would be the greatest slaughter."

Date of First Invasion of Korea by China: 19 October 1950

The 13th Army Group of the Chinese People's Volunteer Army (PVA) crossed the Yalu River in secret.

Date of Public, First Phase Offensive by China: 25 October 1950

The PVA's 13th Army Group launched the First Phase Offensive.

Date of Surprise Attack by China on U.S. forces: 1 November 1950

The Chinese won this encounter, then unexpectedly withdrew into the mountains. It is unclear why they did not press the attack and follow up their victory. MacArthur's UN Command in Seoul concluded that this was not a general intervention by China.

I flew Navy Grumman F9F-2 Panthers from USS Valley Forge (CV-45). The Essex-class aircraft carrier was home to Air Group 5: two squadrons of F9F Panther jet fighters and two of propeller-driven F4U Corsair fighter bombers.

On 16 November 1950, General MacArthur ordered me to take gun-camera pictures (film) of three specific locations during reconnaissance along the Yalu River. Each was a quadrant of ten by ten kilometers. I was chosen due to my previous successes in precision aerial photography. Film was to be delivered personally to MacArthur and was not to be processed on board the Valley Forge. (I did not know this at the time.)

Date of aerial reconnaissance photographs: 18 November 1950

This was the last sortie before the <u>Valley</u> <u>Forge</u> was scheduled to return to San Diego for overhaul.

Five other pilots and I departed the <u>Valley</u> <u>Forge</u> at 0640 on 18 November. Three of the Panthers remained in orbit over the carrier for "top cover." The other three jets reached their initial intersection position at 0713. For me, this was the first of the three locations I was to film. Using hand signals, I waved off my wingmen. They would proceed southwestward along the Yalu, seeking MiG-15s and other targets of opportunity and would return in 120 minutes. The two jets dropped away. I nosed down from 24,000 feet and aimed for the corner of my first quadrant. While my Panther was armed, my mission was neither attack nor defense. Leveling at 1,200 feet, I started the camera. After less than a minute of orientation footage along the west side of "Box 1," I clicked off and started a visual appraisal of the North Korean terrain. I made a right-turn circuit of the 100-square-kilometer target, turning on the camera again for a four-minute segment.

I climbed away and headed to the southwest at 10,000 feet for "Box 2." Ten miles out, I reduced power and descended toward the southeast corner of my new target. As I reached 1,200 feet, I turned right and followed the east side of the quadrant. I held down the camera button and looked left as I made my initial circuit. Nothing. Supposedly, there were thousands of Chinese troops along the north side of the China-Korea border and some already across the Yalu River to the south, but, so far, it was all "no joy" for me. No men, no nothing. Full power.

One more to go. I aimed for my last target and climbed to ten grand once again to avoid small-arms fire. I plotted "Box 3," six minutes away. Down again. I pulled back on the throttle. This time, as the first, I decided to make a right-hand circuit. The rising sun would help light the hilly terrain when I'd round the corner for my final pass to the south. So far, I hadn't seen anything out of the ordinary. The third time had to be the charm. I'd take my time on all four passes, especially the fourth. I was abeam the southeast corner of the quadrant, the starting point, just as I leveled at 1,200 feet and headed west. I peered out the right side of my canopy. I'd ramped up my concentration. This was my last chance to find something. If there <u>were</u> anything, that is.

A denuded mountain, a few skinny trees, a faded green all. Even at my slow, near-stall speed, the vertical sticks flashed past. Then, a bump to my peripheral vision. When I looked, it was gone. I had less than a minute before my turn to the north. I looked back. Nothing but the trees. As I rolled into a right turn, another bump caught my eye, something white but not snow. When I finished the turn, I was a thousand yards beyond whatever it was. I decided to complete the circuit as planned. Right turn, around the north end, toward the east, but nothing along the way. When I began the turn to the south, I realized I hadn't activated the camera. I did so immediately, with an eyes-upward thank-you. I hadn't missed anything yet, or so I hoped. My airspeed was borderline. I wished I could stop, get out, and investigate on foot. I peered to my 12 to 2 o'clock position. All of a sudden, there they were. Dozens of very tall men. Men? My mind raced. These "creatures" were much taller than humans. My means of measurement was limited, but my best guess was at least half again as tall as an adult male. Eight, nine feet maybe? Jesus! My aircraft started to shake, a sign of an imminent stall. I advanced the throttle. I didn't know what I had seen or if my camera had captured the scene. I made a wide 180-degree turn and reoriented the camera. My second pass found the "men" again, still standing motionless. I stared. No, they didn't look like soldiers in winter uniforms. They looked like huge gorillas in white fur, standing among the bare trees. I knew the trees in this area averaged four to six inches in diameter. These stocky, upright creatures were definitely at least seven feet tall. They weren't trees. I saw their eyes and hands. I made a third pass, just to make sure I had detailed photographic evidence. The "men" never moved. I rendezvoused with my flight. When I landed on the carrier, my film canisters were removed and sent directly to General MacArthur. I asked but didn't learn what was concluded from my mission. At least not then.

Rotation of the USS <u>Valley</u> <u>Forge</u>: 20 November 1950

The <u>Valley</u> <u>Forge</u> sailed from the Sea of Japan for San Diego for overhaul on 20 November 1950. However, upon arrival in California on 1 December, the carrier was immediately ordered back to Korea. The UN Command had finally confirmed that the 1 November Chinese intervention was indeed an invasion and not simply an incursion.

Post-military career: American Airlines (1965-1985)

After my retirement from the Navy in 1965, I became a pilot for American Airlines. I was based in New York and Chicago and flew BAC 111s, Boeing 707s, Boeing 727s, and McDonnell Douglas DC-10s, both as a first officer and as captain.

Halsey stopped reading.

"Mrs. Byars, I'm sorry to have read so much right now, but this is fascinating."

The woman smiled. "Take all the time you want, Captain."

Halsey nodded. "I have to get back to something, ma'am, the 'puzzle' question. You said your husband had solved it. Maybe he didn't want to tell you at the time, but why didn't he write about it?"

"Oh, I'm sure he did. He just didn't put it with these papers."

"Meaning?"

"Meaning I think there's another safe."

CHAPTER 25

McAlester, Oklahoma

General Thomas Benning waited impatiently for the call. He toyed with a paperweight Oklahoma's governor had presented him at last fall's annual ceremonial "inspection" of MCAAP. It was a Lucite cube containing miniature flags of Oklahoma and the Army. He glanced at his watch. They were ten minutes late.

"God <u>damn</u>!"

Benning positioned the cube on his desk. "I despise waiting. Especially <u>now</u>!" he barked. The three trucks had left after dark on Sunday. They had armed escorts. They should have arrived on time...and safely. His work was succeeding, he reassured himself. He <u>had</u> to succeed. This would be his legacy and surely worth another star.

The phone rang. It was line five.

"Report!"

"They're gone," a man moaned. "They're all <u>gone</u>."

Benning jerked upright.

"What?"

"Nothing in the trucks. They were empty. All 433 have been taken! Stolen! They've just disappeared!"

Benning's brain started shorting out. He couldn't maintain a coherent thought.

The man went on. "Every one of our 'chips' is gone, General. Gone! Jesus Christ. Oh, Jesus Christ!"

Benning tried to speak, but he couldn't connect his brain to his mouth.

"Did you hear what I said?" the man pleaded.

"Shit, yes!" he exploded. Everything suddenly focusing. He slammed down the handset. His mind was attempting to connect the dots. Someone had taken his prize "creatures." But how? He knew the escorted trucks were to follow a circuitous route to Aberdeen. They'd left 36 hours ago, and security was everything. For Christ's sake, where could they have been intercepted? He took a deep breath. From McAlester eastward, the first and best place would be in the vast, untracked forests of southeast Oklahoma, along narrow two-lane roads in the so-called Oklahoma Triangle. That's where they were headed immediately after they left MCAAP, and that's where most of them had been captured. It's where they had to be. By God, I'll find them and the bastards who did it! He pulled open a desk drawer and found a number. He punched it in and waited for acknowledgment.

"Thank you for..." a recorded voice began.

Benning hit "7785" and hung up.

"I'll hunt you down and kill you all, you sons of bitches! Just watch me!"

CHAPTER 26

McCarran International Airport, Las Vegas

TUESDAY, 29 January – 6:55 P.M. PST

Located on the northwest side of Las Vegas' airport complex was a small array of hangars and buildings operated for the U.S. Air Force by EG&G, a national defense contractor named after its 1930s MIT founders Harold Edgerton, a pioneer of high-speed photography, Kenneth Germeshausen, and Herbert Grier. During and after World War II, EG&G increased the range of its technical services to the U.S. government, most of it classified.

In 2002, the defense and services sector of the company was acquired by defense technical services giant URS Corporation. In December, 2009, URS announced its decision to discontinue the use of "EG&G" as a division name. URS stated that by January, 2010, it would discontinue using secondary corporate brands, including the EG&G name and logo. The EG&G Division became URS Federal Services. However, its assignment and activities were still officially headquartered at McCarran and remained the same as before. And just as secret.

The main building was called the "Janet Terminal." Its principal operation was the launch and retrieval of aircraft, both Boeing 737s and props, engaged in classified Air Force flights. It is not known where the name "Janet" came from.

Each flight went by a Janet call sign. The "airline" became better known to the public once it was discovered ferrying workers and supplies between Las Vegas, Groom Lake (also known as "Area 51"), Tonopah Test Range (TTR), and other unspecified destinations.

TTR was a small-scale Department of Energy operation until 1982, when the base was modernized and an enormous hangar complex constructed. That facility, located in "Area 30" on the Nellis range, 140 miles northwest of Las Vegas and controlled by the USAF's Air Combat Command, consisted of 72 specially built hangars for secret and other aircraft.

Janet's principal activities today were centered at TTR where two 737-600s were being fueled and readied for a flight to McAlester, Oklahoma. The original manifest showed they were to be carrying 240 special troops, most with high-tech equipment such as 3D/HD night-vision goggles, pressure and temperature sensors for air drops and ground positioning, and devices that could track the movement of a caterpillar from a mile away. However, there had been a change in plans: instead of the men, the planes would carry several hundred tons of classified equipment in large wooden crates. The revised manifest simply read, "photographic equipment."

The loading required a little more than an hour, the planes pushed back from the hangar and onto the apron right after sunset, and both were airborne within seven minutes.

When departing Las Vegas, Janet aircraft maintained their civil call signs until they neared their destination. If they had been flying from McCarran tonight, they'd have been called "Janet 710" and "Janet 721." At TTR, they were immediately dubbed "Hawk 25" and "Racer 25" and would maintain these designations to McAlester and back.

The 737s made a gentle turn into the night, to the east-south-east. Hawk 25 and Racer 25 climbed to 39,000 feet, in trail. Their estimated time en route was two hours and five minutes.

CHAPTER 27

Houston Ship Channel

WEDNESDAY, 30 January - 10:30 A.M. CST

Two men waited in the spacious fifth-floor observatory at the tanker anchorage of the massive Sinergy Petroleum refinery at the Port of Houston. They were alone.

Telescopes on tripods pointed around the western half of the compass from the north, the Turning Basin, to the south and Galveston Bay. Immediately before them lay the Houston Ship Channel, one of the busiest conduits of ocean-going vessels in the world. Arrayed behind the men was an ultra-modern complex, the biggest refinery in the United States.

Sinergy, a Chinese government-owned company, had purchased a rusting leftover from Venezuela in 2008 and spent $5.1 billion over half a decade on its resurrection. It was nearly five square miles of state-of-the-art technology, three times the size of the old facility. The dedication was a national celebration, a moment to point out America's "superiority in energy matters." Twenty congressman, five United States senators, and the President himself had attended. He lauded the Chinese commitment to a "green" future and to the employment of some 3,700 highly skilled U.S. and other employees who would "make us all proud."

One of the men in the observatory looked through binoculars and pointed to the south.

"There, behind the tanker."

The other man looked at his watch and raised his binoculars. "Got it."

"How many 'pigs'?" the first man asked.

"All of them. We took a chance on one shipment with Customs and Border Protection. It worked."

The first man smirked. "If nothing else, the Americans are predictable. They so want us to succeed. The refinery, I mean." Both men laughed.

"One plays by the rules, and one can write the rules," his associate mused.

The smaller ship edged closer to the dock. The first man lowered his binoculars.

"Off-loading, six hours. Arrival of the 'hummingbirds,' two weeks. Mating, one week. Pipeline delivery to the targets, end of February."

The second man kept watching the smaller ship. He grinned.

"End of February, end of the U.S.A."

2.

BURIED TREASURE

"Fear has many eyes and can see things underground."

–<u>Miguel</u> <u>de</u> <u>Cervantes</u>

CHAPTER 28

Fort Worth, Texas

FRIDAY, 1 February - 3:00 A.M. CST

"Tom, c'mere," Scott Murphy called across the aisle at the Lockheed Martin Flight Services hub in Fort Worth.

"You gotta see this."

Tom Gaffney, his supervisor, scooted his rolling chair to Murphy's desk.

"What's up?"

Murphy pointed to the lower portion of his large flat-screen monitor.

"Rivers MOA, covering over 2,500 square miles of southeast Oklahoma, is to be active from 0600 local today through 2359 local Sunday. And get this: surface up to and including Flight Level Three-Niner-Zero! That's supposed to be an 8,000-to-18,000-foot <u>occasional</u> block of airspace, once in a blue moon for maybe as long as 24 hours. Why the hell do they need 2,500 square miles up to 39,000 feet for 66 hours?"

"And who is 'they,'?" Gaffney wondered out loud. He squinted at Murphy's screen and considered the oddity.

Military Operations Areas were special-use airspace, and they were usually activated for a few hours at a time here and there in order to separate high-speed military traffic from civil IFR flights. MOAs were marked on aviation charts and were different for separate parts of the country. VFR pilots were not prohibited from entering active MOAs, but they had to exercise extreme caution for the military traffic, everything from refueling, combat training, formation flying, to extremely low-level flying. Night "lights out" flying also takes place there and can be extremely hazardous to the unaware pilot. All pilots transiting "hot" MOAs were strongly advised to check with the local controlling agency before attempting such flights.

"Almost three days?" Gaffney asked in a near-whisper. "We've done some infrequent 12-hours-at-a-time stuff at Rivers. But this? It doesn't make any sense." His voice returned to normal. "Let me check." He wheeled back to his desk and picked up one of his telephone handsets. Five minutes later, he was back at Murphy's side.

"It's true, an extraordinary, almost unprecedented Department of Defense NOTAM, and it is for sixty-six hours. Whatever's going on, it's serious stuff. They said they'd even considered making the MOA a prohibited area."

"Jee-sus," Murphy responded. "Okiedoke, I'll get the advisories out, but this is weird. Really weird. Who's the controlling agency, Fort Worth Center?"

"You're not going to believe this: MCAAP."

"'Mack-App'?" His jaw dropped. "What the hell do they have to do with airspace? Rivers MOA is Fort Worth's responsibility."

"Don't ask. Just do."

Murphy sighed and entered the notice on his computer.

"Strangest special-use airspace I've ever had to deal with," he mumbled. "An area bigger than Delaware and over seven miles high. What the shit are they launching up there in Oklahoma? A space shuttle, for Chrissake?"

Murphy pressed the "send" button.

CHAPTER 29

Laconia, New Hampshire

FRIDAY, 1 February – 5:00 A.M. EST

Halsey yawned and opened his laptop on his motel room bed. It was early, but he was too unsettled to sleep more than a few hours at a time. He had waved off his return flight Monday after his initial meeting with Mrs. Barney Byars. It was not only because of the treasure trove of information left behind in the barn safe by her late husband, it was the promise of even more.

He had hit a potential intelligence gold mine. He figured that what he'd already seen was ten times beyond what the Navy had known about the so-called "creatures" and their clandestine pursuit by the Army. Anything more would be like winning a mega-jackpot in Vegas.

Halsey immediately noticed a flashing alert at the upper right-hand corner of his laptop screen. It was an ONI-urgent message, not a "critical" which would have been sent to him on his encrypted satellite phone for immediate action. All wireless data to and from his computer was also encrypted. However, it was usually not stored after it was received and read or composed and transmitted, just in case his computer and its messages were ever to fall into the wrong hands. He tapped open the alert. It was a Notice to Airman affecting special-use airspace for a military operations area in Oklahoma. It was headed, !MCAAP RIVERS MOA AIRSPACE.

"Urgent?" Halsey saw the telling exclamation mark before the title. "And that's damn near everything in Oklahoma southeast of McAlester! What the hell's going on out there?" He continued reading out loud.

"Activation time: 1100 Zulu. That's 6:00 A.M. Central, seven o'clock here. Less than two hours from now, and no usual advance warning? What are they <u>doing</u>?"

He ran his finger down the screen to the vertical limits line of the MOA.

"Surface to 39 grand? Double damn, this is TFR stuff." He'd no sooner said it than a second alert popped up, a Temporary Flight Restriction for the Rivers MOA. Same horizontal and vertical limits and timeframe. Halsey sat back. "This is a <u>major</u> event, like an Air Force One visit. Only bigger."

In McAlester, Anoli saw the new MOA as soon as it popped up on her computer screen. She and Fritz had kept an eye on local aerial traffic ever since the previous August, looking for curious operations, especially those south and southeast of town. It was still dark. She had thought about going into her office later, out of growing curiosity or fear or both. She frowned and read the entire notice, line by line. Anoli knew what "hot" MOAs were, but they'd never been issued by MCAAP. Mostly, in Oklahoma, they were requested by Tinker Air Force Base in Oklahoma City or Vance AFB in Enid, places with aircraft in training. The timing and altitude limit of this MOA just didn't make any sense. Why were they planning to fly over an area of hundreds of square miles and up to seven miles high?

She called her husband.

A low, steady whooshing sound came from his encrypted phone, not unlike that of air passing through a room ventilation register. It was designed to fit into the ambient noises of a small room, to sound harmless. Halsey clicked on.

"MOA activation for this area," Anoli began. "Big time. 'Rivers,' all the way up to 39,000 feet, this morning through Sunday."

"I saw it," Halsey interjected. He rolled onto his stomach.

Anoli went on. "What the hell are my little bomb-builders up to out there? And what does a 'hot' MOA have to do with these so-called 'creatures'?"

"It's all part of a major Army effort," he mused. "Totally 'black ops,' and we obviously know little about their big picture. As you and I have talked, the Navy's best guess is they're primarily after a way to capture and control some sort of creature to create the 'perfect' soldier. Now, this. Everything's been centered at MCAAP recently, so it's probably part of that. But this is not only 'black ops,' it's totally off the grid. We're getting nothing of substance. We have to get ahead of this. I'm planning to stick around here for another day or so, but that depends on what ONI decides, especially given today's news about the MOA."

"Remember fishing with your nephews last summer?"

Halsey hesitated then nodded. "Yeah, that was our first evidence of the aerial part of the equation. I've reread my report a dozen times." He remembered the event once more. He'd repeated it to his wife often, for reinforcement and maybe a helpful insight.

On a still farm pond a mile south of the McAlester airport, Halsey and the two boys sat in a rowboat, fishing poles in hand. Their red-and-white plastic bobbers hadn't moved in an hour, yet hopes of wriggling perch focused them on the muddy water. The late August sun kept afternoon temperatures in the humid nineties.

"'bout how much longer, Unc?" one of the boys asked.

"Patience, Robbie." Halsey smiled. "That's what fishing's all about."

The boy sighed.

Three thousand feet overhead, scattered summer clouds held their positions in the calm atmosphere, casting a ragged checkerboard of shadows over the hot and hilly southeastern Oklahoma countryside.

"Yeah, but aren't the fish <u>ever</u> hungry?" the boy persisted.

"It's too <u>hot</u> to eat," grumbled his older brother, Austin.

Halsey pointed to the northern sky. "It's a lot cooler up where they are." The boys looked and heard the puttering of an airplane engine. A small aircraft climbed toward them from the airport.

"What kind of plane is that?" Robbie asked.

"Looks like a Cessna 152," Halsey replied. "Carries two people, mostly used for training. If you'd like, we'll go flying someday."

"Really?" Austin turned and stared at his uncle. "In a Navy jet?"

Halsey grinned. "Probably not, unless you become a Naval aviator."

Austin frowned.

Abruptly, Halsey held up his hand and cocked his head. "Shhh!"

The boys thought a new story was about to begin. They both spoke to encourage him.

Halsey tapped his index finger against his lips. The boys saw he meant it.

Halsey squinted toward the sky, searching between the clouds. He cupped his ear. The boys wanted to ask what he was listening for, but they remained quiet. After a few seconds, they heard a faint whine, like a jet engine. Halsey's head moved ever so slowly with the sound, which grew louder from the east. Suddenly, two large jet aircraft dipped beneath the clouds, a half-mile away and in trail, and extended their landing gear. Painted white with a single red stripe the length of their fuselages, they were on a westerly heading.

"But there's no airport over there," Austin objected as the planes continued their rapid descent. "Just the Army base."

Robbie frowned and looked at Halsey.

"Uncle Fritz, are those Army?"

Halsey watched as the planes disappeared behind a ridgeline to the west.

"They're Janet 737s." He grabbed the oars. "We gotta get out of here."

CHAPTER 30

Laconia, New Hampshire

FRIDAY, 1 February - 5:25 A.M. EST

Halsey had focused on the Byars records since his arrival. He had scanned and forwarded many of them to Suitland for further analysis. Because of what was probably here but still hidden, ONI was assembling a technical team to come to New Hampshire to conduct a sophisticated search of the entire Byars property. The men would be disguised as landscape architects and workers, and they'd be here tomorrow. However, right now, Halsey had a new problem: trying to figure out what the hell was going on in the sky near his hometown. He was sure the MOA was solely an Army project since it was issued by MCAAP, not to mention all of the suspicious activities Anoli had discovered at the base, especially recently.

Halsey entered the classified number for the ONI director on his secure telephone. As he waited, he toyed with a wrinkled 3x5 card from Captain Byars' notebook. On it was typed, "Although I inquired several times, I never learned what was officially concluded from my special mission for the General over North Korea. Once, in 1953, a man slipped up behind me in a crowded Tokyo railway station. He punched his finger into my right shoulder blade and told me in a menacing voice to forget the whole MacArthur thing or forget my family. I immediately knew what he was talking about, but, just in case, he even used the code name for our mission, 'Gypsy.' Then he was gone."

CHAPTER 31

McAlester, Oklahoma

SATURDAY, 2 February – 6:05 A.M. CST

In the final moments of the cold pre-dawn darkness, while most of the nearby community remained asleep, the main eastside doors of MCAAP's massive hangar slowly rolled open. The process was silent and took less than two minutes.

No lights were visible inside or within 100 yards of the cavernous structure. Almost immediately, a low hum came from within the building. It rapidly grew into a sound resembling the beating of the wings of a thousand bats. All of a sudden, small objects began darting toward the approaching dawn. More than a hundred altogether. Eleven waves of ten "birds" each. All were 1,000 feet or more above the terrain before they even reached the perimeter of MCAAP, traveling at more than 100 m.p.h.

The first outsider to notice the strange exodus was 22,236 miles away, a new Navy reconnaissance satellite nicknamed "Chaperone," high above southeastern Oklahoma in a geostationary orbit.

CHAPTER 32

Suitland, Maryland

SATURDAY, 2 February – 2:25 P.M. EST

Halsey arrived in Washington from New Hampshire shortly after noon. The command-performance meeting was set for 2:30 P.M. in the ONI director's secure Annapolis Room. Halsey was advised to bring a change of clothes, usually a guarantee of at least a two-day sequester.

Vice Admiral Raymond Collins' aide waved Halsey into the walnut-paneled room whose walls were adorned with large and lighted original oil paintings of famous Naval scenes. One of the most valuable was that of John Paul Jones, the "Father of the United States Navy," at the Battle of Nassau. It was twice the size of the others, and it hung on the far wall opposite the entrance. It was what the director saw from his seated position at the table.

Navy captains Pierre Archambeau and William Edwards and three other captains whom Halsey didn't recognize were already in their places at the polished conference room table. Crystal glasses etched with the Navy ONI logo and pitchers of ice water rested on two silver trays on the table.

Collins walked from the side of the room and shook Halsey's hand. Before the door was closed, another officer slipped in. Halsey recognized Rear Admiral Roberto "Shiv" Ochoa, C.O. of the Naval Special Warfare Command in Coronado. As a ten-year-old, Ochoa was brought to America from Cuba by his parents in the Mariel Boatlift of 1980. His father had been born in Puerto Rico. "Shiv" was a graduate of Annapolis and was now the leader of the SEALs. The two friends exchanged nods. Given what Halsey was expecting to talk about, Ochoa's presence was a surprise. He wondered what the SEALs had to do with the Army and their "creatures."

"This is both a briefing and a debriefing," Admiral Collins announced as he sat down. He didn't introduce the three officers Halsey hadn't met.

"The first part is a review of what we know and surmise about the secret Army program, and we'll begin with the news of this morning's launch of 110 UAVs from MCAAP in Oklahoma."

Collins tapped a button on a console to his right. A screen lowered at the far end of the table, and a projector clicked on. Collins tapped another button. A high-resolution, night-vision aerial view of a massive surface installation appeared in wide-screen, then the picture tightened and focused on a large hangar, its doors open.

"The McAlester Army Ammunition Plant," the ONI director announced matter-of-factly. "This morning at 12:05 Zulu, 7:05 A.M. Eastern, compliments of <u>Chaperone</u>, our new eye-in-the-sky."

His audience leaned forward. Suddenly, a ragged fog appeared from the entrance of the MCAAP building and seemed to blow to the right of the screen at a rapid rate.

"Did you see them?" Collins asked. Without waiting for a response, he pointed a penlight laser at the hangar entrance. The video recycled, this time in slow-motion. The men saw the unmistakable shapes of unmanned aerial vehicles. Halsey guessed that the digital camera speed was probably 100,000 frames per second. He'd been told that <u>Chaperone</u>'s rotating prism could record at speeds in excess of 250,000 fps. He suspected the recon satellite's classified upper limit was closer to a million.

"The UAVs were flown in eleven formations to a point some fifteen nautical miles east-southeast into the western edge of the Rivers Military Operations Area, then they broke ranks, spread out, and started covering assigned grids at various altitudes, sometimes utilizing zig-zag courses. Their main mission covered the entire MOA, more than 2,500 square miles, and took three hours, seventeen minutes. All 110 of them were back in the hangar by 15:22 Zulu, 9:22 A.M. local. Remarkable control for what purpose we don't know, but we suspect they were looking for their 'creatures.'"

"Creatures," Collins repeated slowly and deliberately. He clicked off the projector.

"Let me introduce our liaisons with the NRO." He gestured toward the three strangers at the table: "Captains Mike, Oscar, and Victor."

Halsey moved his hand back and forth across his mouth, covering a smirk. Well, well, well, he thought, what do we have here, the ICAO alphabet trio? Wonder where "Juliette" and "Whiskey" are? He appreciated his inside-baseball sense of humor. No, these guys were definitely not Navy.

Collins went on.

"These men will continue to monitor and report on what we believe will be an expansion of the Army's search area. For the final 45 minutes of today's flight, all of the UAVs moved from the southern portion of the MOA to the northern. Some flew beyond, into a triangular area bounded by the Spiro Mounds near Ft. Smith, Arkansas, then southwest to MCAAP, southeast to Honobia, a tiny town located at the northeast corner of the MOA, then back to Spiro. Immediately before the aircraft returned to MCAAP, many more started shifting to this new area. It's a place some 'bigfoot' researchers and lots of common kooks call the 'Oklahoma Triangle.' The Army apparently thinks it merits a lot of their attention. That means it's a place we have to pay attention to also."

Several of the attendees were taking notes, even though they knew no paper transcriptions would be allowed to leave the room. Writing during such meetings was an old practice. It often led to questions that needed to be answered.

"Now, the search in New Hampshire. The first 'find' there, in a barn on the property, was of Navy and American Airlines Captain Barney Byars' Korean photog evidence and comments. We've evaluated most of what we've found so far. It was what really motivated us to start to tail the Army and their current efforts. As Captain Halsey knows, we're now looking for a second cache of materials on the Byars property. The first only dealt with matters during Byars' career with the Navy. There's a lot of good material. However, we're hoping the next discovery will go well beyond. We should have something to report within days.

"Any questions so far?" Collins looked around the table. No one responded.

"All right, two more items. The death of the secretary of the Army last month and a report from North Korea. As to the former, we are virtually certain it was a hit. It may or may not have anything to do with what we're discussing today, but, personally, I think it was part and parcel of it all. We expect to have more to report soon. Finally, as for North Korea, one of our SEAL teams learned on 24 January that the DPRK is assembling, or attempting to assemble, nuclear materials for transshipment through China. Where and why, we don't yet know. We have an informant in one of their prison camps who has been spot-on with intelligence in the past. His code name is 'Eve,' and he is probably our best source ever in that kingdom of darkness. The SEALS will be back in North Korea shortly to attempt to gather additional information.

"Oh, one more thing," Collins added with a raised finger. "The minisubs. To date, there's no evidence they've taken out any of the 'creatures.' At least not through the Gulf from Houston. We've pretty well closed that down."

As Collins took his chair, he noticed Halsey's raised eyebrow.

CHAPTER 33

Laconia, New Hampshire

TUESDAY, 5 February - 8:00 A.M. EST

The Navy "workmen" began their fourth day on site at the Byars property. So far, they had not found what they were looking for: a second hiding place with additional records from the late Navy and American Airlines Captain Barney Byars. Only numerous stacks of rebar rods, animal bones, and assorted rocks and fossils lay clumped every 100 yards or so across the 160-acre expanse. Regardless, they'd have to begin actual landscaping soon, just to cover their activities.

Lieutenant Commander Dwight Billingsly was in charge of the 17-man unit. He'd called for a meeting in the barn to plan the day's activities. His men crowded around him.

"There's one place we really haven't searched: the house."

"Skipper, sir," one corpsman spoke as he raised his arm. "We've been in <u>every</u> room there, and more than once. Nothing."

"Attic?"

"Yes, sir."

"Basement?"

"Yes, sir."

"No...you haven't," Billingsly corrected. The men frowned and looked at one another.

CHAPTER 34

Houston, Texas

WEDNESDAY, 6 February – 9:00 A.M. CST

Thousands of refined petroleum products pipelines underlie and crisscross the United States in a wide swath from Seattle to the tip of Florida, including all points south of Canada and north of Mexico: Boston, New York, Philadelphia, Miami, Chicago, Dallas, Houston, Denver, San Francisco, and Los Angeles. Not to mention the country's dozen major harbors and its airports and 100 scattered military installations. Most Americans were no farther than a few blocks from one of these silent suppliers of essential energy for their daily lives and the survival of the country.

The ultimate U.S. nexus for crude oil on its way to the refineries to produce the critical finished products was 45 miles west of Tulsa, just outside rural Cushing, Oklahoma, a mostly unacknowledged "center of the oil and gas universe." If Cushing were to fail to deliver crude to the refineries, America would be crippled.

Product pipelines of every diameter from the refineries were America's arterial structure, necessary for its commercial life and survival. They carried gasoline, kerosene, jet fuel, heating oil, naphtha, and a dozen other finished petroleum products, twenty-four hours a day, seven days a week. No time off for weekends or holidays. They provided the lifeblood of the country's economic engine. Virtually every American depended on them. If they ceased to exist, modern America would die.

The Chinese were particularly interested in one type of U.S. pipeline, the large "interstate" that transported refined petroleum products to major population centers, harbors, and military installations.

All of this was a major topic of today's opening of the annual Houston Petroleum Pipeline Conference, sponsored this year by China's Sinergy Petroleum. More than 40,000 were expected to attend the four-day event. Most were individuals interested in the industry. Major corporations sent groups of a dozen or more. The Chinese delegation was 156.

Sinergy not only owned and operated the largest refinery in the U.S., it also owned an elaborate system of pipelines that radiated across the land with many tie-ins with other pipelines. Without question, Sinergy had its thumb on America's energy pulse. Some believed its presence was more ominous.

CHAPTER 35

McAlester, Oklahoma

THURSDAY, 7 February – 6:00 P.M. CST

Halsey returned home to be with Anoli for what both felt might be the last time before things really began to get interesting. Mostly, they had used the word "unravel." It might even be their last time together for weeks or more. The Navy needed Anoli on site at MCAAP, and Halsey had business in a dozen other places.

This time, he had flown into Tinker AFB in Midwest City, a major suburb of Oklahoma City. Halsey appeared to be just one of the many military types hitching a ride from Andrews, although he wasn't making a particular effort to be incognito. From Tinker, he rode an Army personnel bus the nearly two hours to MCAAP in McAlester. Anoli met him at the drop-off shelter inside the base. He grinned when he saw her passenger.

"Uzi!" he shouted. "Anoli, you brought our baby!"

His wife laughed and started to get out of the car.

"No, no, you drive." He waved her back inside. "I want to cuddle our little one." She rolled her eyes.

Uzi jumped out of his oversized Dean & DeLuca tote in the passenger seat and wagged his tail furiously. Halsey had bought the bag in Georgetown for Anoli to transport the pooch. Uzi was their purebred bulldog. They had bought him as a puppy. He was now two, often a terrible time for parents of children of that age but nothing but joyous days for the Halseys. At least that's what Halsey told everyone. He suspected that Anoli might have a slightly different take. She took care of Uzi whenever he was out of town, which was now most of the time. Whatever, Uzi was their "baby."

The drive home from MCAAP took 20 minutes. Halsey wrestled with Uzi all the way.

Shortly before dinner, Halsey went upstairs. They had three bedrooms: the master, a guest room, and his old retreat when he was in high school, the "bunker," he'd called it. Uzi ran ahead and jumped on the bed, reversed himself, and waited for his master. Halsey sat down next to his dog. It was the bed he had slept in before he went to the Naval Academy.

"Uzi," he said as he massaged the squirming dog's thick neck, "Maybe we should have called you 'Bull,' as we'd planned, after my great uncle." Uzi's eyes closed, and he slowly relaxed. He looked as if he were smiling.

Fleet Admiral William Frederick Halsey had always been Catman's hero. Uzi had Uncle "Bull's" countenance, but he and Anoli had finally decided that "Bull" wasn't an appropriate honorific of the Halsey family these days, not that "Uzi" was, either. However, in addition to the name of a submachine gun, Uzi in Hebrew was generally accepted to mean "power, strength" or simply "to be strong." So, that was his name.

Admiral Halsey was the Navy leader who had planned America's initial response to Pearl Harbor. He commanded numerous fierce battles across the Pacific during the Second World War. In 1945, the Japanese unconditional surrender took place in Tokyo Bay on his flagship, the USS Missouri. Yes, Catman reflected, "Bull" Halsey was the "face of the Navy," and Uzi always reminded him of his beloved uncle. He looked down. His dog was asleep and already snoring.

He and Anoli hadn't changed anything in his old room, yet. His mother had kept his prized possessions: the winning football from the state championship, his track trophies, and, fortunately, his baseball cards. Many mothers throw out their sons' baseball cards when they move away. His were valuable, although they weren't worth what his best friend and classmate once owned. Jody told him he had two that would command a quarter of a million dollars each, if only his mother hadn't tossed them into the trash.

Halsey thought about Anoli. He smiled as the recollection took shape. He remembered one summer when they were dating. He'd arrived at the McAlester city pool mid-afternoon. The place was full of families and singles, many of them from MCAAP. Children ran in all directions.

He saw Anoli at the poolside bar. She looked better than attractive in her micro-bikini. He really hadn't noticed her evenly tanned skin and incredible figure before. All right, he admitted to himself, he had, but he'd only been able to imagine what her body looked like through her Sunday best or Army fatigues. He lowered his head and stared over his sunglasses. She was indeed an eyeful. Not one ounce out of place. One-hundred-percent female. Halsey again mused that this just might be the woman for him.

He stepped to a lounger near the deep end of the pool, with an empty one next to it. He sat down, arranged his towel, lay back, closed his eyes, and waited. The trap was set.

"Hey, handsome," came the familiar caramel drawl, "Are you with anyone?"

"No," he answered without opening his eyes. "My gay lover's out of town."

She'd slapped him on the leg and sat down and squirted SF15 oil across his chest and down his thighs. Her hands completed a quick and rotating generous massage, including outside and inside the top of his trunks.

"Mmmm," Halsey hummed as he rubbed his face, his eyes still closed. "So, your boyfriend dumped you?" Anoli had laughed, held his face between her hands, and kissed him.

Not much had changed between them, other than getting married. And older. Honesty and humor, always with love. Lots of love. He smiled again. He loved this woman more than he could put into words.

After a few more minutes of reflection, he started back downstairs. Uzi tumbled after him. Halsey's childhood home always had a calming effect on him. It was, first and foremost, home. And it was perpetually a safe refuge.

Halsey was born in McAlester. His father had located here in the sixties to work for the Navy, eventually becoming the commanding officer of what was then called the McAlester Naval Ammunition Depot. Halsey became a Navy brat. When the Army took over the base in 1977, and renamed it MCAAP, Halsey remained Navy.

Now that his parents were gone, Halsey and Anoli owned the place. He didn't know what he would eventually do with it, but at least for now it was his. Theirs, he corrected himself.

"Dinner!" Anoli called from the kitchen.

"Coming." Halsey stopped at the bottom of the stairs and looked out the living room windows. It was starting to snow.

He walked into the dining room.

"What a night for..." he began, with a knowing grin. He approached her with open arms.

"My famous Choctaw Hunter's Stew!" she completed his sentence, her way.

He rolled his eyes and gave her a kiss. That's when he noticed she was wearing the 22k gold St. Christopher medal pendant necklace he'd given her last Christmas, to protect her.

"Yes, I wear it everyday now," Anoli whispered.

He gave her another kiss.

They sat down. Uzi coiled and settled beneath the table at Catman's feet. Halsey said the blessing. At the end, he added, "And dear Lord, please always protect us from evil."

Anoli reached over and took his hand.

"Amen," they said simultaneously. She squeezed then released her grip. They started eating in silence. What both were contemplating was hard to imagine, let alone verbalize. Halsey knew the night ahead promised hours of serious talk instead of lovemaking.

CHAPTER 36

Hwasong Labor Colony No. 16, DPRK

SATURDAY, 9 February - 5:00 A.M. KST

Yuk-sa Lee remembered peering through a ripped slat in a wood fence as 64 naked and shackled male and female prisoners were marched from the barracks of Camp 16 in the northeast quadrant of the Democratic People's Republic of North Korea. The temperature was well below zero. The wind was fierce.

Some of the condemned were too weak to stand, let alone walk. Those were immediately shot in the back of the head. The rest were hit by rifle butts and shoved into two nearby unheated wooden buildings. Hand-printed signs over the doors read, "Health Examinations." Yuk-sa Lee knew that term was a euphemism for medical experiments, assuming that the "patients" lived long enough. The pace of prisoners accelerated over the next few weeks. He knew selection for his own last journey was inevitable.

As he shivered in the bitter cold, Yuk-sa Lee wondered again if his work for the West had achieved any traction. He didn't count on it, but it was a slim hope he hung onto, In truth, he fully expected to die within the DPRK without ever meeting anyone from the United States, especially not his indirect contacts in the U.S. military.

The Navy knew him as "Eve." Someone had concocted his nickname from the first letters of his name, Y, S, and L. Those were also the initials of the famous French fashion designer Yves Henri Donat Mathieu-Saint-Laurent, known to the world as Yves Saint Laurent. "Eve" was a shortened version of the pronounced "Eves." Yuk-sa Lee had no idea who his namesake was. He did figure that there was some sense in giving him a decidedly female code name, for possible misidentification. Not that it would make any difference if he were caught aiding the United States.

Barely six thousand feet from Camp 16, at the base of 7,234-foot Mount Mantap, was the drilling and construction site for the DPRK's first nuclear test in 2006. The excavation had begun three years earlier. Yuk-sa Lee would never forget the horrors of his year on site. A thousand prisoners from Camp 16 were forced to dig tunnels and carve out underground facilities in the rock mountain, using shovels and other cheap implements and often their bare hands. More than half either starved or froze to death. Most of the rest died in vicious beatings by the guards.

The 76 who survived were later lowered by buckets into vertical tunnels at various distances from the epicenter of the scheduled atomic explosion. Eve was one of those who had to wait for uncounted hours in the cold and darkness of a 24-inch hole deep below the surface. He wasn't told anything about what was to happen or when. Suddenly, a crushing force nearly collapsed his skinny body, and he lost his hearing. There was no light, but a rapid climb in the temperature took his breath away. He dropped to the bottom of the bucket and lost consciousness.

While in a North Korean "hospital," Yuk-sa Lee learned that, in addition to a dozen other serious maladies, he was also suffering from a mild-to-moderate case of radiation poisoning, although that's not what they called it. But at least he was alive. He was told by an orderly that there were five survivors, not counting the "creatures" that had received more than four times the radiation than the men who died at the test site. It was a year afterwards before he found out what the "creatures" were.

His reward for living through the ghastly period at Mount Mantap was a scribble-on-paper promotion by the DPRK to be a guard at the camp. His new title was no triumph in an insane world. He figured that he'd just have to suffer longer before escaping in death.

CHAPTER 37

McAlester, Oklahoma

MONDAY, 11 February – 8:00 A.M. CST

Halsey was ordered back to Washington at dawn Central Time. He was to rendezvous with a Navy aircraft at Tinker by noon, as its sole passenger.

Anoli stood in the doorway of their bedroom as he collected his clothes.

"What about Benning?" he asked. He tossed extra underwear into his suitcase.

"As I told you, I'm being cut out of the loop over there," she said matter-of-factly. "They're suspicious of anyone outside their inner circle. I still have my access to most parts of the base, but heaven knows how long that will last. They just don't like me."

"I'll see what I can do. We have to keep you there, but I'm worried. We'll keep in touch. Our secure line. Let's make it noon and midnight. Central time."

Anoli stepped into the room and reached for his back. At her touch, Halsey sighed and relaxed.

"I love you, Babe," he whispered.

"And I love you more than you can ever imagine."

CHAPTER 38

Northwest Caribbean Sea

WEDNESDAY, 13 February – 11:40 A.M. EST

The first man, other than possibly an unfortunate member of the crew, to know about the explosion on board the Chinese cargo ship Zhou Enlai was an observer in a bunker control room a thousand miles away at the Sinergy Petroleum facility on the Houston Ship Channel. He was alerted at 0.45 seconds. The next to know was a monitor in Beijing when klaxons sounded at 0.71 seconds after the event. The third was the United States Navy, also at 0.71 seconds.

The newly commissioned nuclear-powered Virginia-class fast attack submarine, the USS Oklahoma, had trailed the Zhou Enlai from its exit at the northern terminus of the Panama Canal to its present position in the northwest Caribbean. It was a hand-off from another Navy sub that had followed the cargo ship over 10,000 statute miles from the People's Republic of China. The Zhou Enlai's passage through the canal was monitored by ultra-high-resolution satellites.

The sub was at 100 feet, slow, to match its prey, and five nautical miles to the southeast when its acoustic monitors alerted the Navy sonar listeners. The data indicated one boom followed almost instantaneously by several others of equal intensity. To Commander John Litton, it sounded like the undersea recordings he'd heard of the destruction of bomb-carrying ships during the Second World War. The $2.7 billion <u>Oklahoma</u> was based at Naval Station Norfolk, the largest Naval complex in the world. He radioed his urgent report.

The Navy knew that Chinese cargo ships made weekly visits to the huge Texas refinery. They shadowed all of them, incoming and outgoing, beginning just outside the PRC's territorial waters at Hong Kong. The Navy had had to board two such ships over the past three years after fires had broken out and S.O.S.s were broadcast. They'd used the opportunities to take a look at the goods aboard. The Chinese hadn't seemed to mind the thorough inspections. As a matter of fact, they actually seemed to welcome them. The Navy had found nothing suspicious.

At periscope depth, the horizon was unbroken. The <u>Oklahoma</u> surfaced and rounded a 1,000-yard perimeter from the last known position of the <u>Zhou Enlai</u>, looking for debris. At first, the lookouts spotted an occasional shard of wood, possibly from pallets. Then, more wood pieces bobbed up, along with what looked like small pieces of orange plastic. They tightened the radius. Much more wood. It was probable that the explosions had ripped the ship's hull from bow to stern, possibly below the water line just above the keel, and the <u>Zhou Enlai</u> had sunk immediately, without survivors. One of the Navy corpsmen stood at attention on the deck and saluted the dead.

CDR Litton concluded that salvage operations would be minimal, at least until it was decided whether or not to explore the sunken remains. That was unlikely, he thought, since the water depth here was more than 13,000 feet. Besides, the <u>Zhou Enlai</u>'s published manifest showed only resupply items common to refineries and other large liquids and processing facilities throughout the world. The Chinese had hundreds of customers like Sinergy. Nothing out of the ordinary, he concluded.

Suddenly, an electronic wail reverberated throughout the submarine, both inside and from hidden speakers outside on the conning tower. It was a unique general alarm. Litton slapped his hands over his ears and pressed hard. The siren was painfully loud.

"Radiation!" The engineering chief's cry was louder than the electronic wail.

"Radiation!" he shrieked again. "No reactor breach, all on-board systems green, but very high rads in the seawater! Off the charts! Close everything, and let's get out of here!"

Crewmembers out of position ran for their stations, the seawater cooling systems were quickly shut down, and all inlet hatches and valves were closed. Litton ordered the <u>Oklahoma</u> to full speed in a 90-degree right turn. In less than two minutes, the radiation monitor faded to normal. To the engineering department, this meant that the hazard was most probably confined to the immediate surface area above the sunken ship. A wide circuit would confirm it.

"What the hell was that?" Litton shouted into his boom microphone.

"Shit, Skipper," the chief yelled. "Sorry, Skipper, but we were in deadly waters there. The boat has to be decontaminated, but we're not showing anything much above normal in our air. Filters can handle that. I've never seen readings that high before. They lighted up everything here, real bright."

The operations division officer handed a message to Litton. "From ComSubLant, sir." Litton took the sheet and frowned. The Navy was already sending a nuclear specialist from Norfolk? To arrive in seven hours?

"Here's another, sir." The communications man was back, holding a folded note. Litton took it. On the outside was the NAVSOC emblem. Special Warfare? The SEALs? What the hell's going on?

CHAPTER 39

Northwest Caribbean Sea

FRIDAY, 15 February - 7:30 A.M. EST

The Oklahoma had repositioned two days earlier to 50 nautical miles east of the Turneffe Atoll off Belize. Its only other choices for a rendezvous nearby, yet removed from the tomb of the Zhou Enlai, were Mexico and Cuba, a slim-and-none option.

The three visitors had been on board the submarine for 31 hours, 30 minutes. All Navy: a "physicist" from the Norfolk base who had flown to Naval Air Station Jacksonville where he joined an "ordnance specialist." Together they traveled to NAS Key West and waited for the third member, a "special ops man," who came in from the U.S. Naval Special Warfare Command at Coronado. They were taken to the Oklahoma on a twin-engine HH-60 Seahawk helicopter, a trip around the western tip of Cuba that required an aerial refueling.

The trio, wearing full-body suits protective against short-term ionizing radiation, were lowered to the deck of the submarine at midnight Wednesday. Ironically, their rad suits had been manufactured in China. The Oklahoma immediately submerged and went silent and deep, as far away from prying eyes as technology could assure.

The meetings Thursday had taken all day. This morning's summation and conclusion was scheduled around a breakfast in the captain's quarters. The visitors would depart before noon. In spite of the virtually zero risk of outside interference, the four had been 'round-the-clock protected by six armed Marines who held everyone else at bay.

Commander Litton, as the host, sat down last, one man at each of the four sides of the table. His plate contained a piled-high helping of scrambled eggs with fresh mushrooms and chives, seven rashers of crisp brown-sugar bacon, and three thick slices of Virginia ham. He noticed the raised eyebrows.

"Hey, don't look at me that way. Navy subs eat well. Low carb diet for me. That's how I maintain my girlish figure."

His guests laughed. It was the first overt display of humor since they met on the deck of the Oklahoma at midnight Wednesday. At that time, as the helicopter pulled away into the darkness, the "physicist" had introduced himself.

"I'm Gilligan." He then motioned to the two other men. "I've brought 'Ginger' and 'Mary Ann' with me." Litton smiled and shook hands.

"So we're 'Gilligan's Island' now?"

"You bet, but for security purposes, you can call me the 'Professor.'" Everyone laughed. Litton pursed his lips and nodded.

"Well, folks, welcome aboard a very big Minnow, and you can call me the 'Skipper.'" Everyone laughed again.

The greeting ceremony ended abruptly when unsmiling Marines stepped forward and motioned the men below.

"Radiation, gentlemen. Please."

The four had bonded over the past day and a half. The subject matter and their close proximity had been the driving forces.

"The Professor" was Navy Commander Paul Gilligan. His doctorate in nuclear physics was from Michigan State. "Ginger" was CDR Andrew Yost, also a Ph.D., who had degrees in chemical and explosives engineering from the University of Missouri. At his introduction, Andy approved of his new nickname: "But based on what I do, 'gingerly' might have been better." The third, "Mary Ann," was CDR Wohali Hart, a Cherokee whose given name meant "eagle." However, at the Naval

Academy, the big man's first name became "Wooly," a handle he bore from then on. He'd become a SEAL, then, after several classified assignments, he was promoted to be one of the group's commanders. Today, Wooly simply told people he was in "management" at the Navy's Special Warfare community in California. His sun-wrinkled face hid a lot of stories.

When they finished breakfast, the dishes were removed, a Marine guard closed the door, and Litton began.

"It's a diabolical pyramid. Let's review."

The others positioned their notepads and looked up. Litton continued.

"We believe the Chinese are assembling the assets to attack the United States in an Armageddon scenario. The end of this country, in other words. Based on what we've discovered, there's no doubt something big is coming, and soon."

The Oklahoma captain looked at one man at the table.

"Professor, it's all yours."

Navy Commander Paul Gilligan stood up.

"We found cesium-137 in the water. That's a lethal but not explosive radioactive isotope. We also found traces of RDX, also known as Cyclonite and Hexogen. Few people call it by its full chemical name, cyclotrimethylenetrinitramine. It's one of the most powerful high explosives ever developed, many times greater than TNT. Its use would be to disperse the cesium. Not good news, gentlemen. Not good at all.

"For security reasons during the Second World War, Britain called Cyclonite RDX, for 'Research Development Explosive.' The substitute name caught on in the United States shortly after the war.

"German admiral Karl Doenitz once bragged that 'an aircraft can no more kill a U-boat than a crow can kill a mole.' That may have been true before RDX was introduced into battle by the Allies, but after RDX torpedoes and depth charges began falling from bombers, the Nazi subs became, as they say, sitting ducks. By mid-1943, the deadly 'wolf packs' had been devastated. The new explosive definitely accomplished its mission."

"So?" Litton asked.

"So, we'd better expect something involving this kind of weapon. Cheap, easily concealed. They'd be foolish not to employ it."

CHAPTER 40

Hong Kong-Macau Ferry Terminal

SUNDAY, 17 February – 5:00 A.M. HKT

The weather was cool. There was no precipitation at the time, although a humid 59 degrees Fahrenheit was officially reported, with scattered clouds in the subtropical darkness above. Small crowds began assembling an hour before the celebration at the Port of Hong Kong.

Today commemorated the second week's anniversary of the launching of <u>DragonFlyy</u>, the world's first intercontinental hydrofoil service, a private, high-speed, luxury craft that plied various oceans and inland waters each way between Houston and Tokyo on a scheduled, daily basis. It was historic, exciting, and a moment to celebrate, again.

At 6:00 A.M., from Hong Kong, the precise launches were in two directions, one four-story hydrofoil coursed away to the east, to Tokyo, and the other powered above the waves and roared away on a westerly course, on its way to Houston. Both "flights" were mostly always full.

<u>DragonFlyy</u>'s two-sided local berth was temporarily at the Hong-Kong-Macau Ferry Terminal and Heliport, immediately west of Hong Kong's main business district. All things being equal, this was the best location until <u>DragonFlyy</u>'s new, $206 million state-of-the-art anchorage was completed, six months from now.

DragonFlyy connected the two international terminal cities of Houston and Tokyo with Miami, Rome, a floating station for the nearby countries in the eastern Mediterranean, Mumbai, Singapore, Manila, and Hong Kong.

The promotional flyer said it all:

- "R and R" just became whatever you want it to be.
- Step aboard our newest and finest ocean-going hydrofoil, for business or pleasure, and savor the travel experience of a lifetime.
- Fast but without the hurry.
- Twenty-seven ultra-exclusive, individually decorated suites with advanced entertainment, HD television, and sound systems, along with high-speed wireless Internet.
- Marble baths, showers, and whirlpools, with every amenity.
- In-room wine and minibars, stocked with the finest selections.
- Five-star dining rooms with international chefs and cuisine.
- All menu and bar desires available in suites 24/7.
- Personal in-room chefs available upon request.
- Fully equipped business and retreat facilities.
- Spa and fitness center.
- Personal butler services.
- Superb comfort.
- Arrive rested and ready.
- Complete and discrete security.
- Daily service each way every day.
- Embark or disembark at port or via private helicopter deck.
- Flag stops en route, by prior arrangement.
- Toll-free reservations in the U.S. – (372) 466-3599

DragonFlyy's service mark was "The most exclusive resort at sea." By eliminating airport transfers, it was nearly as fast as jet travel, time elapsed, but it was not an inexpensive journey.

Passage for one person for the entire first-class trip between Houston and Tokyo was $18,500, not including meals, special lodging arrangements, wine and liquor, and tips, which could easily double the basic fare.

However, for the two men traveling from Hong Kong to Tokyo this morning, cost was no object. Their conversation was not about money. They stood on the empty swaying deck as the hydrofoil accelerated erratically into the chop of the approaching dawn. Both gripped the railing and stared out to sea.

"I need the timing," the North Korean insisted. "The final mating schedule."

His Tokyo-bound Chinese compatriot forced a smile.

"As I have repeatedly told you," he spoke calmly, "all of the 'hummingbirds' we need are there, together with the spheres."

"What about last Wednesday?

"Wednesday? You presume to ask me about Wednesday? That was your screw-up, your so-called 'final shipment.' You are in charge of assembly. The Zhou Enlai explosion could have ruined everything. As a matter of fact, we're still not sure it didn't. You kept insisting on one more temptation of fate, one more tweak of the devil's tail. We'll soon find out what the Americans learned from your little gambit."

The North Korean started to say something. The Chinese man quickly held up his hand.

"If you and I were in my country at this moment, you would already be dead."

CHAPTER 41

Suitland, Maryland

TUESDAY, 19 February – 9:00 A.M. EST

Halsey had been back at the Office of Naval Intelligence for a week. It was a frenetic, don't-look-at-the-clock stint. Meetings, phone calls, and more meetings. Halsey had the authority to ask questions and demand answers from a myriad of sources within the military. Several times he'd looked out the window expecting sunshine, only to see darkness. His timing was off by twelve hours, again. Other than his own office, he had a cubbyhole on the director's floor with a sofa for occasional naps, and the men's room for a bathroom. Not literally; it had a shower. Halsey yawned and shuffled toward the umpteenth meeting in his boss's office.

"Three agenda items this morning," Vice Admiral Raymond Collins, ONI director, said as Halsey sat down. It would be another one-on-one, with most of the answers being Halsey's responsibility.

Collins nodded at a pen and a yellow pad at the edge of his desk. Halsey picked up the pen and positioned the pad in front of himself. Collins began.

"More on the Chinese boat explosion last Wednesday, update on our North Korean informant, and a necessary intercept. Basically, it's 'China day.'"

"Intercept?"

"Third item, Captain. Patience."

Halsey had a feeling that Collins had a surprise for him with that third item. It wasn't a guess. It was his gut.

"First, bottom line on the explosion?" Collins asked.

Halsey clasped his hands on the desk and began.

"I've spent most of the past seven days going on the entire scenario. We have enough of the puzzle to know it's very troubling. With the discovery of cesium-137 and RDX, it's unquestionably dirty-bomb stuff. Those two components are all one has to have to reach my conclusion. Chinese ship? That's icing on the cake."

"Your conclusion?"

"The Chinese are planning an attack on U.S. soil."

Collins squinted.

"How?"

"That ship was bound for their Houston refinery. Sinergy transports refined products all across the country, underground in pipelines. Easy to send dirty-bombs in separation spheres, all across the country."

"Shit!" Collins exclaimed. "Defense?"

"No ready or effective protection against such an attack. Never been attempted before. It's our Number One overlooked vulnerability. Once the spheres are in a pipeline, they're off the grid to anyone, except possibly to those who launched them. No way to tell which ones are threats and which are not. There could be a thousand or more."

Collins sat back and gripped the arms of his chair. He stared at Halsey and pulled himself forward.

"More?"

"Yes, sir, and it relates to North Korea, your second agenda item."

Collins motioned. "Go on."

"The North Koreans began harvesting radioactive cesium-137 shortly after their first uranium 235 fission event at Mount Mant'ap, or Mantapsan, on 9 October 2006. Transshipments of the deadly isotope by way of China began in mid- to late-2007. Possibly even with the triggers. However, there were numerous delays, some serious, during the initial transportation phase, over at least two years. We believed they might have been having major infrastructure challenges, such as moving heavily shielded assets over primitive roads and railways. Maybe some of the explosives detonated accidently, what probably happened to the cargo ship.

"By way of emphasis, let me say that what the DPRK was dealing with nearly a decade ago was, and to this day remains, an extremely deadly fission product nuclide. So-called 'atomic bombs,' both uranium and plutonium, produce cesium-137 in copious quantities. This 'death child' of these explosions, by itself alone, poses a persistent hazard to human life. Contamination by cesium-137 can render an area uninhabitable for decades.

"Our best analysis is that the quantity of cesium-137 powder that could be contained in and dispersed by a box the size of ordinary laundry detergent could kill 100,000 human beings within 30 days. And not one of them by a nuclear explosion. What we envision are many, quick, and massive spreadings of a fine cesium-137 powder over an area about the size of an acre of land, something that could occur with an explosive dispersive and render the area uninhabitable for a very long time. In my opinion, the explosion that sank the Zhou Enlai was an unintended revelation of the importation by the Chinese of the components of dirty bombs to be used against the United States, most probably utilizing our underground pipeline network.

"We're woefully unprepared for such an accelerating threat. It's worse than Pearl Harbor for 'shock and awe' and far more deadly. It's a potential nation-killer."

Admiral Collins stood up. He pointed at Halsey.

"And that's why you're going to Oklahoma immediately. I was informed an hour ago that MCAAP's General Benning has a covert, unauthorized, and highly suspicious rendezvous tomorrow in Tulsa with three Chinese People's Liberation Army agents. Your 'necessary intercept.' Get anything you can on what he's up to. I've called Commander Byrne. He's already out there. Take him with you for the intercept."

He handed Halsey an envelope.

"Here're the particulars. There may be more tonight from our men and equipment aboard the <u>DragonFlyy</u>. We're focused on both the Chinese and MCAAP."

As Halsey departed, he shook his head. Chinese agents and Benning? An inside job? A Rubik's Cube would be child's play.

CHAPTER 42

Tokyo Harbor

TUESDAY, 19 February – 11:30 P.M. JST

The Navy had a lock on surveillance aboard the <u>DragonFlyy</u>. Most of the high-resolution cameras and sensitive microphones were installed as regular "safety equipment" during the hydrofoil's construction. Navy specialists had adapted the signal transmissions to be uplinked in real time to an orbiting military satellite through the National Reconnaissance Office in the Pentagon. It was all part of the Navy's strategic "Rimpac pivot," its new focus on the Pacific region, especially China and North Korea. In case the secret transmitters for the cameras and microphones were ever discovered or otherwise compromised, the Navy had its own "eyes and ears" system that was retrofitted during regular maintenance checks of the boat.

As the <u>DragonFlyy</u> docked at Tokyo, 18 hours after leaving Hong Kong, ONI language analysts in Suitland were completing the deciphering and translating of the audio recordings from the 1,797-mile trip. They were the more important for immediate intelligence needs. The video would be matched with the sound within six hours.

There was a lot of small talk in Mandarin between the two men targeted. Then, they spoke in riddles, mostly short poetic selections from celebrated Chinese writers. But what riveted the analysts' attention was the repeated occurrence of seven words or phrases: "MCAAP," "Benning," "creatures," "three plus one," "tomorrow 1300 local," "Tulsa," and "Professional Styling." The transcript was sent immediately to Halsey whose newly formed task force had its own secured offices a floor above the ONI director's.

Suitland, Maryland

TUESDAY, 19 February - 9:30 A.M. EST

Halsey dashed into his office and waved his secretary to follow. He started checking off on his fingers.

"Get me to Tulsa this evening. Commercial's OK. I'm traveling as myself. Contact 'Bolter.' Tell him to pick me up at the airport. I'll stay wherever he is. There's a Navy Reserve security function out there tomorrow. That'll give me a reason to be in town. Bolter's officially on the agenda in the morning. Have him buy me a plain winter jacket and a ball cap, something so I fit in. For himself, too, if he doesn't have them. Tell him this could be a breakthrough. I'll fill him in when I get there."

Ten minutes later, his secretary was back in Halsey's office.

"American in an hour and 55 minutes. Reagan. Here're your boarding pass and carry-on bag. The car's downstairs."

Halsey grabbed the items and winked his thanks as he sprinted past her.

CHAPTER 43

Tulsa, Oklahoma

WEDNESDAY, 20 February – 1:00 P.M. CST

One hundred yards north of Saks Fifth Avenue, Professional Styling was a princely, eight-chair barber salon in Utica Square, Tulsa's upscale shopping center. From ornate ceilings to the Persian rugs, every millimeter was museum quality. Architectural Digest had featured three laudatory articles over the years, and The New Yorker wrote a 23-page piece in its Style section about the establishment's worldwide clientele and reputation.

Elegant Professional Styling was where anyone who was anybody came regularly for the artistic magic of Casey Thomas who'd moved from Hollywood in 1980. In Tulsa, he'd sculpted Elvis, Rick Nelson, Ronald Reagan, Garth Brooks, Matt Damon, Johnny Depp, and dozens of other notables. His starter razor cut began at $150. Thomas had regular customers who arrived in sleek Gulfstream V's and VI's for the unique experience. His institution was one in a million.

Precisely at 1:00 P.M., three lean, oriental-looking men in padded jackets and baseball caps entered the tony salon. All wore dark glasses. A fourth man, who held open the door, was similarly dressed. He hurriedly motioned his comrades inside. He was heavy-set and had pasty-white skin.

Fifty yards away, across a tree-lined parking lot, two men sat in a black SUV with darkly tinted windows. The vehicle's

Oklahoma tag was phony. Both focused binoculars on the door and waited.

"That's <u>gotta</u> be them," Halsey whispered after the four men entered the style shop together. "Should have had that place bugged, but we'll catch up with them when they come out. Hope to get some good pix."

Only an occasional patron arrived or departed while Halsey and Byrne watched. Most of the customers' faces were at least partially covered by scarves or the high necks of their winter coats. The two men continued to wait.

"Been fifty-five minutes, Catman."

The driver said nothing. They continued their vigil. Nine customers had entered and departed the salon in the last hour, but the three who'd arrived at one o'clock and the man who got there just before hadn't left.

Halsey raised his Black Ops Luminox and kept its sweep second hand in his peripheral vision as time ran out.

"Sixty minutes. Let's go!"

Both pushed open their doors, jumped out, and jogged across to the sidewalk in front of Professional Styling.

U.S. Navy Commander Chris "Bolter" Byrne was five steps behind Captain Halsey, his boss. As former Naval aviators, they were still known by their "handles." Both wore nondescript jackets and caps similar to those of the men they were following. Oklahoma casual, for want of a better term.

Halsey held up his hand as they drew closer to the salon. Both slowed to a walk and rounded the corner to the front entrance. Two customers departed as Catman entered the beveled glass door ahead of Byrne and walked to the receptionist. He tucked his hands into his pockets and smiled. Bolter followed. He picked up a copy of Elite Traveler magazine and stood by the door.

"Do I need an appointment?" Halsey asked the young woman behind a rosewood and glass desk. He removed his cap.

"Yes, sir," she replied. "All of our post-New Year's customers are coming in. Plus, we're closed Mondays."

"How about Mr. Thomas?"

"Mr. Thomas?" She looked surprised.

"If possible, please," Halsey responded.

"Oh, my." The woman hesitated then tapped her keyboard.

"Mr. Thomas is extremely busy. He's conducting a private seminar at Bellagio in Las Vegas next week. Let me see. Maybe ten o'clock a week from Tuesday?"

Halsey withdrew an iPhone from his jacket and punched in a few commands.

He nodded. "That'd be perfect. My name's Burlingame. Steve Burlingame." It was one of his three dozen, and frequently rotating, aliases. Each was employed for a specific mission. If someone attempted to contact him using a particular alias, Halsey would know the caller had taken the bait for that mission. No other Navy "spook" ever used any of Halsey's aliases.

"Telephone number, sir?"

"I'm at the Hyatt Regency downtown. Room 1120."

She added his room number to her database, then filled out an engraved appointment card and handed it over.

"Thank you, Mr. Burlingame. Mr. Thomas will see you a week from Tuesday. Ten o'clock, for one hour."

Halsey smiled his thanks.

"By the way," he asked, "may I use your restroom?"

"Certainly, sir." The woman pointed. "Through those doors with the brass handles and to your right."

He nodded and went in the direction she indicated.

Once he was beyond the carved wooden doors, he made a swift reconnoiter of the seven rooms in the back. Five were dedicated to washing, shampooing, and hair styling, and two were executive suites with polished boardroom tables and leather chairs, large HDTV flat-screens, full bars, and interactive high-tech AV.

Strange, he thought. For a hair salon?

He also found two large carpeted and marbled restrooms, the men's with shoeshine services. The faucets and sinks looked to him like 18-karat gold. A double-decker storage area was accessible from a sliding glass door off the restrooms, electronically operated.

Within two minutes, and without attracting scrutiny, Halsey searched everything. Cabinets, closets, windows, walls, and storage facilities, with enough time left over to check for trap doors and escape hatches. No sign whatsoever of the men. Halsey was pissed. Three Level Ten national security "persons of interest" and their host had simply vanished.

"We definitely should have bugged this place," he grumbled.

Catman sauntered back to the reception area, smiled at the young woman, and followed Bolter out the door. They walked to their SUV.

Halsey got in, pulled the door shut, and tightened his harness.

"Shit!" he yelled. He slammed his palms against the steering wheel.

"He walked right past us!"

Byrne frowned. "Benning?"

"Yes, Benning! 'Three plus one,' Chris! That 'one' was MCAAP's General Benning himself! He held the goddamn door. We were so focused on the three oriental men who went in that we didn't pay any attention to the non-oriental customers who left when we were in there. He must have walked right past us. Simple as that. Would have been nice to have ID'd him in the company of some very bad people. Yet we lost them, too. Must have met with Benning, probably exchanged something, money, papers, whatever. Then they all somehow left, separately, probably in different directions. We were so cautious not to spook anyone that we were just sitting on our asses out here. Then we forgot about that 'local-looking' man when we went in. Hell, he could have been parked right next to us. Shit!"

Byrne cocked his head and squinted.

"The guy I saw didn't look like Benning to me, at least not like his picture. The man at the door as the three Chinese dudes went in was the same man I saw walking out as we approached the salon. Pale white skin, yes, but big nose and ears. 'bout my size otherwise."

Halsey stared at Byrne for a second.

"Did you hear him speak?"

"No."

"A frikken disguise. It <u>had</u> to be him. I know in my gut it was. Who else was supposed to be with the three Chinese? Hell, he was their <u>escort</u>!"

Halsey thought for a moment.

"I'm going to go back in. Ask a question or something. I saw a lot of high-tech security cameras around the place. Maybe we can find out what kind of system they have, hack in, and still ID him. And his friends."

"Good afternoon, Hyatt Regency Tulsa. How may I direct your call?"

"Steve Burlingame, please."

"One moment, sir."

The room number rang. After five unanswered rings, the operator clicked on.

"May I leave a message for Mr. Burlingame?"

The caller disconnected.

CHAPTER 44

McAlester, Oklahoma

SUNDAY, 24 February – 3:45 P.M. CST

Donny Ray Pritchard leaned back in his office chair, his legs crossed on top of a battered wooden desk. It had been his father's, and he had used it for a couple of decades. It had brought "home" to his office. He stared outside without focusing. The hilly terrain five stories below was mostly brown and featureless on this clear and cold Oklahoma winter afternoon. The sun was already low in the sky. He usually didn't work Sundays, but this was going to be a busy week.

Pritchard was warden of the Oklahoma State Penitentiary. His new fifth-story office faced the southwest. At the horizon, above a barren tree line, he could make out the tops of several tall water towers at MCAAP, ten miles away. That is, he could if he wanted to, which wasn't very often anymore. His eyes filled again.

He had sat like this and contemplated a hundred times. He'd tried to forget what started on that day four years ago, a day with consequences that never seemed to end. He had finally taken ownership for his unforgivable sin because he had allowed it to happen twice more since "that day." He reached for the tumbler of vodka he had just poured, his fifth of the day. One telephone call, and lives had been ruined. He wiped at his face with his free hand.

Pritchard's job was mostly as a glorified civil servant. A furnished home with a car, occasional driver, and a decent salary for the two of them, then.

He thought about Norma. Her image used to engender warm feelings. Had for most of the 21 years of their marriage. Today, there was nothing. Thinking of her didn't fill the emptiness anymore. Couldn't, wouldn't, especially from the moment she'd moved out, exhausted. It was probably a year or so ago when both finally realized the emotional breach was irrevocable. It was ordained from that day. <u>That</u> day. He drank the remainder of the vodka in the glass.

Thank God their three children were grown and gone and had kids of their own. <u>They</u> still had a future.

"Prichard!" he heard himself yell. That and the fire alarm thought of the first telephone call combined to shake him out of his reverie. He remembered answering the call loudly with his last name, as he usually did. He had cradled the handset against his left shoulder and ear and motioned to Opal, his secretary. He'd asked her to report for work today. As warden, he was accustomed to these incessant, annoying, virtually always worthless, last-minute pleas from family and friends of the condemned before executions. Not that this one would be unique, although he sensed it would be. His secretary insisted it was important.

"It's about Jemison, right?" he asked, closing his eyes.

"Yes, sir, but not what you think."

Kenny Jemison of Tulsa was the devil personified. He had killed, dismembered, and eaten most of his wife, their two-year-old twin daughters, seven boys and eleven men over a five-year period, all within 50 miles of Tulsa. He was convicted in 2007 and was on Oklahoma's death row, his plea of insanity rejected by the courts. A nondescript bookkeeper in a small Tulsa firm at the time of his arrest, Jemison was suspected of murdering a dozen others whose bodies were never recovered.

Fifteen of his murders were committed in public areas, ranging from a shopping center parking lot to a high school baseball stadium. Three of his victims had been stalked for miles before they were seized, killed, and consumed in rural areas. No incriminating evidence of the perpetrator was left at any of the scenes. Jemison was arrested and convicted only after he was struck by a vehicle while fleeing his final killing. The DNA of his last victim was identified from Jemison's stomach contents. Truly, Pritchard had concluded, an evil man not of this world.

Jemison's neighbors told reporters the killer was a quiet man who lived alone and never had a problem with anyone. "We had no idea a monster lived in our midst," one woman said on camera.

Jemison had no known living relatives. His execution was set for five days from now.

Prichard picked up the handset and punched the flashing button. "This about Jemison?"

"Yes, sir," the caller, a man, replied calmly. "But I'm not an attorney, on either side. I'm with the Pentagon. We have to meet tomorrow morning. Ten o'clock, your office."

Prichard closed his eyes and turned in his chair. "Who the hell is this?"

"I'm Army Colonel David Walker. It'll all be explained to you in the morning, Warden Pritchard. This is a matter of national security. Believe me, sir, at the highest level."

For a second, Pritchard was silent. A toxic brew of anger and fear boiled up inside. He knew it was "that call," the fourth time around. He tried to say something, but words eluded him.

"Simply be there," the voice continued. "If you're not, sir, you'll be held in contempt and considered a Federal fugitive." Pritchard was stunned. He didn't hear the colonel hang up.

Pritchard's mind raced. He seemed to have no control over his reaction or emotions. The colonel's call had pierced his soul. Not just the words or the ominous tone of the man's voice. Pritchard knew exactly what was going on: It was the devil knocking again, and he had no strength to resist.

CHAPTER 45

McAlester, Oklahoma

MONDAY, 25 February – 10:00 A.M. CST

Pritchard had gotten to work early, even though he knew he wouldn't be able to do anything meaningful until the Army colonel arrived. He tried to accomplish some prison work, but all he could do was worry.

At ten sharp, Opal escorted Colonel David Walker into Pritchard's office. Two armed soldiers accompanied him and stood guard outside. The colonel was all business. At the door, he shook hands perfunctorily and brushed away the warden's offer to sit down.

"Warden Pritchard, I'll make this quick." He handed over a folded document. "That is a writ of mandamus from the Federal District Court for the Eastern District of Oklahoma and a immediate transfer order to the custody of the United States for one of your prisoners, Kenny Jemison."

"What the hell is this all about, Colonel? Jemison's on death row, scheduled to be executed at 5:30 Friday afternoon. There's no way…"

Walker interrupted. "Our van and armed escort are in front of the death row unit right now. The marshals are at the entrance there also. We expect to be finished here and on our way in…" he looked at his watch, "twenty minutes. So, Warden Pritchard, chop chop!" He made a cutting motion with his hands in the silence that followed. Pritchard thought he detected a smirk.

The colonel was off his schedule by a minute.

When the entourage of black SUVs departed the prison, Pritchard sat down and unfolded the legal documents. He assumed that everything was in order. It was, although there was no destination or reason given for the sudden "extraction." Not that they needed either. They never did explain anything, and Pritchard had always complied.

Pritchard's life began unraveling from the day he'd given up the first prisoner. His moral strength drained a little more each time. He hadn't resisted the taking of his prisoner today, the fourth. He had little choice, he reminded himself, but he did attempt to fill in the blanks in the immediate hours afterwards, initially from the Oklahoma Department of Corrections and the governor's office. The latter told him it was apparently a classified Homeland Security operation, on the Federal level, so there was little or nothing the state could do. The D.O.C. feigned ignorance but promised, oddly, to issue a statement about a delay in the execution of Jemison. That it did a day later, citing a lack of lethal drugs for the procedure. The department did not release a revised schedule or estimate for the execution. The governor was asked only once about the "snafu," an old acronym the media used generously for the postponement. She mentioned a pharmaceutical quality-control issue and went on to another subject. The reporters accepted her simplistic explanation. She never challenged the use of the word "snafu." Pritchard's calls to the U.S. attorney in Muskogee were not returned.

As the hours passed, Pritchard continued to ask himself questions. Why had Jemison been taken, and where? This removal was cloaked in Federal legalese, the first time for that. He remembered that he'd asked these questions after the first man was taken, a loner "lifer" without family who was never returned to the prison. Same for the second and third ones. All were blind alleys until the McAlester newspaper reported that a "creature" had trashed a local woman's home and nearly scared her to death. While he wasn't a conspiracy theorist, Pritchard was intrigued by the local whispers and blogs that "reported" suspicious activity at MCAAP involving the development of methods to control the activities of hominids, both human and nonhuman. He'd learned from a snitch that his three prisoners had indeed been transported to MCAAP, never to be seen or heard from since. He wondered what the connection was between Jemison and the puzzling activities at MCAAP. Actually, in his heart, he knew.

As time passed after the first taking, Pritchard, simply by living in McAlester, learned of, among other things, the comings and goings of sophisticated vehicles, the landings and takeoffs of various unmarked aircraft on a hastily constructed runway, and aerial surveillance of vast areas east and southeast of McAlester. The "base," as many locals called MCAAP, had indeed become a very busy place, and Pritchard's concerns only grew.

Pritchard was a law-and-order man, and he supported the death penalty. Nonetheless, his prisoners, even those on death row, deserved to be treated as human beings. He lived by that belief, and his gut told him that Jemison was being abused as part of the secret operations at MCAAP. He had only suppositions, but his gut was usually right. If what he'd heard was true, Pritchard had provided fodder for the devil's altar. Piece by piece, he began to accept that.

Jemison had been on his mind virtually all the time since the third man was taken from the prison. Pritchard knew Jemison was the perfect "subject" for Benning. His imagination only worsened his concerns. Over the past year, Pritchard's supervisory responsibilities visibly suffered and drew increasingly negative comments from a few of his associates, even among some of his friends at the Department of Corrections. He had also begun drinking on the job, at first at the five o'clock hour, then earlier and more heavily. His conduct was excused for a while because of the "pressures" on him that people had acknowledged. Pritchard's secretary Opal had been with him for more than a decade. She admired him, and she was able to cover for him, most of the time. At a banquet in Tulsa, Pritchard stumbled and slurred through a speech. Opal excused his performance as a serious flu virus he had acquired. Fortunately for the two of them, they were exonerated, at least socially, when Pritchard was hospitalized in critical condition the following day from a medically diagnosed and life-threatening flu virus. But there was no covering for him at home. Norma's father had been a drunk. Her patience with her husband finally ran out, and she filed for divorce. Being thrown out by the love of his life called for a toast, so he ordered more vodka, now by the case. His hallucinations waxed and waned. But mostly waxed. The precipitating trigger for his rapid descent into madness was today's seizure of Jemison and the real or imagined horrors that occasion entailed.

The vodka had extinguished Pritchard's psychic fires temporarily, yet it sank him further into depression. However, there was always another day, he'd tell himself before falling again into a stupor across his office desk. Each time was going to be his last, he'd always promise himself. However, this time he would keep his word.

Pritchard unlocked a door on the right side of his desk and pulled out a drawer. He lifted up one of a dozen fresh quarts of the clear liquid and poured a full glass. Time to put my promise in writing, he concluded, and he began a smooth cursive message. He finished it just when his glass was empty. He knew what he had written, but he couldn't read the swimming characters. No matter, he thought, it's done. They'll understand even if God won't.

Pritchard reached back into the drawer and felt around. He passed over the vodka bottles and found what he was looking for. He wrapped his hand around the grip of his Smith & Wesson .357 Magnum and withdrew it. He started sobbing.

He knew that God's creation was perfect and at peace. It had no cares. His own mind was the opposite: troubled and corrupt. Suddenly, without warning, the memory so well repressed overwhelmed his consciousness: he had personally offered Jemison to Benning for the "experiments." The other three prisoners just seemed to disappear. To MCAAP, he was sure. Of <u>course</u>, he was sure. Benning had thanked him repeatedly. The awful thoughts tumbled over themselves. He had seen the pictures and heard the audiotapes. His heart raced. There could be no forgiveness for him, ever. He hurriedly laid the barrel atop his tongue and pulled the trigger.

MONDAY, 25 February – 8:40 P.M. CST

It was getting late: going on nine o'clock. Anoli sat in her medical office and attempted to piece together the additional suspicious activities at MCAAP. Other than her desk area, most of the rooms were in the dark. If anyone came snooping, she'd say she was trying to catch up on paperwork.

She rested her head against her left palm and stifled a yawn. She gazed at her notes and shifted to her right palm. Her eyes closed for a second, then she jerked upright. She looked at her watch.

"Damn, they should have arrived by now," she spoke to herself. "I am <u>so</u> wiped out." As her eyes closed again in the quiet, she heard increasing and decreasing whines of jet engines. They were growing louder. She jumped up from her desk and ran to the long window of her office. Her view of the base was limited to a 150-degree sweep on the north side of MCAAP.

In the darkness, she saw lights of two aircraft approaching from the northeast. They were spaced for landing and descending at a steep angle. As she watched, two Boeing 737s touched down from right to left, east to west, along the north perimeter of MCAAP, on its medium-length runway. Both were white with a red stripe along the fuselage. With full flaps and thrust reversers, each aircraft slowed rapidly and taxied into a specially designed hangar built into a hill. The heavy doors closed.

"Uh-oh. More Janet flights. Second time in a week. Fritz was right." The first of the jets had arrived the previous summer and were observed by her husband and the boys from the pond south of MCAAP. At that time, the planes had landed on a flat grass strip. Today, they were welcomed by a special metal mat secured over the grass that extended the full width and length of the runway.

Anoli dashed to the northwest door of her building where she exited after displaying her credentials. She walked briskly toward the large hangar. She had tried to gain access earlier but was immediately blocked by a dozen armed guards. She hoped that the intervening months since last summer had lulled the security forces into a lower level of alertness.

Two protective zones blocked her path. At the first, she only had to show her base ID. At the second, she explained that she was the chief medical officer for the entire MCAAP complex of some 45,000 acres, an area larger than the District of Columbia, and that she possessed all clearances required to carry out her duties.

She was emphatic. She was here to make official the occasional transit of personnel and cargo at MCAAP between military aircraft en route across the country. Health and HAZMAT were her main concerns. The soldiers carefully read the front and back of her identification cards. They made verification calls on their cells. Surprisingly, they cleared her.

Anoli walked to the hangar. A small door marked the entrance. She went inside.

The hangar was cavernous. At least 100,000 square feet and 60 feet high. Two white Boeing 737-600s, their forward stairs extended, were parked next to each other. They gleamed in the metal halide lights from above. No markings were on the planes. The building appeared empty otherwise. Anoli walked around the two aircraft. She boarded first one, then the other. The window shades were up on both, and the planes had a full compliment of seats, so she figured that passengers, not cargo, would have been aboard. A quick guess was 150 each. She stepped outside the second aircraft.

"Are you finished, ma'am?"

Anoli saw an armed Army guard at the bottom of the stairs, his hands on his hips. His right palm rested on the top of his black sidearm.

"Almost, but I do have a few questions. Why weren't the passengers cleared as usual?"

"Ma'am?" He sounded annoyed.

"As the chief medic here, I'm supposed to be told who and how many are on these flights."

"Just technical stuff, ma'am," the Army guard said. "Classified cargo. No passengers."

"Really?"

The man glared at her.

Knowing that an argument would be fruitless, Anoli thanked the guard and left the hangar. She walked past the perimeter guards and returned to her office. Her curiosity was running amok. She wanted to contact her husband, but that was out of the question, given her immediate circumstances, not to mention his. She thought for a minute, then decided to visit the base dispatcher's office, where her friend Colonel Brandon Freeman was in charge. She glanced at her wall clock.

"Geez, it's after ten. Can't go now. He's been gone for hours." Anoli sighed and stretched out on her sofa. "I'll catch him first thing in the morning. Maybe I can get some sleep in the meantime." She closed her eyes.

All of a sudden, a crushing weight smashed her into the sofa. She could barely breathe. Before she lost consciousness, she smelled a dizzying odor.

As she awoke, Anoli's mind wandered in and out of awareness. She hurt, especially across her chest. She had no idea what had happened. She winced at the pain.

Her body motionless, she squeezed open her eyes. Her breathing was shallow. At first, nothing registered. She seemed to be on the floor and alone in a room. The lighting was dimmed. She slowly raised her head and saw that the enclosure was approximately ten feet by ten feet. Then she noticed the brass door handles. She lay back.

"Goddamn Benning."

She closed her eyes.

"Preening, arrogant, egotistical ass!" she mumbled before she lost consciousness again.

When Anoli awakened the second time, she recognized the detainment room adjacent to General Benning's nine-room HQ complex. She had seen it before, but not under such ominous circumstances. She remembered hearing about guards who had seized suspects and prisoners from Benning's office and had dumped them here. She looked up at the small window in the door. That's where they watched. It was her only source of light.

Anoli glanced around her cell. There was one chair. No other furniture. No pictures on the walls, no other windows, nothing else. Just a boring Army-green room. She sat in silence.

She knew it must now be very late, but they had taken her watch. She just wanted to sleep, but there was no place to lie down, except on the floor. She tried several ways to fashion a resting position against the wall, but none worked comfortably.

Finally, as she started nodding off, with her head on her arm draped over the chair seat, noises outside grew louder. They sounded like boot steps and voices. The door was unlocked and pushed open.

"Get up," a female voice commanded. Anoli heard but didn't initially comprehend.

The woman yelled again. "Get up!"

Anoli opened her eyes wide and slowly pulled herself up the chair legs. Three armed MPs surrounded her, two men and a woman.

"General Benning's ready for you," a man said. He was all business.

He motioned toward the door with his automatic weapon.

"Let's go."

Anoli squinted.

"Why have I been brought here?"

The MP indicated the door with his head.

Anoli stood up and followed her escorts down the hallway. Their pace was brisk.

Benning's office was two doors and 30 yards away. They entered. Only one of his three secretaries was present at this hour. The woman raised her eyes from her computer. A hand pushed Anoli forward into an adjacent room.

"Doctor Summerfield," Benning said in a patronizing tone as they filed into his oak-paneled command post. His use of her medical title rather than her military rank was intentional. He thought she was a disgrace to the uniform. "How nice to see you. It's been a while." He waved away her guards.

"Cut the crap, General. Why all the police-state stuff?"

"Now, now, doctor. Please be seated." He motioned to a leather-covered chair. "I'm sure we can clear things up in a few minutes. Then, you'll be free to be on your way."

"I look around and ask a few questions, which is my job, incidentally, and I get treated like a terrorist."

"My apologies," Benning replied. "After 9/11…"

"Screw the 9/11 security speech, General," Anoli interrupted. "That's been going on for nearly two decades now. Why the hell am I being treated this way?"

"OK, my dear, let me cut to the bottom line. We had a breach, of sorts, and no one's above suspicion. Detaining you was obviously an overreaction. Please accept my sincere apologies."

"What kind of breach?"

Benning simply stared at her.

Anoli pressed on. "All right, then, I have few questions. Will you answer them?"

"I'm afraid not, little lady. At least not until we have a better handle on things."

"But if…"

Benning cut her off.

"No, nothing. Sorry, Doctor Summerfield." He stood. "Oh, one more thing. I'm reminding everyone these days of that old adage, which is always good advice: 'Curiosity killed the cat.'" He walked toward the door and opened it. A soldier stood outside.

"We'll stay in touch," he said with an outstretched hand and a smirk. "One way or the other."

Anoli's fury rose. She wanted to hit him with an ashtray. What infuriated her even more was Benning's parting piece of political correctness: "Have a nice day."

She glared at him. "That's it? All of this for some Mother Goose shit?"

Benning had already sat down at his desk and begun to sort papers. A hand grabbed her shoulder. She jerked away.

"I'm going," she snapped, "but you can bet this isn't the end of this." She was really pissed, mostly at herself for losing her cool.

Anoli walked briskly back to her office. She found her purse under her desk where she'd left it. Not that it hadn't been searched. She palmed her keys. At her car, she opened the door and got in. The drive home in the light night traffic would take twelve minutes, another six to reach Fritz on a secure line. That'd be close to their regularly scheduled check-in time at midnight anyway.

Approximately halfway to town, Anoli decided to call her husband anyway. Her only thought was, this can't wait. She punched in their confidential number and code on her cell. Almost immediately, she heard a siren. She glanced around but first saw nothing. She then looked in her rearview mirror. It was a patrol car but not one from the local police department. Red and blue flashed from its rooftop light bar. She pulled over and waited. She looked at the side mirror. A military policeman approached. Military? Great. She lowered the window.

"Ma'am, are you Lt. Colonel Anoli Summerfield, and do you work at MCAAP?"

"Yes. What's this all about? Just minutes ago, I was an involuntary 'guest' of General Benning."

"May I see your ID, please?"

"It's in my purse under the seat. May I get it?"

The MP wrapped his hand around the butt of his semi-automatic.

"Yes, but very slowly."

Geez, "international terrorist captured," she thought out loud, but she dared not smile. She reached underneath and retrieved a small zippered purse.

"My ID's inside my billfold."

"Get it out," the MP said.

Anoli opened her billfold and handed over her base ID.

The MP looked at it carefully, both sides. He handed it back, then said, "Ma'am, you are to follow us to the base. Orders from the commander himself."

"Benning, again?" she asked incredulously, not really expecting an answer. The MP was already halfway to his car.

Anoli closed her eyes and rested her forehead on the steering wheel for a second.

"What the hell?"

She swung her car around and followed the MPs. They didn't stop for security at the main gate as Anoli had to do every time she went to work. Armed guards near a series of buildings 100 yards beyond waved her into an "MPs Only" parking lot, to follow the car that had intercepted her in town. Another guard in white gloves pointed to a space. She pulled in and stopped. The two MPs in the patrol car were at her door almost immediately.

"Get out!" one of them ordered. Anoli had no intention of defying him, but she was apparently too slow to comply. He grabbed her door handle. "Get out!" he repeated.

"I'm coming!" She shut off the engine and lights and grabbed her purse.

The second MP indicated with his thumb. "This way."

All of a sudden, she felt like an idiot, even, curiously, self-betrayed. The second time in less than six hours to be called in by the principal. Both times against her will. This time, it was definitely her cell call to her husband! She shook her head. At least this "interview" with Benning would take place in an off-site locale.

They walked briskly toward what looked like a modified Quonset hut. The seriousness of the occasion hit her again. She knew she wasn't prepared. She hadn't planned for this, at least not this early in the game. But, then, she really didn't know how far intel was into Benning's game.

Anoli was marched into the metal structure to the stares of other male MPs. One of her escorts was ahead of her, the other behind. The lead MP stopped at an open door and motioned her inside. She walked in. The MPs followed.

Another bare bones stockade, she thought. A plain wooden desk with an old "executive" chair on small rubber wheels, an open metal folding chair facing the desk, and a battered wastebasket. No pictures, no windows. She knew her place. She sat down. The MPs left and closed the door.

Anoli looked around the room then at her wrist. She sighed at her watch's absence. Oh, well, must be at least 4:00 A.M. Occasional footsteps sounded outside the door for, she guessed, at least a half-hour. She was still angry at getting herself into this fix. She had walked right into it! No pushing. Just a cell phone call at a thoughtless moment. That's what triggered the highway intercept.

The door opened. She knew who it was without looking. General Benning walked to his desk and sat down. He opened a file folder.

Anoli remained quiet. No need to start another futile conversation.

Benning stared at her for several seconds. The silence was oppressive.

"You don't have many friends, do you? Not here, or anywhere."

She had no idea where he was going with this. She shrugged.

"Your mother's not in the hospital. She's dead, right?"

"General, maybe I can help you out. What in the <u>hell</u> are you really asking?"

"You've never been known as 'Donna Wilcox.'"

"What? No."

"'Dottie' was a figment of your, or someone's, imagination."

"No clue, General." She shook her head. "Do you actually have a real question floating around that beady little brain of yours?"

"Why the call, and whom were you calling? Was it your husband? He's been quite busy at our expense."

Anoli took a deep breath. She didn't answer.

Benning leaned across the desk.

"Oh, you'll answer, Doctor Summerfield. For someone supposedly out in left field, just an Army lady doc in the sticks, you have contact with some very high-up operatives in the United States intelligence community, and way beyond your husband's level. We're tracing that telephone number you called. Probably to him. It's extremely well covered, at the highest classified level. You're part of something very sophisticated, but our people are the best, with unsurpassed computers at our disposal. Oh, we'll crack your codes and expose whatever it is you're up to. Your hubby, too. I'll give you one more chance. Why the call and who to?"

Anoli simply stared back.

"All right, Doctor Summerfield, or whatever your real name is, you're about to take a little vacation with some of our finest truth-detectors. You'll like them. They're doctors, too."

Benning leaned over his desk, and his tone of voice changed from toying to menacing.

"Whether or not you come back alive or in a barrel is entirely up to you, and, little lady, my money's on the barrel."

CHAPTER 46

Enid, Oklahoma

WEDNESDAY, 27 February – 5:00 A.M. CST

In the pre-dawn blackness, the Beechcraft T-6 Texas II trainer banked from a right base and lined up with Runway 35C one mile ahead at Vance Air Force Base south of Enid, Oklahoma.

"Roger, cleared to land, three-five-center," the pilot acknowledged the tower's instructions. His passenger looked out at the lights of the city ahead and tightened his jaw.

The Air Force turboprop landed and turned for the apron outside the base operations building. Once the plane was shut down and chocked, the travelers were met by an airman who escorted them inside.

"Welcome to Vance, Captain." An Air Force major stepped forward and extended his hand to the pilot. "Major Sweeney. Who's your passenger?" He nodded toward the civilian.

"Charlie Reeder," the forty-something man replied in a husky voice with a moderate Oklahoma accent. They shook hands. The major smiled. He knew that would be all he would probably learn about the man's identity. And Reeder was most assuredly not his real name. All Sweeney really knew was that the flight had originated at Andrews Air Force Base. Why they used a trainer common to Vance was something else he wondered about.

"Well, Mr. Reeder, let's get you out of that flight suit and on your way." The major gestured to a side door. "Your clothes are in Locker 407, fourth row. Here's the key."

Halsey gave him a layman's sloppy salute and went into a combination ready room and prep area. The lockers were angled, and the fourth row of units opened toward a wall, a semblance of privacy. He opened 407, unzipped and peeled off his suit, and took out the coveralls the Navy had left for him. He put them on. There was a winter work coat and an OU ball cap as well. Keys to the pickup were in a pocket, along with a wallet with his new driver's license and other identification. There were various papers and credit cards in his pseudonym and $255 in old bills. Even a rabbit's foot on the key ring. He smirked. "Nice touch, boys." Halsey knew from the briefing in Suitland the previous afternoon exactly where the pickup was parked. Changes of clothes and toiletries, all scrubbed of traceable evidence, would be in a suitcase in the cab. An encrypted cell phone was fashioned as part of an armrest.

Halsey left the ops facility and walked directly to a scuffed Chevy with numerous dings. His main job when he got to McAlester – his only job, as far as he was concerned, was to find Anoli. She had missed two calls with him. Now, as of midnight, three. He was arriving disguised as a worker at MCAAP for the replacement of a large water tower. That would get him into the facility where he intended to find, or rescue, his wife.

The 205-mile drive from Enid to McAlester would take nearly four hours in his fully fueled but 100,000-mile-old "loaner." It looked the part for Charlie Reeder, seasoned water tower construction technician with a lot of time on projects of 200 feet or more. He departed the Air Force base and headed home.

With 800 employees, Choctaw Steel Fabricators, Inc. was the second-largest employer in McAlester, next to MCAAP. It had been in business since 1978, when it was formed as an Oklahoma corporation by a firm secretly owned by the U.S. Navy as a post-transfer entity. The Navy wanted to keep an eye on the Army after being "forced" to give up MCAAP. Ninety-nine percent of the employees over the years, mostly members of the Choctaw Nation, thought they worked for a solid, closely held construction company that manufactured and installed oil tanks and water towers and had consistently done well across five states. Only a handful knew that Choctaw Steel Fabricators was today a part of the Navy's TF-7456 über-classified operation, whose boss was blue-collar, aw-shucks "Charlie Reeder."

As Halsey drove south on I-35, he reviewed, again, what was ahead.

He had flown into Vance AFB to avoid Tinker, his usual jumping off point. If he were under surveillance, and the Navy assumed he was, they'd surely be watching for him at Tinker. The pickup and his supplies had been delivered to the secure, lighted Vance parking lot by another "workman" a day earlier, and the Navy, which also trained pilots at Vance, had the armed personnel to guard it well.

Since MCAAP had an operating 7,300-foot runway that accommodated aircraft as large and heavy as a fully loaded Boeing 737-600, the Army decided to topple a 150-foot water tower that the FAA considered too close and a possible hazard. A larger, 200-foot structure would be built a quarter-mile away. Choctaw Steel Fabricators was selected to down the one and construct the other. Halsey was tasked to inspect the old tower before it was brought down. This would give him a bird's-eye perch for his initial assessment of MCAAP's complex of office buildings where Anoli might be imprisoned. Much of MCAAP was now off limits to most, even military personnel. That policy was less than a year old, and it bothered Halsey. He could understand a ban on the most dangerous sites where explosives were mated with bomb and missile casings, but offices?

He made the turn from I-35 South onto I-40 East at Oklahoma City. One hundred and thirty miles to go, a little over two hours, if his pickup held up. He was to report to work at noon.

As he drove toward the bright sunrise, he donned his aviator Ray-Bans. He continued to assess the challenge.

"What if she's not being held in an office at all?" he asked himself out loud. "There are hundreds of storage bunkers out there where she could be hidden. And what about the rumored underground facilities?" The more he thought about it, the worse he felt.

Halsey pulled into McAlester right before 10 o'clock. He'd stopped on the way to check his tires, but he was still early. He had time to drive around town and to have lunch before reporting in at noon. He shifted gears and motored for a drive-in restaurant. He hadn't been to Arby's in a while, so that's where he headed. Afterwards, he'd check in at Choctaw Fabricators to help the men get organized for the day's work ahead. He resisted the urge to seem too curious while motoring through his hometown. He was just one of the employees of Choctaw Steel Fabricators, an ordinary grunt. He'd sleep on a bunk at the facility tonight.

CHAPTER 47

McAlester, Oklahoma

THURSDAY, 28 February – 5:00 A.M. CST

The Choctaw Steel Fabricators bus pulled away from the company's yard east of McAlester right after 5:00 A.M. "Charlie Reeder" and two dozen other workers were on board. Today, they were scheduled to topple a large old water tower at MCAAP. Three explosives experts were also on the bus. Bringing down the structure would require four hours of their careful preparations and six seconds once the button was punched. The complete breakup of the structure would take two days.

"Hey, Charlie!" a man in back yelled. "Where ya been? Haven't seen your ol' ass in a while. Chasin' chicks as usual?"

Halsey, up front, recognized the voice. It was Ben Callingbird, his old Indian buddy during most of his undercover days at the fabrication facility. He grinned and gave a thumbs-down sign behind his head.

"Buildin' better stuff in higher-class places than you, Injun," Halsey, in his best Okie-slang voice, yelled back and looked over his shoulder.

The 63-year-old dark-skinned Choctaw who was sitting in the last row had no fear of heights and was perfect for this particular job. The Indian laughed and responded, "Injun? Is that a white man's term for 'Thank-the-Great-Spirit-these-savages-don't-have-tomahawks-today-or-I'd-never-need-a-haircut-again?'"

Halsey shook his head. "You old bastard. How ya been?"

Callingbird guffawed. "Chewin' tobacco and stayin' alive's 'bout all. You?"

Halsey shifted to face the rear of the bus.

"Done seven or eight towers up in Kansas. Almost got myself killed at Salina last fall. Damn strap snapped, but I caught myself on one of the riders and slid down. My gloves were really smokin'."

"Reeder," Callingbird yelled back, "you're so full of shit, you'd have contaminated two counties if you'd hit the ground and split open."

Halsey made a fist and pumped his arm twice. The older man returned the compliment and laughed.

The bus chugged up to the security gate at MCAAP, and the driver handed over his papers. After a brief perusal, the guard waved them on. The bus shifted into low gear and jerked forward.

The construction staging area was a mile inside the MCAAP complex, north of the main east-west access road. The bus braked to a stop on a newly laid gravel surface. "This is us!" the driver announced. He opened the door.

The men stood and started filing out. Halsey was the first off the bus. He jumped down and assessed the area. The doomed water tower was to his right, about a hundred yards away.

The aging metal tower, on a cracked concrete base, was darkened by vertical striae of rust. Originally, it had once held a million gallons of potable water, but it hadn't been in use for several years. It was definitely a hazard today. Without doubt, it couldn't be repaired.

"Let's go!" an assistant foreman called as he waved the men toward their project. "It's empty. Check the base structures, climbers up, secure the top. You know the drill. Everybody report back here in an hour."

Halsey was one of the three climbers. He tightened his harnesses and ventured forward. Two other men came alongside. He didn't recognize either of them.

"Piece of cake, eh, Charlie Boy?" the younger one said with a smirk as he rotated his head and shoulders in a stretch exercise and secured his straps. He repeated "Charlie Boy" in a mocking tone. Then he made some quick "I'm one tough S.O.B." muscle flexes. Halsey didn't like the man's attitude and obvious problem with authority. He didn't know the man's name, and he really didn't care. Might pollute his brain.

"Say your prayers, buddy, then say them again," Halsey cautioned.

"Right. You, too, <u>buddy</u>," the man retorted in a menacing tone.

"Charlie, I'm Bobby Ray," the other man introduced himself and extended his hand. He had a firm grip. "Ray's my last name. People think it's Bobby Ray something."

"Glad to meet ya, Bobby," Halsey replied with a nod. "Ready?"

The three scampered for the metal ladders at the base of the tower. There were two ladders at ground level with one-foot rungs, extending from the surface upwards 125 feet. The top of the water tower itself was an additional 25 feet beyond. It had its own set of access ladders.

Halsey and "Tough Guy" ascended the first ladder, hand over hand, as fast as they could. Bobby climbed the second ladder. All were in position at the 125-foot catwalk within minutes. Halsey would be loath to admit it, but the rapid ascent winded him. His fellow climbers were fifteen or more years younger and did this kind of work all the time. Desk duty definitely took its toll.

Halsey had never been a fan of heights. He was now at the very top, 150 feet above the ground. He exhaled and chose not to look straight down. He had work to do. After a moment stabilizing himself, he planted his hands on the metal surface and looked off into the distance.

To the north were miles of hills, trees, and scrub brush where, for years, hunters had brought down deer and other game native to the area. To the immediate south, left to right and paralleling the access road, was the new east-west runway where jets and other unreported aircraft had been landing. Beyond that was the massive MCAAP complex, larger than Manhattan in total area. To the right was the new aircraft hanger, then its complex of structures. An array of new three-story brick buildings with odd façades lay immediately to the south of the hangar. Maybe a dozen, Halsey figured. One had loading docks for trucks. Another had its own contingent of strategically positioned and heavily armed guards. Something or <u>someone</u> there was apparently worth the extra protection.

To the horizon and in a sweep from the east to the west were at least five hundred Quonset-like bunkers, mostly for explosives storage. There were supposedly hundreds more underground. Halsey noted several clusters of low-slung buildings under construction across his field of vision. He had no idea what they were for.

"Reeder?" It was Tough Guy. "Where the hell <u>are</u> you?"

Halsey looked around. He couldn't see the man.

"Here, on top," he answered. He intended that his voice sound annoyed.

"And what are you doin'?" the man pursued in a singsong manner.

"Checking to figure where this pile of crap might fall."

"Hey, Charlie Boy, get a clue. We already <u>know</u> where it'll go. Is that all you're doing with your lazy ass?"

Halsey was increasingly irritated that a man with such a chip on his shoulder could get, let alone keep, a job with Choctaw Fabricators, and he intended to find out when this job was over. He was about to chew out the worker when he noticed a flanged access port into the tank about ten feet away.

"Gimme a second. I see something."

Halsey carefully started shifting toward the port, step by step. It was on the downside of the round top of the tower. One slip and he'd tumble off the structure. He positioned himself so that if he rolled he'd at least have a chance to grab one of the metal hinges to stop himself. Hopefully, his safety harness would do the rest.

It took him ten minutes to descend to the sealed opening. He held onto one of the flanges and jerked open the seals and lifted the heavy two-foot-wide door. Almost immediately, he was nearly overcome by a noxious odor. Decay, like dead bodies.

"Why don't you join your buddies, Captain?" a laughing voice immediately behind him yelled.

Before Halsey could react, he was shoved into the opening. He fell and splashed into a warm, fetid pool inside the tank. He could see several floating corpses, many of them well decayed. Their continuing decomposition kept the lumpy soup tepid. Then, more laughter from above, and the heavy door slammed shut. Everything went black.

CHAPTER 48

McAlester, Oklahoma

THURSDAY, 28 February – 6:00 A.M. CST

"He pushed him in!" a man yelled from above. It was Bobby Ray's voice. "Shit, he cut his safety line and pushed Charlie into the tank!"

Callingbird had nearly completed connecting and tightening the 24-inch flexible hose at the base of the water tank.

"Bobby? What'd you say?"

Callingbird cocked his head and heard sounds of a scuffle and blows being struck.

"What the hell's going on up there?" he shouted.

All of a sudden, he saw a figure tumble past, arms flailing. The man hit the frozen ground headfirst. His skull exploded into a thick mist of blood, and his legs splayed awkwardly.

"Holy shit!" Callingbird looked away. "Holy shit!"

"That's him," Bobby yelled over the edge. "That's the son-of-a-bitch who threw Charlie into the tank. He'd probably have done the same to me if I hadn't knocked him over the catwalk from his crouch next to the opening. The guy was just looking down at Charlie and laughing."

"What about Charlie? Can you see him? Is he all right? Is the tank empty?"

"No. Uh, I mean, yes. I think Charlie's OK, so far, in about 15 feet of smelly muck. Looks like he's unconscious, but he's floating face-up. We gotta get him out of that liquid crap, or whatever it is, now! Might be no oxygen at all down there."

Callingbird knew he had only seconds.

The final step before toppling the water tower was to open a two-foot-wide drain valve at the bottom of the tank to allow any remaining liquid to be released through the hose to a tank truck nearby, often called a "honey wagon." He needed to get Charlie out as soon as possible, even though the initial hundred-foot drop might kill him. Unless...

"Pull the connection from the truck!" he boomed so all the men could hear, his hands cupped around his mouth. "Stretch out the hose. As the tower drains, let everything flow across the ground! Across the ground!"

The Choctaw Steel Fabricators men responded instantly.

Callingbird directed them to lay the exit end of the hose across a flat portion of the ground that was covered by occasional patches of dormant grass. The hose would extend approximately fifty feet horizontally from the base of the tower. The bend from the vertical to the horizontal just might slow Charlie's fall and save his life.

"Charlie will be coming through the hose fast, along with several hundred gallons of really bad shit! Get ready to first-aid him. He probably won't be breathing."

Callingbird prayed that Charlie's body would get properly positioned during the rapid outflow. He didn't know what he'd do if Charlie's bulk were to block the exit.

He yanked at the handle of the rusted valve. At first, it didn't budge. After several additional attempts and a couple of strong whaps with his wrench, it yielded, an inch at a time. Finally, it broke free, the drain cap swung away, and a gusher of liquid roared downwards into the hose. Callingbird choked at the smell. He bent over and attempted to catch his breath. During the 60-second release, he heard and saw through the translucent hose four separate plugs of something large descending with the liquid. He looked toward the exit end of the hose near the tanker truck.

"Holy shit!" one of the men suddenly cried out as the flow diminished to a trickle. "Three mostly complete but decomposing bodies plus Charlie!" A Choctaw Steel medic ran to the filthy but gasping man. Another worker quickly surveyed the area around Charlie. "Good God, there are pieces of fingers, and ears, and watches, scraps of clothing, and other stuff in here also!"

"Bobby, are you still up there? We have to get back to the yard with Charlie."

"On my way down."

Callingbird saw that Bobby was already about ten rungs from the bottom. He started down himself.

"Reeder?" Callingbird called out.

"Partially hosed off and already on his way to the bus," the medic reported. "But I wouldn't recommend sitting next to him." He wrinkled his nose.

"That dead son-of-a-bitch?" Callingbird asked when he ran up to the truck.

A man pointed. "Over there, in a garbage bag and ready for the bus storage bin. Looks like a road grader ran over him."

Callingbird signaled for the men to get onboard.

Minutes later, the Choctaw Fabricators bus and tanker truck passed through MCAAP's main exit without incident. Callingbird took a deep breath and exhaled slowly as they drove off the base. Job uncompleted and abandoned, for now. He wondered if plausible explanations could be found by Benning and his fellow conspirators and how much time they had to formulate them. Probably only minutes. They may even have rehearsed their excuses. Yeah, he was sure they had. He looked over his shoulder at "Reeder" who gave him a wink. Callingbird turned back to the front of the bus and suppressed a smile. If anyone already had answers, it was his Navy buddy. Yep, "Catman" would figure it out. He always does.

CHAPTER 49

McAlester, Oklahoma

THURSDAY, 28 February – 6:45 A.M. CST

Hands thrust into his pockets, MCAAP's General Thomas Benning paced back and forth across his office's thick carpet with its intricate inlay designs from the history of the Choctaw Nation, a gift of the tribe. His private telephone rang. He glanced at his watch and walked toward his desk. The screen indicated it was a secure call from the second rollover of his unlisted number. He picked up the handset and tapped in a code.

"So?"

"He's history. Dumped into the tank by Stipe. No way he could survive. Not only from the fall but also from the gases inside. Either way, he's a dead duck. You can cross that bastard off your list."

Benning frowned.

"You <u>saw</u> this?"

"You're damned right. I was observing from the top of the hangar, as you and I planned. He and one of his comrades, together with our man, climbed to the top of the tower. Stipe pushed him into the tank, just minutes ago. He reported he saw him hit the water, or whatever you want to call it. But Halsey's history, baby!"

"What about Stipe?"

"Thrown off the catwalk by one of their fucking guys. Dead, I'd guess."

"You don't <u>know</u>? Did they recover his body? Did he tell them anything?"

"Hell, they had trucks, trees and other shit blocking my view. I saw him fall, but not hitting the ground. The 150-foot fall to concrete-hard frozen soil had to kill him. I'll find out."

"But Halsey's in the tank, right? You're sure of that?"

"Yeah."

Benning exhaled. A mixed message at best.

"You going over there?"

"Have to. 'Local Emergency' call. You know the drill. We're on our way now. About five minutes to be on site. Full search. I'll call you back."

Benning wasn't finished. "Who called it in?"

"How the hell should I know?"

"What else don't you know that you're not telling me?" Benning's voice was rising to the "pissed off" level his subordinates knew was the tipping point before an uncontrolled explosion. The caller had planned not to report the departing vehicles until he had personally checked the site.

"I asked you a question!"

"Calm down. Supposedly they took some of their equipment off the base, not long after our man fell, or was pushed. I just learned that from the front gate. I'll find out when I get there."

Benning felt that the man was still holding back.

"Do I have to pull all your goddamned teeth individually?"

"All right, shit, it was the bus and the tank truck. Maybe a winch truck or something. That's all they took. They told the guards they'd completed the first phase and needed some additional or different equipment."

"And that they'd return shortly. Yada yada, right? For Christ's sake, you numbskull, they have Halsey, dead or alive, and they surely have our guy also. They're way ahead of us in this connect-the-dots game. Lots of DNA, too. Get me some answers.

For starters, where did they hide the bodies, so to speak? Or, better, literally. You have one hour."

"Yes, sir."

Benning disconnected. He stood erect and considered the implications and possibilities. Halsey was dead, probably, and our man Stipe had no history to discover. Didn't exist until he went to work for Choctaw Steel Fabricators. If Halsey were really dead, whether or not they had his body, now was the most opportune time to deal with his meddlesome little Army wife. Might be a two-fer. He lifted the handset and tapped three buttons.

"Bring her to my office!" He hung up.

Suddenly, Benning's office doors burst open. Three well-dressed men walked in with business-only expressions. His distraught secretary followed, waving her arms.

"General," she stammered, "I'm sorry, but these gentlemen insisted on seeing you immediately." She gestured awkwardly. "No appointment." The three had already formed a half-moon stance around Benning's desk.

"Thank you, Dolores," Benning said smoothly. The woman hesitated then nodded and left, closing the doors behind.

Before Benning could greet his visitors, the man closest to his desk extracted and opened a small leather folder with a photograph and a gold ID badge. He held it out so Benning could see it.

"We're United States Army Counterintelligence. I'm Special Agent Thomas Dunn, and these are Special Agents Phillips and Emmons. Where is Dr. Summerfield?"

For a few seconds, Benning was uncharactistically without words.

"Uh, oh, you mean our <u>physician</u>? And what might the little lady have done to merit this visit by Army Counterintelligence? She's a talented professional, you know."

"Sir, we have a warrant for her arrest. Where is she?" Dunn was all business.

Benning was taken aback at the speed of the encounter and the fact that they had a warrant. His smile turned into a frown. His mind caught up. A warrant? Arrest?

"Uh, she's here. At MCAAP, I mean. As a matter of fact, she'll be in my office momentarily. I've had my own suspicions, gentlemen, for a long time. Troubles. What is she charged with?"

"As base commander, you're entitled to know," Dunn replied. "But it doesn't go outside this room for now. Understand?"

Benning nodded vigorously as he sat down at his desk.

"Do you understand?" Dunn demanded with a finger pointed at the general.

"Uh, yes, of course I understand," Benning replied. Then he smiled. "Secrets are my business."

"For starters," Dunn began, "treason, espionage, and subversion."

"Holy fucking shit!" Benning exclaimed then frowned. "Excuse the language."

"Sedition and possibly a couple of other charges," Dunn added, "Several with the death penalty. We won't know until we get her back to D.C. Where is she, general?"

Benning punched his intercom.

"Dolores?"

"Yes, sir, they're getting off the elevator right now. Another minute or so."

"Talking about timing," Benning said. "I was just bringing her here for more questioning. As I said, I've had my doubts about her for a long time. Yes siree, a long time. And I'd get to the bottom of it."

Dunn stared at Benning who quickly averted his eyes. The other CIs made mental notes of their surroundings.

Benning's office doors opened and Anoli stepped forward, supported by her armed escorts.

Dunn held out his arm to stop her. He peered at her face.

"Dr. Summerfield?"

Anoli looked confused.

She nodded slowly. "Yes, I'm Doctor Summerfield."

"Ma'am, I'm Special Agent Thomas Dunn, United States Army Counterintelligence, and you're under arrest. You're charged with espionage, treason, sedition, subversion, and several other serious crimes against the United States of America. Do you understand what I am saying? Do I need to read you your rights?"

Anoli closed her eyes. She looked as if she were going to faint.

"No, sir, I know my rights."

Dunn held Anoli's arm as another man cuffed her. They left Benning's office and walked briskly for the elevator then the parking lot.

Benning watched from his office window as the three Army agents put the woman into their car and drove away.

He started to grin. Two problems solved. He really wanted to enjoy this, but something gnawed at him.

CHAPTER 50

McAlester, Oklahoma

THURSDAY, 28 February – 7:15 A.M. CST

The worker bus, a large diesel sewage suction vehicle, and a winch truck had pulled into two open bays at one of Choctaw Steel Fabricators' remote sites, for security. The unmarked building's doors were immediately lowered. Twenty-two men disembarked from the bus. The drivers stayed inside their cabs. One man ran to the bus from the sewage vehicle and, with Callingbird on board, helped Halsey get out of his seat.

"Did you get samples from whatever else was floating around in that tank?" Halsey asked as he shuffled toward the exit.

Callingbird helped him down the bus's steps.

"You know something? You beat all. You're nearly killed, I save your ass, you stink, and you're worrying if I sampled the ingredients of some Wolfgang Puck recipe gone awry. Well, screw you! I was a little busy."

Halsey scratched his sticky head. "How does some primitive Indian know about Wolfgang Puck?"

Callingbird put his face a couple of inches from Halsey's.

"He's famous, Kemosabe. We plan to eat him."

Halsey jerked away and smirked.

"Well, anyway, I gotta get out of this shit, literally."

Both men walked toward the company's locker room where hot showers awaited. Halsey continued to feel light-headed.

He was peeling off his clothes and looking at the inviting sprays when Callingbird was summoned outside by his cell phone's Lone Ranger ring tone. He'd wanted the Tonto version, but one wasn't available.

"Yeah, he's with me," Callingbird responded. "What?" Callingbird listened for a few seconds. "Geez, hold on." He ran back into the shower room and reached into the strong stream and grabbed Halsey by the arm.

"It's for you," he yelled over the noise of the shower. "You need to take it."

Halsey frowned. "Who the hell knows I'm here?"

He grabbed a towel from a pile on a rack, wiped his face, and wrapped his waist.

Callingbird handed the phone to his friend and grinned.

Halsey held the phone to his ear.

"Yo, Reeder."

"This is St. Jude's Hospital," a woman's voice stated in a monotone. "The family wishes to inform you that your sister delivered a happy and healthy girl this morning at 6:45 A.M. Central. Both are doing well. We will have more information shortly." The caller clicked off.

"Oh, Sweet Jesus!" Halsey gasped. He slumped onto a bench and clutched his chest. He felt dizzy. "Anoli!" His heart was racing. Tears welled in his eyes.

"Thank you, Dear Lord."

3.

-March-

ASHES. ASHES.
WE ALL FALL DOWN.

"The worst fate for the survival of a people would be the surprise unleashing of a Hydra for which no one was remotely prepared. A multiple-headed monster attacking across the land that, as in Greek legend, could grow two new heads for each one cut off. And this time, there would be no Hercules to save civilization."

–Author unknown

CHAPTER 51

Washington, D.C.

FRIDAY, 1 March – 12:50 A.M. EST

For Anoli, the previous 18 hours had been a toxic tangle of despondency and euphoria. She was exhausted. The Gulfstream G550 from Tinker Air Force Base eased onto the runway at Andrews precisely two hours after the wheels were in the well in Oklahoma. It was shortly after midnight, Eastern Time.

Looking back, she was already numb when the Army CI car rolled toward MCAAP's eastern border yesterday morning. Counterintelligence Special Agent Phillips drove, SA Emmons rode "shotgun" (Anoli had forced a smile at her apt analogy), and SA Dunn, the apparent chief of this mission, sat next to her in the back seat. The three men were grim-faced. She remained handcuffed.

"I suppose you're taking me to Lawton where they have the best brig this side of Leavenworth," she commented lightly to her captors, not really expecting a reply. She didn't get one. The right turn south on U.S. 69 confirmed her suspicions. The usual route between the two cross-state Army installations was either north or south from MCAAP then west to Fort Sill on one of three Oklahoma state highways. Some 200 miles and three-and-a-half hours, depending on conditions. She knew it by heart. She'd driven it dozens of times herself in all kinds of weather.

They'd been on U.S. 69 South for less than ten minutes when Dunn's cell phone buzzed. He retrieved it from inside his jacket, peered at the call screen, and answered.

"Yes, sir?"

He slowly slid bolt upright. He listened for a full minute before saying anything.

"Are you <u>sure</u>?"

The caller continued for another few seconds.

"<u>Yes</u>, sir," Dunn replied. "We're on our way. I'll report upon delivery." He tucked the phone away and slapped his hands on the back of the front seat.

"Make a one-eighty. North on 69 to the McAlester airport."

He waved away the men's questions and turned toward Anoli.

"Please lean forward, ma'am, and I'll take off those brace lets." He looked embarrassed.

Anoli could hardly believe what was going on. Dunn quickly removed the restraints and pocketed them. He angled toward the front seat so both Anoli and his men could hear.

"The charges against Dr. Summerfield were strictly pro forma, as was her arrest by us, although we thought it was the real deal." He looked at Anoli. "Sorry, ma'am, truly am, but we were only following orders. Those who arranged this extraction couldn't risk exposure of their plan to get you out of MCAAP as quickly as possible. You're not charged with anything. It was all a cover."

Anoli's eyes began to tear. She tried to tamp away the liquid with her coat cuff. Finally, she looked over at Special Agent Dunn.

"Sir, do you have a Kleenex?"

SA Emmons reached around from the front seat and handed her a small pack of tissues.

"Here. I've been fighting a cold, so I have plenty."

"Thank you," Anoli whispered. She extracted one and pressed it to the corners of her eyes. "I could just kiss you guys!" she said haltingly. The three men smiled.

"You might want to save that for your husband, ma'am," Dunn offered. "He has his own wild tale to tell. We're taking you to an Army helicopter that should be at the McAlester airport within minutes, if it's not already there. It'll take you to Tinker Air Force Base where a jet's waiting. You'll be reunited with Captain Halsey in a few hours. Seems as if you two are genuine Homeland Security VIPs." Anoli's eyes overflowed with tears.

Minutes later, the Army car turned off the highway and headed for a hangar where a UH-60 Black Hawk helicopter waited. It bore no identifying marks. Two pilots in flight suits without name tags or ID patches stood on the tarmac, plain white helmets tucked under their arms. They were airborne seconds after their special patron was on board. The 98-mile trip to Tinker was scheduled to take 34 minutes.

A Gulfstream G550 business jet descended through 39,000 feet over northeastern Oklahoma. Its identifying "N-number" was fictitious. An Army general in civilian clothes was its lone passenger. He would have company for his return to Washington. He had a thousand questions for her.

Four and a half hours after leaving McAlester, Anoli was in a suite at Fort Belvoir, Virginia. She had every amenity but a cell or landline, for her protection and security. Those who watched over her smiled and were most polite, visibly proud to have her in their care. All of them were armed.

Anoli's sense of anticipation grew all Thursday afternoon and evening. The solid knock on the door came nearly two hours after midnight. She said a short prayer, closed her eyes, inhaled deeply, and depressed the bronze handle. When the door swung open, her husband immediately wrapped his arms around her, lifted her off her feet, and held her so tightly she could hardly breathe. She finally tapped his back enough times to gain her release. They shared a long, passionate kiss that almost made up for all the missed connections over the past week. Finally, one of the military policemen in the hall outside cleared his throat. Halsey winked at the man, then he hugged his wife again.

"Are we ready?" Halsey asked the MP.

"Sir?" the soldier responded.

"To send you nice people home. Mrs. Halsey and I have some business to attend to." Everyone smiled and nodded as Halsey closed and locked the door and resumed directing his attention to his lovely Anoli. They kissed again and held each other tightly. Halsey looked at his watch.

"Omigosh, Sweet Pea, I have a meeting in six and a half hours. I mean, <u>we</u> have a meeting in six and a half hours."

"Then we'd better get started," Anoli purred.

Walter Reed National Military Medical Center

FRIDAY, 1 March - 2:05 A.M. EST

Noises, then words, but nothing intelligible. Or had he heard them, or something like them, before? Halsey couldn't be sure. Consciousness was an occasional thing. Memories? Dreams? Nightmares? He didn't know, nor did he have the energy or desire to force himself to wake up. His eyes remained closed. He hoped to find Anoli again in the darkness.

CHAPTER 52

Apostolic Palace, Vatican City

FRIDAY, 1 March – 6:55 A.M. CET

Several dozen yards northeast of St. Peter's Basilica, in the dark and overheated sacristy three stories above the snowy Courtyard of Sixtus V in Vatican City, Archbishop Auguste Desautels paced, mused, and glanced again at the large, ornate grandfather's clock next to the door. It was one minute before seven. The pontiff should have been here ten minutes ago, he fussed, vesting for his regular 7 A.M. Mass.

Desautels was a diminutive Frenchman of 80. It was both his personality and his job to worry. He was the Pope's private secretary.

Desautels sighed and resumed his pacing. The pontiff was late. He was <u>never</u> late. He usually arose by 5:30, dressed, and, no later than 6:40, arrived at his private chapel adjacent to the sacristy in order to pray, alone. At seven o'clock, for Mass, Desautels would join Pope Pius XIII, along with his personal valet, two secretaries, an occasional invited visitor, and four Italian lay women who worked in the papal apartment.

The antique clock chimed seven times, at three-second intervals.

Desautels opened the door to the chapel and peered inside. He hadn't done so earlier, out of respect for the Pope's privacy during his few minutes of personal morning prayers. The pontiff was bent over his kneeler in front of the altar, his face buried in his hands. Desautels stepped into the chapel and walked hesitantly toward the Pope. He leaned forward and whispered.

"Is there a problem, your Holiness?"

After a long silence, the Pope replied without moving. "Lepanto, Auguste. It is now our turn." Before Desautels could ask what he meant, the pontiff lifted his head and opened his hands. They were bloody.

Desautels immediately noticed the pontiff's face. He gasped. It, too, was covered with blood, flowing in tiny rivulets from an irregular ring pattern around the Pope's head at eyebrow-level. Desautels didn't remember collapsing.

CHAPTER 53

Walter Reed National
Military Medical Center

In 2011, the Walter Reed Army Medical Center was consolidated with the National Naval Medical Center in Bethesda, Maryland, to form the tri-service Walter Reed National Military Medical Center, the largest military medical complex in the United States. WRNMMC occupied buildings covering 1,219,680 square feet of floor space and providing 5,500 rooms for patients. In one of them, struggling to regain consciousness, lay Navy Captain Frederick William Halsey.

Halsey had been at Walter Reed for nearly 24 hours. He was in a special VIP facility within an unmarked, unnamed, and well-guarded compound built for and outfitted with the finest of medical and surgical equipment. One could undergo the most elaborate of procedures without having to venture to other parts of the massive hospital complex. The secret center was completed during the second term of President Clinton. Halsey was in Suite Three of six.

The staff knew from his monitored vitals that "Patient Echo" had drifted into and out of awareness for the previous five hours. He had suffered two severe concussions during his rapid, uncontrolled descent from the water tower at MCAAP the previous morning, and he was knocked out completely when he fainted and fell in a shower afterwards. Now, his eyes still closed, he moaned and spoke in slow, disconnected sentences. The only word he repeated was "Anoli."

Specialists, nurses, and other skilled attendants tightened the circle around Halsey's bed as their patient's recovery continued to advance. His vitals were increasingly acceptable to the physicians.

"What's he been saying?" one doctor asked as he came into the room.

"Mostly his wife's name, Anoli," a nurse stated.

All of a sudden, Halsey opened his eyes and jerked upright.

"Where is she?" he demanded.

A nurse quickly placed her hands on his shoulders and tried to press him back against the pillows of his hospital bed.

"Anoli!" Halsey cried out. He fought the nurse's effort. "What's going on? Where am I? Where's my wife? I was just with her!"

Doctor Harold Fielding took Halsey's hand and squeezed it. He reached around with his left arm and supported his patient.

"Captain Halsey, you're among friends." Fielding spoke with the calmness he was known for. "You're at Walter Reed. I'm Dr. Fielding. You're safe."

Halsey scanned the physician's face anxiously, looking for grounding, for reality, for Anoli.

"Now, why don't you lie back, sir, and let's talk." Fielding smiled warmly.

Halsey stared at the older man for a few seconds, then he settled backwards.

Fielding pulled a stool alongside and sat down.

"We're expecting Admiral Rourke momentarily. In the meantime, let me bring you up to date."

Halsey interrupted. "Start with Anoli. Is she all right?"

Fielding maintained eye-to-eye contact. "We don't know anything yet about your wife. We don't know where she is. We don't know the circumstances of her disappearance."

Halsey struggled to sit up again. The doctor gently pressed him back.

"But she was taken from MCAAP by Army intel," Halsey insisted, "then flown here. The phony arrest charges were just to get her out of Benning's clutches. She told me herself."

Fielding frowned. "None of that ever happened, Captain. You suffered two serious concussions on site at MCAAP and another in a shower afterwards that knocked you out and caused worrisome intracranial bleeding. You were in a deep coma when the Navy flew you to Andrews yesterday on board an Angel Flight Learjet. You've probably experienced some powerful hallucinations, but they weren't real. You're lucky to be alive."

Halsey shook his head. "I can recount her rescue, second by second. I saw it clearly. Benning's office. I know who was there and what they said."

Fielding squeezed his hand.

"You weren't even close to Benning's office yesterday morning, Captain. How could you have seen what happened and remembered conversations if you weren't there? It didn't happen, sir. It was all a dream, brought on by your concussion."

Halsey fell silent for a second.

"But I talked with a woman at St. Jude's Hospital about Anoli's rescue. She said it was carried out at 6:45 that morning. Yesterday. My old friend Ben Callingbird answered the call, got me out of the shower, and gave me the phone. Call him!"

Fielding waited for a second before he spoke. He maintained his calm demeanor.

"You didn't take a shower. A medic hosed you off on site and accompanied you to the McAlester airport where you were met by a Navy physician and airlifted to Tinker, then flown here. Callingbird last saw you unconscious on the ground at MCAAP, about the time you 'remember' being in Benning's office."

Halsey lay immobile, incredulous. He fought the reigning confusion, a maddening mixture of fact and fiction. He knew what he knew and saw and heard, or at least he thought so. It was all so <u>real</u>.

"But you just said that I received a third concussion in a shower afterwards that knocked me out and 'caused serious intracranial bleeding'!"

Fielding took Halsey's hand in both of his.

"No, Captain, I said you received a serious concussion in the fall through the tube. You did <u>not</u> take a shower in McAlester. You were never injured again after the fall from the tower. What you're 'remembering' is the brain's attempt to make sense of part nightmare and part reality, a common condition during recovery from a severe cranial insult. Don't worry, sir, you'll segregate the two in time.

"I <u>have</u> to find her," Halsey said quickly.

Dr. Fielding leaned forward. "You <u>will</u>."

"God...help...the...bastard...who...took...her." Halsey's words were like a metronome.

CNO chief Admiral Donald Rourke stepped into Halsey's hospital room at 7:40 A.M. He pulled off his winter gloves and tucked them into his overcoat. Two nurses were on duty, one on either side of Halsey's bed. Dr. Fielding was still sitting and talking with his patient.

"How are you feeling, Catman?" Rourke began.

Halsey shifted into a full upright position again and gave a thumbs-up. A handshake with his boss followed. It wasn't perfunctory. The two men genuinely liked each other. Fielding stood up.

"I'm Dr. Fielding, Admiral." They shook hands. "Captain Halsey's been pretty well banged up. Severe concussion, but, incredibly, no broken bones. He wants to be discharged today." Fielding put his hands on his hips. "In similar cases I usually advise three days for observation. However, from his present and improving medical condition and from what I perceive to be the importance of his mission, because of his being in this special suite and all, I'm going to allow him to leave in the morning, with some restrictions and daily reporting back to me tomorrow and Sunday. I understand his personal motivation as well, so I think he'll take care of himself."

Rourke looked at Halsey.

"Did you hear that, what your doctor said?"

"Yes, sir, but what about Anoli and today's meetings?"

Rourke sat down on Fielding's stool and scooted in.

"Listen to me, hot shot. We need you. Anoli needs you. But you <u>have</u> to be in top form. I can override the doctor's orders and keep you here longer if that's appropriate, so don't argue with me. <u>Listen</u> to me." He leaned closer.

"You stay in the rack today and cool it. Rest, let them keep doing their diagnostics and treatment, I'll handle the meetings and get you a complete report. I'll see you at our breakfast in the morning at the Pentagon, then on to the meeting with the President. Agreed?"

"Anoli?" Halsey asked.

Rourke thought for a moment. Then, he squinted and lowered his voice.

"We have a plan. That's why I need you out of here."

"No need to say anything else, sir," Halsey replied. "I'll behave myself and see you in the morning."

Admiral Rourke stood, placed his hand on Halsey's shoulder, nodded, and departed.

CHAPTER 54

The Pentagon

FRIDAY, 1 March – 8:00 A.M. EST

Army Lieutenant General Terrance King was punctual. He was usually in his Pentagon office at or before 8:00 A.M. weekdays, occasionally even on weekends. The chauffeured drive from his home in Alexandria took a maximum of 30 minutes, unless there were a major accident on Interstate 395, or as King had called it since he was first posted in Washington, the "Shirley Highway." Snow and ice delayed him a few times each winter. He always swelled at the thought that he was one of those "essentials" who didn't have to stay home on "snow days."

King's direct phone rang. It wasn't an everyday thing. He frowned, sat down, and picked up.

"King," he answered in his official monotone.

"Terry, it's Dick Barnes." King's jaw tightened. The Army chief of staff didn't make social calls, especially not on this line. He sat up.

"Yes, sir?"

"Airborne and Special Forces will be testing two new man-portable explosive launch devices at Fort Bragg. I want you down there as my personal rep. They know you're coming, special assignment. Formal orders are being cut. Take your aide. Look at the ordnance critically and outside-the-box. Ask them anything and everything. I want your honest evaluation. Report back to me personally upon your return. All right?"

"Certainly, sir. When do I leave?"

"Car's waiting. It'll take you to Andrews. They're starting the tests this afternoon. Sorry about the short notice. I just received the time confirmation myself."

King was surprised at the urgency, not to mention the mission itself. He once had only four hours to prepare, but never anything like this. That is, if he'd heard correctly.

"You mean...<u>now</u>?"

"I mean <u>now</u>." Barnes hung up.

CHAPTER 55

En Route to Suitland, Maryland

FRIDAY, 1 March - 8:45 A.M. EST

When confirmation came that General Terrance King was on his way to Andrews Air Force Base then to Fort Bragg, Army Chief of Staff Richard Barnes was in the backseat of his limousine en route from the Pentagon to the Office of Naval Intelligence in Suitland, Maryland, for the 9:00 A.M. all-day meeting with the Navy. He sat next to his aide, Colonel Bernet.

Barnes knew that King and his aide were already without their principal contacts with the outside world: their cell phones. That was the first order of business in assuring their insulation and isolation for the remainder of the "mission," a period Barnes initially estimated to be two weeks. He couldn't imagine that it would take longer, although circumstances were fluid. If the combined Army-Navy intelligence proved reliable, King might find himself using pay phones in Leavenworth for 20 or more years as he contemplated his betrayal of his country. Time would tell.

Barnes tapped in the direct number of another officer under his command, that of Brigadier General Thomas Benning at MCAAP in Oklahoma. The chief of staff had waited until General King was assuredly unavailable before he made this call. He knew that Benning's first call after they talked would be to his immediate superior, King, for information and guidance.

Barnes held the phone to his ear. He glanced at his watch: 7:45 A.M. in McAlester. The connection required two rings.

"Uh, Benning," a voice answered.

"Tom, Dick Barnes," the Army chief said brightly.

There was a pause.

"Why, yes, General," Benning replied, easing into his best Oklahoma drawl, "and how is everything on Mount Olympus?" He pronounced the word everything "ever-thaing."

"Tom, I'm placing you on a special, personal assignment for the next few days."

"Certainly, General, whatever you want. What ever."

Barnes ignored the faux syrup.

"Fort Sill is set to test the 10X-21 shipment you sent them on Tuesday. I want you to be there, on my behalf. That ordnance is critical for several of the scenarios we're looking at. It'd damn well better perform at or above specs."

"Oh, it will. It will, General," Benning replied with a forced southern lilt to his last word. To Barnes, it sounded like, "wheel."

Barnes continued. "The tests begin today. They know you're coming as my representative. Take your aide, as usual. I want your honest assessment. Dig in and get all the specifics, outside-the-box analysis. You know what I want. Call me as soon as you have something."

"Will do, General." Benning replied. "And just when should we leave?"

"Car's outside right now. It'll take you to the McAlester airport. A helicopter is standing by. They're starting the tests at Fort Sill this afternoon. Sorry about the short notice. I just received the time confirmation myself."

Benning was surprised. He'd had no time to prepare for any of this. He hesitated for a few seconds.

"So, uh, that's it?"

"Tom, you'd better be off that base and on your way to Lawton within 15 minutes."

Barnes terminated the call and slipped his cell phone into a side pocket. They were seven minutes from ONI.

CHAPTER 56

Suitland, Maryland

FRIDAY, 1 March – 9:00 A.M. EST

The arrival and handling of the seven VIPs was expedited. Four armed Marines with iPads and earpieces quickly identified and waved the men past the security portals and into the Annapolis Room of the director's complex of the Office of Naval Intelligence. The usual protocol involved a more thorough physical screening for briefings, but today was far from usual.

The United States Army was represented at the table by four-star General Richard Barnes, Chief of Staff, and four-star General Ralph McNerney, Vice-Chief of Staff. The Navy had four-star Admiral Donald J. Rourke, Chief of Naval Operations, and three-star Vice Admiral Raymond Collins, Director of the Office of Naval Intelligence. The third group represented was the United States Special Operations Command, headed by four-star Admiral Arthur W. Cabot. Under Cabot were 70,000 special forces, including the U.S. Army Special Operations Command, led by three-star Lieutenant General Tyrone "Ripcord" Washington, and the U.S. Naval Special Warfare Command, whose chief was two-star Rear Admiral Roberto "Shiv" Ochoa.

As soon as the men were seated, Admiral Collins rose. Two large blank video screens occupied half of a wall. A lectern stood in the center. The entry door was closed. Jets of pressurized air were audible as the door's seals were secured. Dimmed lighting shrouded all but Collins who had taken his position beneath two spotlights. Out of habit, he tapped the microphone with his index finger.

"Good morning." His voice was low-keyed. "I'm Ray Collins." The introduction was superfluous. Everyone knew who he was.

"This may be one of the most important meetings you will ever attend as a member of the United States military. I ask that you give your undivided attention to what is said and shown here today. Gentlemen, the safety and security of our nation are in grave peril.

"The Army and the Navy are on joint status with this. I will open the meeting with a short statement. Then, the Army will conduct its part of the briefing, led by Chief of Staff General Barnes. We'll break for lunch at noon, followed by the Navy's analysis at 1300.

"Navy Captain Halsey was to have been with us, but he's hospitalized at Walter Reed after the events in Oklahoma. We'll discuss those in the Navy's part this afternoon. I'm hoping he'll be able to join us at tomorrow's breakfast meeting before our appointment with the President. Halsey is responsible for probably half of the Navy's current intel for this operation. He's essential to our overall effort. Disturbingly, his wife Anoli, an Army medical doctor and head of the medical staff at the McAlester Army Ammunition Plant, has disappeared and is presumed to have been kidnapped."

Collins looked around the room. He made eye contact with each participant.

"It is the conclusion of the United States Army and the United States Navy, from information from multiple sources, that a major attack against the United States may be imminent."

The electricity in the room was palpable. Even Admiral Rourke winced, and he already knew most of the big picture.

"What we have learned over the past 60 days is that the People's Republic of China and other anti-American interests, particularly North Korea, and a renewed and united force of former Taliban, al-Qaeda, and other Muslim bad actors, are in a position to attack and paralyze this country at a time of their choosing this month or next, possibly even within days. What they have in mind, if carried out, would effectively neutralize every significant defense of America and render the nation powerless to protect herself. In my opinion, there has never been a graver threat to our survival."

The only sound in the room was the whisper of heated air passing through the ceiling-level registers.

Collins went on. "This, gentlemen, is a threat worse than Pearl Harbor or 9/11, its consequences are far more deadly, and, unless we can unravel the details of the enemy's plan over the next 36 hours and prevent it or counterattack effectively, the United States may not survive."

His audience sat mute. Collins stepped from the podium and gestured.

"General Barnes."

Army Chief of Staff Richard Barnes stood and walked to the microphone.

"First, you need to know how we got here. Even if you've heard some of the "accurate" scuttlebutt, part of this is going to sound like science fiction, but I assure you it's anything but."

General Barnes clasped his hands together and rested his elbows on the podium.

"On Monday, 8 July 1991, at a top-secret meeting in the E-ring of the Pentagon, the United States Army formally reaffirmed and reestablished General Douglas MacArthur's Korean War curiosity about and pursuit of the ape-like cryptid Yeti, as part of a comprehensive Defense Department analysis for manpower requirements in a post-Soviet world.

"The Army had considered a myriad of possibilities to augment 'force projection' in light of the new realities. Several classified comprehensive studies concluded that the eventual elimination of the Cold War standoff would lead to a larger U.S. involvement in conflicts that had been stifled for decades by brute Russian fiat and other political repression. The studies warned that these struggles would return and metastasize with a vengeance. Most of the Army leadership agreed, seeing no possibility of any reduction in American forces but, rather, a probable need for an exponential increase in U.S. worldwide presence, especially requiring specialized troops for the multiple and varied life-or-death missions the brass worried that lay ahead. The U.S. media and a large portion of the political class, to the contrary, celebrated the so-called 'peace dividend.'

"General MacArthur was a brilliant military strategist and leader but a deeply superstitious man. From the first time he heard tales about a large, elusive man-like creature, reported by societies for hundreds of years and called 'Yeti' or 'Sasquatch' or 'Big Foot,' his imagination was irretrievably captivated, and he speculated broadly about the opportunities for the Army, possibly even using some form of these animals as troop replacements. This 'creature' had supposedly never been captured, and most people doubted that it even existed, but MacArthur and a number of his cohorts believed that that was only a matter of time and an iron commitment to accomplish the mission. It was a statement the Army now made its own.

"Army Special Forces secretly trapped their first Yetis in January of 2002: two large males in a vast British Columbia provincial park northeast of Vancouver. Over the next decade, an additional 807 creatures were located and seized at a dozen sites across North America. One of the greatest yields came from the 'Oklahoma Triangle,' an area of some 1,750 square miles east of the city of McAlester where 233 of the animals were discovered. All were sent to the Army's Aberdeen Proving Ground in Maryland. The project was considered of the highest priority and classification, and its hundreds of operatives comprised an elite team of secret-keepers whose scientific effort and significance to the security of the United States, they believed, was rivaled only by the Manhattan Project more than 60 years earlier."

His audience members were shaking their heads. Barnes continued.

"After Los Alamos in the 1940s, no other military development facility rose as rapidly to the top of innovation and sophistication in the development of cutting-edge weapons as had Aberdeen. By 2005, fully one-fifth of the Maryland installation was off-limits to anyone outside the need-to-know research personnel and their directors. Aberdeen was considered to be the crème de la crème in the applied pursuit of military miracles. On a much broader scale, it was to the armed forces what Kelly Johnson's vaunted Lockheed Martin 'Skunk Works' was to the development of futuristic aircraft. Then, in 2006, a major sister site was set up at Oklahoma's McAlester Army Ammunition Plant, or MCAAP, pronounced 'Mac-Ap', until that time a prosaic builder of bombs for all branches of the military. Within three years, MCAAP became a Skunk Works on steroids. It eclipsed Aberdeen in all biotech areas, was massively funded, and took over most of the work on the Yetis. None of this was ever made public."

General Barnes recounted what the Army knew about the activities, rogue and otherwise, at MCAAP, the production and disappearance of the still-missing "creatures," and the unauthorized coordination with the Chinese of clandestine activities at MCAAP. He distributed copies of reports with highlighted sections. Finally, he reported the forced sequestration of Generals Benning and King and the initial plans to breech MCAAP.

"And we will make every effort to locate and rescue Captain Halsey's wife. She has been our eyes on the ground in Oklahoma. She's indispensable."

A discussion period followed. Even though approximately a third of the questions were deferred to the Navy part of the briefing because of overlapping data, a new "team" had been molded. The grave nature of the threat bonded the men. The hottest fire does indeed make the strongest steel.

CHAPTER 57

Northwest Caribbean Sea

FRIDAY, 1 March – 12:00 noon CST

The fast attack submarine, the USS <u>Oklahoma,</u> returned to the northwest Caribbean where the <u>Zhou</u> <u>Enlai</u> had exploded and sunk on 13 February. Its orders were to sweep a large area from the site of the sinking toward the southwest. A continuing analysis of the currents indicated that any lighter debris might have moved toward the Yucatan Peninsula and the eastern coast of Mexico. With luck, some of it may have been deposited on the beaches.

The sub had crisscrossed a ten-square mile area without success when it received word that Navy agents in Belize had located and collected dozens of small orange polyurethane pieces, the largest of which showed an outer curvature which, if extrapolated, would indicate that it was part of a large sphere. The agents estimated that the intact sphere had an outside diameter of approximately 30 inches.

Additional on-site analysis confirmed that the spheres were potential "dirty bombs": debris from them contained RDX, cesium-137, imbedded shards of specially treated Lucite, and telltale pieces of lithium-ion batteries. The agents could not estimate the magnitude of the overall threat, but at least ten spheres exploded almost simultaneously in the hold of the <u>Zhou</u> <u>Enlai</u>. It was anybody's guess how many spheres could already be in the United States. Satellite imagery of the Sinergy refinery showed at least 140 of the color and type. Others could be stored in covered warehouses or already inside pipelines en route to their destinations.

A Navy helicopter dispatched from <u>Gravely</u> collected the debris in radiation-safe containers and flew it to the U.S. for a thorough analysis.

CHAPTER 58

Suitland, Maryland

FRIDAY, 1 March – 12:55 P.M. EST

The seven attendees of the strategic meeting between the Army and the Navy and their special ops units returned to the Annapolis Room after a catered luncheon in the dining room next door. Much of the discussion at their meal was about Captain Halsey and his wife Anoli and what they had mutually uncovered, and suffered.

Rear Admiral Roberto Ochoa and Admiral Donald Rourke walked back together and stopped just outside the entrance to the meeting room. Ochoa eyed his boss.

"'Strict-9'?"

The CNO shrugged.

"Something Halsey and his inner circle cooked up as a nickname for their group," Rourke replied. "He thought it was good for bonding and morale."

"So, it's 'Sierra-9?' Whatever happened to our usual two-letter designator 'TF,' for Task Force, and three numerals?" Ochoa held up his hand. "I know, I know, it's good for 'bonding and morale.'"

Rourke wanted to wrap up the conversation.

"Halsey's original command was of Task Force 7456. So now it's called 'S-9' So what? Matter settled. Back to the meeting."

"Did he choose that number also?" Ochoa held his boss's arm.

Rourke frowned.

"As a matter of fact, he <u>did</u> suggest it. He said 7456 was a personal motivator for his new job, that it represented an attitude he and his team needed in their encounters with the bad guys."

"Like getting-in-someone's-face-big-time attitude?" Ochoa asked. "Someone who means serious business, on a life-or-death mission?"

"I suppose." Rourke reached for the door.

Ochoa laughed.

Rourke cocked his head. "What's funny about that?"

"The numbers 7456 in Mandarin, <u>qi si wu liu</u>, sound like the Chinese expression which means, 'You piss me off.'"

Rourke closed his eyes and exhaled. "Jesus! Well, works for me if it works for him." They walked for their chairs.

Admiral Collins took his position behind the podium as the others sat down.

"This half of the briefing will be a summary of the Navy's findings to date and our conclusions. Captain Halsey is rapidly improving and should be with us at our breakfast tomorrow."

Everyone focused on the Director of Naval Intelligence.

"As the Army pursued its bio-engineered soldier-substitutes, the Navy was on what turned out to be a related track, from separate intelligence. The Navy had heard rumors of the Army's 'Super Soldiers,' but we had information from contacts in North Korea that went well beyond and hinted at involvement by the Chinese in a sophisticated asymmetrical attack against America that might also make use of such creatures.

"The Navy's endeavor was bolstered by the discovery of journals kept by an F9F Panther carrier pilot, now deceased but who, in 1950, flew the photographic mission for General MacArthur that validated the presence of the 'creatures' in North Korea. Barney Byars, Navy captain and later American Airlines skipper, also wrote about his years of further research into the mystery and stonewalling, and warnings, he had faced from military higher-ups. The 'Byars Notes' were a multi-thousand-page treasure trove of information gathered over 40 years, with photographs, dates, drawings, and transcripts of significant interviews. They convinced the Navy that the Army was indeed onto something, but the potential Chinese involvement promised to magnify the threat by a factor of 100."

Collins left out the fact that the Navy had not yet found a second Byars safe that was believed to contain an equal amount of vital information. He went on.

"Strange but very public events began happening at MCAAP. They drew Navy Captain Frederick 'Catman' Halsey back to McAlester, his place of birth where he and his wife Anoli, an Army physician assigned to MCAAP, maintained a residence, the home he had inherited from his parents. Catman's father had been the last Navy commander of the 'base' before it was turned over to the Army in 1977.

"The arrival of unmarked transport aircraft, dozens of stainless steel trucks, the launching of hundreds of UAVs, and other classified, off-the-book 'activities' rang all the right bells with the Office of Naval Intelligence. Earlier sightings of empty coffin-size minisubmarines in the Gulf of Mexico raised the specter of a planned clandestine evacuation of finished 'creatures.' The Navy believed that MCAAP would be the likely source of the shipments, and Halsey was ordered to get to the bottom of the enigma. His effort was expected to do as well as Task Force 157, one of the most successful military intelligence operations in American history.

"Additional information, both direct and indirect, was received from North Korea that heightened the Navy's concern about a possible hostile Chinese operation within the United States. The Chinese had purchased from Venezuela's PDVSA an old, rusting petroleum refinery at Baytown on the Houston Ship Channel and had transformed it into the largest, state-of-the-art such facility in America. Today, it processes 730,000 barrels of crude oil each day. Sinergy Petroleum, China's state-owned oil company, spent $5.1 billion in improvements and was now the owner and operator of the envy of the energy world. The nearly four-square-mile refinery complex was the hub of thousands of miles of pipelines radiating across the country, carrying incoming crude oil and outgoing refined products. Sinergy was indeed in the catbird's seat with regard to the American economy. John Kerry, Secretary of State under President Obama, had welcomed Chinese investment in rebuilding America's infrastructure. The Chinese were happy to oblige.

"Navy SEALs have made several recent incursions into North Korea, officially known as the Democratic People's Republic of Korea, or DPRK. The SEALs were regular visitors to that insular hell-on-earth country. Over the past decade, they have been physically present across that nation more than 700 times, all undetected. The SEALs have recently collected proof, both data and chemical samples, of the North Korean involvement to supply radioactive materials that were transshipped through China. The purpose and ultimate destination were unknown. One of their contacts, nominally a guard at Camp 16, a prison camp close to the DPRK's 2006 initial nuclear test site, passed word that the Chinese were involved in a project to assemble 'dirty bombs' within, or at least to be directed against, the United States. The SEALs' most recent visit to a nondescript building near the Taedong River at Namp'o confirmed the threat.

"Supply ships make weekly visits from the Far East to the Sinergy refinery at Houston. Most make passage from the Port of Hong Kong in China, via the Panama Canal. All are 'shadowed' by United States Navy submarines. On its last voyage, as it entered the northwest Caribbean, the Zhou Enlai exploded and sank almost immediately. Its 'chaser,' the newly commissioned nuclear-powered Virginia-class fast-attack submarine, Oklahoma, surfaced and quickly discovered the presence of radioactive cesium-137 in the water. The Navy flew specialists to the Oklahoma within hours of the incident. They determined that the explosive RDX, more powerful than TNT, was also present in the deadly debris. The entire panoply of the events that night was enveloped in a fog of national security secrecy that remains in place today.

"In less than a month, Halsey's covert task force has grown to more than 30, all professionals he has known and trusted for years and personally selected for this mission. Now, he had the 'muscle' he needed to fight the diabolical forces behind the effort to destroy America, or so he hoped. Halsey remembered Christ's biblical prayer: 'Forgive them for they know not what they do.' Today, he was convinced that certain people knew exactly what they were doing. He prayed that he was ready to find them.

"The more the Navy analyzed the situation, the more we realized the massive scope of the threat. The Navy had tracked malefactors from around the globe, dozens at each 'marker' or terminus. From conversations of travelers on DragonFlyy, a luxury hydrofoil from Hong Kong to Tokyo, to whispers between and among freezing prisoners in North Korean barracks, we listened in. Our intelligence footprint was broad. Regardless of the sins of the National Security Agency, we were grateful for its services.

"Over several weeks, it became obvious that Catman's wife Anoli had fallen under the piercing gaze and suspicion of MCAAP's commander, General Thomas Benning. There were many reasons: He didn't like her in the first place, her marriage to a meddling 'Navy intel ass,' her incessant questions that were supposedly none of her business, and a dozen other just-because suspicions. All told, he considered her a mortal threat. Benning ordered her detained. At first, he wasn't sure what he was going to do with her, but he didn't care. Having her out of the way was really all that mattered, for now.

"When Halsey learned that Anoli had been captured, he immediately returned to McAlester from Washington via Vance AFB in Enid, Oklahoma, this time in disguise. 'Charlie Reeder' had worked undercover before at Choctaw Steel Fabricators, an 800-employee company secretly owned by the Navy to keep an eye on the Army's post-1977 operations at MCAAP. Reeder, whose credentials averred that he was a seasoned water tower construction technician, reported for duty in order to help demolish an old tower for a new, taller one. It was Halsey's intention to use his access to start the process of locating his wife and to expand his search on our behalf across the entire complex. Unlike the old days, much of MCAAP was off-limits to most, even military personnel. He had to play this one by ear.

"Halsey, as Reeder, was part of a team of 25 workers that included three explosives experts. He made it to the top of the tower but was attacked by one of Benning's confederates who shoved him into the tank that contained a gumbo of decaying bodies. We got him out, but not before he was knocked unconscious. Major concussion. He's at Walter Reed. Hopefully, he'll be able to be here in the morning.

"We're well into the planning to breach MCAAP and uncover the criminal activity there. I want Halsey's input for the particulars.

"Let's discuss the panoply as we understand it, from both perspectives, Army and Navy."

A red light flashed on the podium. Only Admiral Collins could see it. He pressed an adjacent button. Seconds later, a Navy lieutenant entered the room and handled a folded note to him. The ONI chief read it, then looked up.

"Gentlemen, we've found the second safe on the Byars property in New Hampshire. We should have an initial appraisal of the contents shortly.

The meeting adjourned nearly three hours later.

CHAPTER 59

Lawton, Oklahoma

FRIDAY, 1 March – 5:00 P.M. CST

Gen. Thomas Benning was furious. His temper had begun to simmer at the moment of his forced departure from MCAAP shortly after nine o'clock. He knew that many of his "black ops" procedures had been known about, supported, and even sponsored by his bosses at the Pentagon, and he took some comfort by reminding himself that Lt. General Terrance King was as culpable as he. However, the more he thought about the immediate matters going on at MCAAP, the higher his level of concern. Obviously, some important excrement had finally hit the propeller, and he was now out of the loop.

Benning had tried unsuccessfully to reach King by cellphone before the car took him to the McAlester airport for the 151-mile, 55-minute helicopter ride to Fort Sill. Worse, as they drove away from MCAAP, the Army agents had confiscated both phones, his and his aide's. That's when he blew up. Benning knew that physical resistance was futile. He was in one car, his aide in another, and three beefy special operations men were in each vehicle with them. All were no-nonsense escorts. His yelling of obscenities for the injustice being done fell on deaf ears.

The Sikorsky UH-60 planted Benning and his aide in a paved clearing outside a remote building on the huge Army base.

From his work overseeing the manufacture of all types of military ordnance at McAlester, Benning was familiar with most of the southwestern Oklahoma Army post at Lawton. However, he'd never seen this structure. It looked impenetrable, or, rather, escape-proof. He knew it wasn't the infamous Fort Sill brig, but that didn't make him feel any better. Immediately before he released his seat belt, Benning peered through a large rectangular window of the Black Hawk helicopter. There, waiting on the tarmac, was his welcoming committee: four armed MPs.

Fort Sill, a National Historic Landmark, was home to the United States Army Field Artillery School, the Marine Corps' Field Artillery MOS School, the Army's Air Defense Artillery School, along with several other brigades. It's also one of the Army's four basic combat training facilities in the United States. All of the heavy ordnance tested here came from MCAAP.

Benning was directed to a third-floor suite in the unmarked structure. He made small talk with the soldiers along the way, but his worry was on the bigger picture: MCAAP and what the brass knew and might do to him. If all of his concerns were correct, at best he'd face a general court-martial and life in a Federal penitentiary.

As Benning's suitcase and briefcase were being placed on a luggage rack in the corner of the living room, one of the MPs handed him an envelope.

"Your orders, sir."

He smirked at the continuing subterfuge. He knew what the bottom line really was: he was being held incommunicado. He had no way to reach anyone, not even his aide. He didn't even think of his family. Hadn't, actually, in a very long time.

The MPs pointed out the various features of the suite: a living room with sofas and chairs and filled bookcases, a large bedroom with a king-size bed, spacious bathroom with a whirlpool, complete kitchen and dinette, two writing desks, a fully stocked minibar, and four flat-screen HD television sets appropriately placed on walls and tables. Comparable to the Ritz

Carlton, really, except for the freedom to come and go. And, of course, to communicate with the outside world.

As the MPs took their respectful leave, Benning continued to think—and scheme. He was good at both. He'd start with Fort Sill's commander and his old classmate, George "Howitzer" Hollings. Time to call in a chit. He couldn't telephone Hollings, so he'd have to start a fire.

CHAPTER 60

Walter Reed National
Military Medical Center

SATURDAY, 2 March – 12:17 A.M. EST

Shortly after midnight, Halsey was gently shaken awake. He mostly had been able to sleep fitfully and had been staring at the muted television set on the hospital room wall, until the last few minutes when he had finally fallen into a deep sleep.

The nurse continued to rock him.

"Captain Halsey?" Her voice was soft but insistent.

"Captain Halsey!" she repeated, louder.

He squirmed and didn't want the interruption to continue. It was only hours before his release from Walter Reed, the Pentagon breakfast, and the meeting with the President at the White House.

The nurse maintained her motions. Finally, Halsey opened his eyes and saw the extended handset near his face. He sighed. No sleep tonight, he figured. He shifted to his side and reached for the phone. It was the secure line the Navy had installed.

"Yes?" he answered.

"Two couriers from New Hampshire dead!" The voice was emphatic. "Both Navy lieutenants. Decapitated. Package or packages taken. Their car was found by the Connecticut State

Police on the Wilbur Cross Parkway about a half-hour ago. No other information." The caller clicked off.

"Oh, Jesus!" he exclaimed.

Halsey held the handset against his ear for a few seconds. He fitted the phone back into its cradle.

LCDR Dwight Billingsly was in charge of the search unit on the Byars property in New Hampshire. Now, whatever he found was gone.

"Shit!"

He rolled onto his stomach, picked up the phone, and punched in a number and a code.

"Halsey," he barked when the connection was established.

Billingsley's cell rang three times. A voice answered.

"Commander Billingsley."

"Ike, did you just call me?"

Billingsley recognized the voice.

"No, Captain, but we found the second safe. It was underneath the Byars' home, in a tunnel off the basement. About half the material of the first one. A lot about the "creatures" and documents in what looks like Korean, plus more notes from Byars. I sent the contents to Suitland with couriers."

"Yeah, well, they're dead," Halsey snapped, more in exasperation than anger. "Dead, Commander. Shipment's gone. Now what?"

"We made copies of everything, sir. Front and back. On CDs. Some DVDs, too. I've already sent them to you electronically, as a backup. Secure, of course. I have the masters."

Halsey sat up. "You just made my day." He glanced at his watch. "And it's not even an hour old yet. Well done, Commander." Halsey's hang-up cut off Billingsley's reply.

Halsey thought about his next steps. Anoli will probably be right in the middle of the forthcoming MCAAP operation. If only he knew where she was and whether or not she was a hostage.

Halsey made another call, this time to his office at Suitland. He needed to start the process of analyzing the second batch from the Byars' estate, immediately. Because of the hour, he left a message for his secretary. She'd contact him within sixty minutes regardless of the time. Hell, she could reach him if he were on a far moon of Jupiter.

And who had called him at the hospital minutes ago?

CHAPTER 61

Las Vegas, Nevada

SATURDAY, 2 March – 1:30 A.M. PST

Three large refined petroleum product pipelines crisscrossed the subterranean world of the Nevada desert basin over which the glittering, phantasmal city of Las Vegas presided 24 hours a day, seven days a week. However, without what lay below, what had been built above could not exist, certainly not in its present form or expanse.

From ten feet below Nellis Air Force Base on the northeast, to the south and underneath downtown and onward to the nether regions paralleling the Strip, with its opulence and excess, to the huge arrays of buried tank farms over which Las Vegas' McCarran International Airport was situated, the 14- to 30-inch steel tubes pumped gasoline, jet fuel, diesel fuel, and other highly flammable liquids, also 24/7. It had been several decades since a pipeline carrying jet fuel had ruptured near Tropicana Avenue, spilling between 50,000 and 100,000 gallons in two hours that ignited, so few of the millions who visited this vacation destination each year were even aware of the hazard. However, several with long memories, and those focused on homeland security threats, were concerned that the past could be prologue. The next time might not be an accident.

Two men from China were completing a week of taking in the sights, sounds, and sins of this decadent metropolis, much as had several of Bin Laden's and other Islamic operatives in the weeks before they carried out their 2001 and other attacks against a debauched America. What these "tourists" had in mind, though, was not the next step in a cleansing process, it was the <u>ultimate</u> step. They nodded and bowed and reaped the respect only money can buy when it's put on the line, win or lose, at the casino tables at this "Mecca" of the gaming world. The men had brought $2 million cash. Without question, they were considered "whales," worthy of the highest deference from the moneychangers. They left most of it behind, happily. That only solidified their moral reputation with their Muslim partners: Lucre in sacrifice to Allah for the uncounted sins of the Infidel, many of whom had to die.

"Mecca" and "gaming." The Chinese men often smiled at the obvious contradiction of the juxtaposition of these two words from entirely different theological perspectives. Actually, they personally didn't care one way or the other. Only that the United States be destroyed.

One of the men spied his watch. "We'd better be going."

The other feigned surprise. "It's about to happen?"

The first man shook his head. He was all seriousness. "No, we have to make our flight. Patience."

The second man started to laugh. Then, both men laughed.

Their fishing, or finishing, tour was over. In truth, it was both. The first man signaled the Bellagio valet director who waved a cab to the curb. He handed the uniformed man two $100 bills. They departed for McCarran. They would sleep well on their way home.

CHAPTER 62

The Pentagon

"Did you get any sleep at all?" the Chief of Naval Operations asked his last arriving guest.

"Two hours, plus or minus." The Navy captain smiled as the men shook hands outside the secure dining room adjacent to the CNO's office. "I'm fine."

"Mostly minus is my guess," Admiral Donald Rourke grumbled. "Sleep deprivation. Just what the docs at Walter Reed ordered, right?" He motioned Captain Halsey inside.

The private breakfast at the Pentagon was a continuation of the gathering of seven, now eight, of the most important U.S. military leaders confronting what could be the most daunting threat against the country in history.

Halsey walked into the room briskly and returned the greeting smiles of the men around the table, all of whom outranked but unquestionably liked and respected him. They had already been fully briefed on what he had gone through in Oklahoma. They also knew about Anoli.

"I got tired of hospital food," Halsey quipped as he sat down in the chair with his place marker. The others were genuinely glad to see him.

Rourke closed the door and took his place at the end of the table. He remained standing, and he squinted at Halsey.

"How are you feeling, Captain?"

"Surprisingly well, sir. I'm good to go."

Rourke continued his appraisal.

"We're facing a 24/7 pace until we eliminate whatever's arrayed against us and get Dr. Summerfield back. No time-outs, no errors. We're already behind and barely prepared to get prepared. There's no comprehensive template to follow. Ad-hoc decisions will have to be right the first time. Are you ready for that pace?"

"Yes, sir," Halsey replied. "And thank you for mentioning my wife."

Rourke sat down, and breakfast was served. After five minutes, the waiters departed, the door was closed again, and the men began to eat. Rourke gave them ten minutes. Small talk was not on the schedule, so most had finished their meals when he began.

"Gentlemen, we have…" He looked at his watch. "Less than two hours before we depart for our appointment with the President. There's a three-item agenda before you. Looks simple, but it's not. Let's begin. Captain Halsey?"

The first item was labeled, "Byars Notes."

Halsey laid his napkin aside and started to stand up.

Rourke interrupted with a tamp-down motion of his hand.

"Please remain seated."

Halsey pushed his plate toward the center of the table and crossed his arms in the cleared space. He had no written notes.

"As you know, the Navy reaped an intelligence bonanza from the first cache of materials we retrieved from the New Hampshire farm of former Navy pilot Barney Byars. We suspected there was a second collection. Less than twelve hours ago, we found it."

Halsey looked around the table. The others were immobile and completely focused on him.

"It's at Suitland right now," he reported. "There were many documents in Korean. Because the late Captain Byars considered these items extremely significant, we've triple-tracked their translation and analysis. I should have initial conclusions by the time we meet with the President. They could have a bearing on the two other items on the agenda."

Halsey nodded to the CNO, signaling the end of his report.

"Questions?" Rourke asked.

"Captain, what's your gut?" It was Admiral Ochoa.

Halsey clasped his hands and rolled them back and forth. He took a deep breath and exhaled slowly.

"That this 'creature' matter is real, but it's not the main event. It's ancillary to something else. My opinion is, based on what we've already discovered, the Chinese are preparing to push radioactive weapons across the country through our petroleum pipeline networks, starting from their refinery in Houston. Baytown, Texas, to be exact. It could come at any time."

"So-called 'dirty bombs,' using cesium-137 as the radioactive dispersant?" Ochoa posed.

"Yes, sir," Halsey replied. "Imagine several hundred of these where they could do the most damage. Not in deaths or destruction but by rendering areas uninhabitable for a century. Manhattan, Chicago, Oceana NAS, the whole West Coast, any place accessible by pipeline. Virtually the entire country. It would be the end of the United States."

No one moved.

"Chilling," Admiral Rourke said, breaking the silence.

There was a collective sigh in the room.

"Seconds count, gentlemen. Item Two: MCAAP. General Barnes?"

Richard Barnes, the Army's chief of staff, looked around the room, glanced at his watch, then began.

"I'll cut to the quick. All of this started with the seizure of hominids in Canada ten-plus years ago, based ultimately on General MacArthur's conviction in the 1950's that such creatures existed, could be captured, and could be made into functioning non-human soldiers.

Barnes summarized the events from the first successful "chipping" of the animals at Aberdeen to the assumption by

MCAAP of the responsibility to supply several hundred operational creatures to the Army. The chief of staff took 45 minutes to mostly bullet-point cover the events at the Oklahoma facility, including the arrival and departure of unannounced and unmarked aircraft, the apparent search or surveillance flights of drones, the comings and goings of dozens of specialized trucks, the work of Captain Halsey's wife, Dr. Anoli Summerfield, her disappearance, and Halsey's "capture" and release. Barnes concluded with the announcement of the removal and detention of Generals King and Benning.

"Next step?" Admiral Rourke asked.

"We're breaching MCAAP early Tuesday morning with Delta Force combat squadrons from Fort Bragg. Our best intelligence is that there is a vast underground facility of some sort, a lab where the creatures were modified. From what we now know of the personal and financial relationship between General Benning and operatives in the People's Republic of China, we're expecting to find unsanctioned and hostile personnel from China and possibly North Korea. How many, we don't know. Best guess is at least a couple of dozen. We have to assume they're paramilitary, or worse, and they'll be ready for our incursion.

"We're going in to secure MCAAP from whoever and whatever shouldn't be there, find the creatures, and, hopefully, rescue Dr. Summerfield. We don't know how far underground we'll have to go, but there is probably access from the surface where we'll start. Those trucks weren't just making 180s inside a large building. We're assuming they were taking in excavation equipment and hauling out dirt. Based on our guess of the number of departing trucks, there's a huge room several stories below. Maybe a hundred yards by fifty, and ten or more feet high.

"It will be a closed assault. There should be no sign on the surface once we begin, other than the swift infusion of our troops. After that, it's all underground. We hope to get it done within 75 minutes."

"Questions?" Admiral Rourke asked again.

General Tyrone "Ripcord" Washington, commander of the Army special ops, raised his hand. "Let me add that every one our men has his specific assignment. We've rehearsed it a half-dozen times."

Rourke nodded. "More questions?" The men shook their heads.

"Admiral Collins?" Rourke motioned to the Director of Naval Intelligence. "Agenda item three: Sinergy?"

"That'll also be Tuesday" Collins replied. "Two simultaneous assaults in Oklahoma and Texas. We're set, but there many be last-minute adjustments based on what happens at MCAAP. We're prepared for 'spill over' surprises. Our Sinergy assault will be further and finally vetted tomorrow at Fort Bragg. It'll be a SEAL operation from start to finish."

Collins wrapped up with a quick recap of the Navy's intelligence timeline on the refinery, beginning with the Chinese purchase of the Venezuelan wreck and ending with the destruction of the <u>Zhou</u> <u>Enlai</u>. The primary suppositions still remained that the facility would be the launching site of remote-activated "dirty bombs." There were dozens of proposals to thwart the effort, but the operative method had not yet been decided upon.

"That's it," Admiral Rourke announced. "Time to go."

All eight officers stood in silence and followed their escorts. It was 8:15 A.M. Their meeting at the White House was set for 9:00 A.M. sharp. A heavily armed convoy of three vehicles awaited them for the quick drive into the District.

CHAPTER 63

The White House

The cold north wind was fierce as a half-dozen uniformed Secret Service officers in winter gear jogged from the gate to keep up, and to attempt to stay warm. Two black SUVs slowed and braked to a stop at the South Portico precisely at 8:55 A.M. A third SUV carrying armed Pentagon security forces remained at the Southeast Gate at Hamilton Place.

Eight military men stepped out of the vans and were shepherded by Presidential Protective Division Secret Service agents toward the White House entrance: Army Generals Richard Barnes, Ralph McNerney, and Tyrone Washington, Navy Admirals Donald Rourke, Raymond Collins, Arthur Cabot, and Roberto Ochoa, and Navy Captain Frederick Halsey. A second group of PPD agents motioned the visitors into the Diplomatic Reception Room where they would meet with the President.

As they walked in and were escorted to their places, the men saw they weren't alone. Already at the table were the Secretary of Defense, Chairman of the Joint Chiefs, the Commandant of the Marine Corps, and the Chief of Staff of the Air Force. The President, Halsey mused, had obviously arranged a full-court press. The two groups recognized and acknowledged each another.

The President walked in at exactly 9:00 A.M. Everyone stood.

"Good morning. Please be seated." He began the meeting immediately.

"Over the past two months, I have become increasingly aware of, involved in, and alarmed by the developments that have brought us together today. Except for Captain Halsey, I have spoken with all of you personally. For a few of you, many times more than once. I have read all of your reports to me.

"Let me summarize what I have learned and am prepared to act on, beginning with the immediate situation, then working backwards in time. At the conclusion, I'd like to hear anything that varies from my narrative and any particulars you feel need to be discussed in more detail. We must be of one mind before we leave this room. No relevant question or concern is too small. The stakes are too high."

The President looked around the room and made sure from their expressions that he had their full attention.

"Today, we face a potential nation-ending threat from a dedicated cabal that includes operatives from China, North Korea, and Islamic militias associated with and/or evolved from the Taliban, al-Qaeda, ISIS, and several other malevolent, anti-Western groups in the Middle East that will not stop short of destroying the United States and the rest of Western civilization, to the last human being."

The room was completely silent.

"With access to nuclear weapons, rapid recruitment of hoards of fanatics, and ample funding from a host of other bad players, combined with many opportunities to act, this is not an 'if' matter, it's a 'when.' Based on current intelligence, from you and other agencies here and abroad, that 'when' could literally begin within hours."

The President paused. No one moved.

"We have to deal first with the tip of the spear aimed at the heart of America and work our way down to secondary threats as fast as possible. From your briefings, I see two simultaneous steps: neutralizing what's going on at MCAAP in Oklahoma and the Sinergy refinery menace in Texas, both within the next two to three days. They are intertwined in ways we don't fully understand, but we can't wait for an academic study. There is more than enough worrisome evidence for us to act now. Studies are a luxury for history. If we don't stop this movement quickly, there might not be any history to write about."

The President's exclusive audience had hands-on control of the military might of the entire nation. Orders from the Commander in Chief through the SecDef to these force commanders would produce fast results. What usually took a massive bureaucracy days if not weeks even to initiate could be accomplished in minutes with a direct communication from any one of these men. Each knew that what lay ahead would demand the highest level of competence, action, and speed.

"My responsibility," the President continued, "is to lay out a strategy; the tactics are yours. However, because of the magnitude of the threat, for this mission I want your involvement in the former as well, and I will expect to be involved actively in its execution. Too much is at stake for us to short-change any part of the operation.

"As I mentioned, there are two principal parts to our focus: MCAAP and Sinergy."

The President stopped abruptly and looked around the table.

"Because of Captain Halsey's role to date, I've asked him to be my liaison, on a par with the combatant commanders. He won't be responsible for designing operations, the strategy, but he will have a strong role in their execution, the tactics. Not quite a "primus inter pares" role, but awfully close. Is that clear?"

The men nodded.

The President looked at Halsey.

"Captain, are you certain you are healthy and ready to participate fully in these activities?"

"I am, Mr. President."

"Very good. I accept you at your word. I want to assure you that the United States will do everything in its power to return you wife to you safe, sound, and soon. To me, she represents all Americans especially since all Americans are threatened by these diabolical forces. I personally will do whatever I can to reunite you with her as soon as humanly possible.

Halsey nodded. "Thank you, sir."

After a few seconds, the President went on.

"Three other matters:

"First, 'Eve,' the North Korean prisoner. He was to be here today, but we couldn't get him out of the DPRK in time. He escaped from Camp 16 and just made it to Honolulu a few hours ago. We have his statements. He's told us everything he knows. He saw the 'creatures' at the 2006 nuclear test site, and he overheard conversations about the Chinese installation at MCAAP where the chip work was being done.

"Second, there has been extensive work done at MCAAP which has continuously tied that facility to Sinergy. A pipeline that was constructed in the 1940s connected the two and has been vastly improved over the years. It's now a 30-inch composite conduit inside the original pipeline. Initially, in the '40s, it brought petroleum products from the Gulf Coast to service the Army facility in Oklahoma. More recently, it was refurbished with what we estimate was at least a quarter of a billion dollars from the Chinese to provide two-way transportation between the two sites. It appears that it now allows the passage of the so-called 'creatures' and other contraband from and between the two facilities.

"The 'creatures' are missing. Although they could still be at MCAAP, they probably have been transported to Texas, to be segregated along with the spheres, pig nukes, possibly even the UAVs.

"We must go forward," the President stated. "What we face today is a second Lepanto." He paused. The first was the battle in 1571 that saved the West from the Ottoman Turkish hoards. The Pope was right. The end of civilization is not acceptable.

"And third, I understand that Boeing is working overtime to modify the P-8As to detect and disarm the 'dirty bombs.' I want to be kept up-to-the-minute with this. Admiral Rourke, will you keep me advised?"

"Absolutely, sir," the CNO replied. "They're well underway at Pax River. I'll give you a report later today."

"Thank you, Admiral. Any further comments about what we've discussed here this morning?"

No one said anything.

The President rose from his chair.

"Then, let's get this show on the road."

CHAPTER 64

The White House

SATURDAY, 2 March – 10:30 A.M. EST

As Army Chief of Staff Richard Barnes walked toward the door of the South Portico, he received a silent vibrating alert. His special encrypted cell phone was reset daily to be accessible only to those who had his unique code. Today there were four individuals on that list.

Barnes quickly extracted the phone from inside his jacket. The red micro-light flashed twice every three seconds. He knew who it was without looking closer. It was a call he wasn't expecting: General Hardesty at Fort Bragg from where the Special Forces would deploy to McAlester. Hardesty was supposed to call only if there were a problem, not a routine update.

"I'm leaving the meeting with the President right now, Roger," Barnes answered quickly. "Special Forces?"

"No, sir. General King just killed himself."

Barnes stopped in his tracks. He was incredulous.

"What?"

"He's dead, sir."

Barnes was shocked. He repeated the message.

"King killed himself?"

"With his robe belt over the showerhead. We don't have video coverage in the bathrooms. Our people found him because he pressed the 'panic button' on the wall more than an hour earlier. He's been doing that every daylight hour on the hour since he got here. All false alarms, probably to condition us, 'crying wolf' and all. They didn't get to him for an hour and six minutes after he missed his last call. Couldn't resuscitate him."

Barnes rubbed his forehead and closed his eyes.

"I'll call you back."

CHAPTER 65

Suitland, Maryland

SATURDAY, 2 March - 6:20 P.M. EST

Five men entered the Suitland Federal Center in Prince George's County, Maryland. Two Navy admirals were accompanied by three senior engineers from Boeing Defense, Space & Security, or "BDS" as insiders called it. All were based at Naval Air Station Patuxent River, 65 miles southeast of Washington. Their full-spectrum, combined responsibilities included research, acquisition, development, testing, evaluating, and support of technologies and systems for Naval aviation. Today's meeting at the Office of Naval Intelligence ranked at the top of any agenda Pax River had ever had.

Halsey stood at the door to the conference room as the group approached. They acknowledged his curt greeting as he motioned them inside. Halsey knew from their forwarded orders that the two Navy were Vice Admiral Lyle Hunter, head of Naval Air Systems Command, known as NAVAIR, and Rear Admiral Jerry Monahan, commander of Naval Air Warfare Center Aircraft Division, NAWCAD. The three specialists accompanying them had led Boeing's Pax River efforts to facilitate the entry of the P-8A Poseidons into the Navy fleet. Four-star Admiral Donald Rourke, Chief of Naval Operations, was the last to enter. Halsey closed and secured the door.

Admiral Rourke positioned himself at the end of the table and welcomed his guests.

"Because of the accelerating developments, we have one hour to get on the same page with regard to all necessary upgrades to the Poseidon. We have one shot at this; there is no second take. I understand that a lot of it has already been accomplished by Boeing in Renton, Washington, and by you gentlemen at Pax River. We have to be assured all of it is covered, understood, and accepted. All modifications have to be installed with full and final testing underway within the next 24 hours.

"Because of Captain Halsey's comprehensive knowledge of and experience with this entire matter, the President has selected him as liaison to coordinate the counteroffensive necessary to defend against and eliminate this threat. He will be the point man to the Commander in Chief for both the Army and the Navy. The President himself will alert Homeland Security and the Coast Guard. This operation will be swift, conducted in a surgical fashion in several locations across a large part of the south central United States, and it must succeed. The actual timing remains classified. All I can say is that it will happen soon.

"Halsey won't be in the higher command structure per se, but he has many unique abilities and insights that led to the President's choosing him for this role. Please give him your complete support." Rourke did not mention Halsey's missing wife.

"Navy Captain Halsey," the CNO announced.

Under ordinary circumstances, addressing a four-star, a three-, and a two-star admiral, in addition to being the spokesman with plans and, supposedly, answers to such a challenge, would have been daunting for any Navy captain. Today, however, was not ordinary, and Halsey was fixated on his mission. As soon as Admiral Rourke sat down, he began without introductions.

"Gentlemen, we have a very short fuse. Renton's already on the line."

Halsey tapped up the volume on a speaker at the middle of the table.

"Renton, can you hear me? It's Captain Halsey."

"Loud and clear, Captain. I'm Dr. Marshall Boseman, Boeing's BDS chief for this project."

"Are your people ready?" Halsey asked.

"Yes, sir. There are seven of us here who've been involved 24/7 with the Poseidon and its Navy introduction and the latest upgrades. We're up to speed with the task at hand, as are, of course, our three BDS engineers there from Pax River."

"Thank you all for being with us this evening," Halsey replied with an acknowledging nod to the Boeing men at the table. "Doctor, please give us a quick update on the program."

Boseman began, "Boeing developed the P-8A Poseidon for the Navy as a special military derivative of the 737-800. It was designed to replace the Lockheed P-3 Orion anti-submarine warfare aircraft that's been in service since 1962. More complex ASW needs called for a larger, faster, and more adaptable aircraft than the turboprop. The new plane was designed to interdict shipping, engage in electronic intelligence and surveillance, carry torpedoes, depth charges, anti-ship missiles, drop and monitor sonobuoys, and to adapt to a myriad of other uses such as carrying, controlling, and monitoring unmanned aerial vehicles. Our first aircraft were operating for the Navy in 2013, and the new fleet is expected to grow rapidly to over 100, possibly as many as 120.

"The original prototype of the P-8 called for the inclusion of magnetic anomaly detection equipment. However, the Navy deleted the MAD requirement in 2008 because of weight considerations. They said the extra 3,500 pounds would shorten the plane's effective range and endurance. The Navy also believed that its new onboard hydrocarbon sensors would be an effective substitute. Boeing engineers, however, were convinced that there were many other uses of the MAD equipment, especially with an improved version. They continued development work separately, without a contract. Within a year, they had produced enhanced MAD composite pod units that measured four feet in length and weighed less than 250 pounds, a minor miracle in the miniaturization of a new and complex technology. The units could be carried within or outside aircraft, including the larger UAVs, and in virtually all ships and submarines, and they could detect and pinpoint within less than a meter tiny magnetic variations from altitudes up to 40,000 feet and through several thousand feet of fresh and sea water. Even better for today, they also have a low-power microwave radar capability, the BLT, for Boeing Laser Tiller. It solved a problem that didn't exist at the time: detecting moving metallic and plastic objects beneath the surface of the earth."

"Like in pipelines?"

"Yes, sir."

"Go on," Halsey urged.

"The Navy has already deployed 17 Poseidons, fifteen of which are still based in the United States. Initially, for our own uses, Boeing funded and produced 104 of the enhanced, specialized MAD adaptors that could be retrofitted to the planes within 24 hours, should the Navy change its mind. In the meantime, Boeing planned to market the P-8A with the new MAD adaptor to foreign governments."

"Doctor, you <u>have</u> those adaptors?"

"Yes, sir, a hundred-plus, maybe 200, here in the same hangar from where I'm speaking. Ready to install."

"Have you tested them with...?"

"Pipelines? Yes, sir. We can find them and see most anything non-liquid in underground transit. We've done a dozen test flights out of Renton. We've even flown in and out of the Sinergy area, fake flight plans, and we've followed some of their pipelines north and northeast for a hundred miles."

Halsey rubbed his face.

"So, you can 'see' the spheres? Locate and track them?"

"Yes, sir, but that's not the problem."

"Meaning?"

"If we find something inside a sphere, we can't tell what it is. It could be the real thing or a decoy."

Halsey exhaled.

"Have you found any in-transit anomalies so far?"

"No, sir. Just hundreds of spheres."

"But Boeing's BLT research for the Navy can be quickly 'battlefield' modified for our new ground-piercing needs, right?" Halsey asked. "The internal analysis of the spheres, at least for locating objects within the spheres?"

"As I mentioned, we can locate the spheres, even up to ten to twenty feet below the surface, but we need more specifics about their contents. They're just blips to us right now. We need something to calibrate from."

"Doctor, if we can give you high-quality 3D pictures of the probable contents of the spheres, can they, the contents, be targeted and destroyed?"

"Yes, sir. Piece of cake. At least the targeting portion."

"Thank you, Doctor.

"Marshall, it's Lyle," Admiral Hunter interjected. "May I pick it up from here?"

"Please do, Admiral," Boseman replied.

"Starting with the Sinergy refinery in Baytown, Texas, we tracked and identified two main underground 30-inch product pipelines owned by the Chinese. One went north to St. Louis and Chicago. The second coursed northeast to Atlanta, then to New York and Boston. Numerous capillaries owned by other pipeline companies, 30 inches in diameter but some smaller, fanned off the main lines to hundreds of communities and other consumers between Sinergy's Chicago and Boston terminals. Petroleum products also went westward from Sinergy but via pipelines owned by other companies. Because of multiple interchange agreements, the Sinergy spheres could reach destinations in all 48 mainland states. Collection basins for the spheres were located in hundreds of 'pens' across the country.

"Right now, we're vulnerable, completely wide open. They might already have bombs in places we don't know about. We have to get a dozen or more 'eyes in the sky' immediately. And God help us figure out how to disable a bomb within a sphere without setting it off."

"That's tomorrow's goal, right?" Halsey offered in an optimistic tone.

Everyone nodded. Dr. Boseman in Renton answered with a wry response.

"Yeah, <u>right</u>."

Gentlemen, this meeting is over," Admiral Hunter stated bluntly. "We have to get back to work...<u>now</u>. Destruction testing begins at 0600."

Admiral Rourke stood up.

"I'll notify the President," the CNO declared. "God speed."

The men departed quickly, each quietly contemplating his own next steps.

CHAPTER 66

NAS Patuxent River, Maryland

SUNDAY, 3 March — 4:00 A.M. EST

The unmarked Navy SUV returned to Pax River at 1:55 A.M. It was a frigid night. The five men who had attended the special meeting at ONI disembarked and walked briskly to their cars. Each went home for a steaming shower and a cup of piping hot coffee. They had to be back in less than two hours to accelerate the pursuit. Home might be but a memory before they finished their work. What lay ahead promised to be, at the least, one very long all-nighter.

The two admirals and the Boeing technicians had been asked to remain at Suitland for several hours after the ONI meeting in order to brief, or to be briefed by, operatives involved in the identification, interception, and destruction of the likely deadly pipeline spheres. In addition, they took time to confirm that the first shift of the appropriate mission personnel would be on duty at Pax River by 6:00 A.M. There were two groups: Navy and civilian. Both specialized in sphere-detection, "bomb" implantation, and "bomb" location and identification. Most of their skills were newly acquired.

Vice Admiral Lyle Hunter met his four recent fellow travelers at the entrance to a massive ghost-grey hangar complex on the southwest side of the Maryland Navy base. They went inside and walked immediately to a high-tech classroom. Groupings of various types of the most-sophisticated and expensive technical, electronic audio-visual, and other "Star Wars" equipment were at each of the four corners of the room. Live worldwide teleconferencing was also available at a round table in the middle of the room. There were sufficient screens for fifty observers.

Once the four had taken their places, Admiral Hunter began. His delivery was alternately agitated and measured.

"They say, microwave radar to detect, laser to destroy, but, gee, there's a problem with the heat. We might be able to detect the damn spheres carrying explosives, but we can't render them inert because the laser's heat will blow them up."

Hunter looked at the ceiling and sighed audibly.

"What kind of bullshit is that?"

He peered at his audience.

"Here're my questions." The admiral ticked off on his fingers.

"First, how much heat does the MAD laser actually produce against a target from various altitudes, at the surface of the sphere and within? And through what? If there's a foreign object inside a sphere, what's the temp there? How do we know? How can we know?

"Second, what's the detonation temperature for C-4 and other garden-variety explosives? Is there one, or do the Chinese rely exclusively on an electrical charge to detonate their explosives?

"Third, how do we target the target, so to speak? Can the laser 'fry' the device without setting it off?"

Hunter looked at his watch.

"When your crews get here at 0600, I want these tests run on the ground first, and I want them completed and reported to me by 1200, along with anything else you may discover. Then," he continued, "we start the airborne operations with four P-8As. I want all actual pipeline runs, mission data, and necessary simulations to be sent through our system algorithms. Everything, gentlemen. This will be completed and the results compiled and delivered to me by 1800 hours. Any questions?"

The room was silent.

The admiral snapped his fingers.

Rear Admiral Jerry Monahan stood up and interrupted the dismissal of the men.

"Keep four things in mind. First, all of the sphere 'imbeds' are probably the same. We have evidence from the <u>Zhou Enlai</u> explosion that there was a lithium-ion electrical source. Engineers don't like to mix things up, to take chances. So, yes, I figure there's an electrical source within each 'dirty bomb.' Second, what is the detonator? For starters, I figure it's some variation of an EBW, the reliable 'exploding-bridgewire.' Let's go with that unless and until we find out otherwise. Third, we know the explosive on the ship was RDX, and fourth, of course, the highly worrisome cesium-137 dispersant.

"Gentlemen, this may sound like a simple task. Believe me, it won't be a cakewalk. There are a hundred variables, and our equipment is untested."

As the men filed out for their offices and laboratories, Monahan whispered under his breath, "Go Navy!" His tone was more of a prayer than a cheer.

Four 138,300-lb. Boeing P-8A Poseidons were carefully pulled from their Pax River hangar at 0500. Standing in the darkness of the tarmac outside were five members of the Nuclear Emergency Support Team. The NEST men had just arrived from Washington. Anyone who had reason to encounter them knew that they were there on the President's orders.

The four flight deck crews and 36 Navy specialists arrived shortly before 0600. All had been briefed on the latest plans. They assembled in what everyone called the "really ready room," the classroom where the others had met two hours earlier. They knew their initial task was to locate the malignant spheres and to kill the lithium-ion batteries. After the short update, one of the Navy pilots muttered, "If they can't do this on the ground, we're fucked."

• • •

Within an hour, the ground sphere-detection tests were underway. The Navy had buried "dummy dirties" in three abandoned pipelines around Pax River, using both empty and mock-explosive contents. The static tests would be similar to the upcoming aerial program. Everything had to go right.

Admiral Hunter walked across the ramp to the Poseidons. He knew the P-8As were exquisitely suited for the mission of locating and destroying targets beneath the surface of the sea, but finding and disabling objects underground was a challenge the plane had not been designed for. Its original sophisticated weaponry of high-frequency sound pulses was useless in piercing solid ground. But, he reminded himself, the P-8A was the nation's only realistic starting point for this challenge.

Surface and subsurface targets had been included in the upgrade process, for both land and sea. The laser range was a full 360 degrees and was determined to be effective in a straight line from altitudes as high as flight level 410, or 41,000 feet. Theoretically, the laser could intercept the horizon as far away as 237 nautical miles. When activated, the laser unit, in a "canoe," would be extended sufficiently to avoid "painting" the under-wing engines during its circuit. But what the new versions could do in the dirt remained to be seen.

Boeing had a facility at Anacortes, Washington, some 40 miles north of its wide-body plant in Everett where it tested advanced automation methods for the 777X and its progeny. In a dozen secret operations and locations, their specialists at Anacortes had already ventured far outside the contemporary needs of current aircraft under contract, which included the further development of navigation protocols that made use of the earth's magnetic field and other esoteric endeavors. Piercing the earth for precision tracking was a related pursuit. Even though it wasn't directly covered by their contract, the Navy finally gave Boeing the green light. Costs would be adjusted. It was indeed a shot in the dark, but the Navy really had no other options.

Boeing and the Navy shifted 63 engineers to Anacortes. All were at their stations within 24 hours of the order. As of today, it had been four weeks.

Based on the threat, Boeing and Navy engineers knew that they were going to have to retrofit at least a dozen P-8As with effective weaponry for the mission, but everything would have to be invented and perfected before it could be installed. Following their understanding of the threat, they had days instead of years to accomplish the task.

The challenge to locate, identify, and render useless lithium-ion batteries in possibly hundreds of pipeline spheres across the country seemed insurmountable. Only a week earlier, the Navy's estimate of the time required for such an effort was eleven months. Now, it had been set at a maximum of two days. Never before in the history of America's quest for a technological miracle had anything been as critical as this. Nor had anything had such a short fuse. By comparison, developing the atomic bomb was a walk in the park.

Hunter came to a stop in front of the four empty P-8A aircraft. He put his hands on his hips and stared. He shook his head.

"Son of a bitch!"

SUNDAY, 3 March – 5:00 P.M. EST

"Nothing!" one of the P-8A pilots yelled into his microphone as he completed his last circuit over an intersection of pipelines at Pax River. "Not a fucking thing!"

He and the three other P-8A crews had been at this all day, and all the men were exhausted. Each of the aircraft carried three pilots and two non-pilot officers, one of whom oversaw the enlisted men at the workstations in the back. All were focused on a mission that looked more hopeless by the minute.

"We've crisscrossed over two hundred square miles a dozen or more times, and we not only couldn't locate anomalies in any spheres in the pipelines, we couldn't even find most of the goddamned spheres in the first place. There's no way we can disarm something we can't find."

"Roger, commander," the tower acknowledged. "Return to base."

CHAPTER 67

Fort Bragg, North Carolina

MONDAY, 4 March – 10:00 A.M. EST

The previous day's suicide of Army Lieutenant General Terrance King was on nearly everyone's mind at Fort Bragg. However, in a separate ten-room enclosure surrounding the base commander's office, King's death was of little or no interest. The forces there had their own priorities, and looking backwards was not one of them. They were about to become even more focused on a place most of them had never visited but where they might lose their lives. Their destination was 950 statute miles due west. Their rendezvous would be immediately after midnight tonight. For them, there might be no tomorrow.

U.S. Army Special Operations Command, led by three-star Lieutenant General Tyrone "Ripcord" Washington, was head-quartered at Fort Bragg. General Washington saw from the door that everyone who was supposed to be at this meeting was there: the senior leadership of the Squadron level of the 1st Special Forces Operational Detachment-Delta, known to the public as Delta Force, their aides, several Army strategists from the Pentagon, and Navy Captain Halsey who would accompany the Delta team.

Halsey had just talked with Pax River for a review of Sunday's surface and aerial tests of the ad hoc sphere detection equipment. The news wasn't good. In truth, it couldn't have been worse. Not only did the Navy P-8As fail to locate most of the spheres in the pipelines, neither ground nor air search efforts could spot any of the hidden mock explosives. But Halsey knew the really bad news was that the Navy had no backup plan whatsoever, and time was running out. He rubbed his face and sighed. For a second, he thought of Anoli, again.

General Washington closed the door and began speaking. He started with a summary. "Ripcord" was a man of few words who expected his audience to have a basic understanding of whatever they were there to hear. He knew these men already had a lot of more than that from briefings over the past few days.

"We're calling this mission 'Operation Fire Ants.' The plan is for two incursions. In the first, Delta Force operators will be airdropped from 20,000 feet and will secure the perimeters, the gates, and all command and control facilities, including the headquarters offices of MCAAP's General Benning. Moments later, a second wave will arrive by helicopters. That one has two goals: the final securing of the base and the breach of the underground facility, which is the most important and, potentially, the most dangerous part of this assignment.

"The insertion of the first has to take place, start to finish, over a period no longer than nine minutes. It will be the ultra-silent portion. The second, with landing helicopters, will be a louder affair.

"Let's go to the details."

Washington clicked on his laser pointer and walked to a large screen. It flashed on.

CHAPTER 68

McAlester, Oklahoma

The late-winter night was clear and cold, barely above freezing. The Moon was in its last quarter. Halsey and 298 Delta Force operators had boarded five Chinook helicopters at Fort Campbell, KY, bound for MCAAP. They, as Unit Bravo, would breach the "base," 958 miles away, as the second of tonight's two-part mission. Time en route was estimated at slightly under five hours.

Two-plus hours later, two Joint Special Operations Command transport jet aircraft, carrying another 300 operators and their equipment, departed for Oklahoma. They would beat the helicopters and parachute in to secure the base minutes before the Chinooks arrived. Theirs, Unit Alpha, was the first part of the equation, and time en route would be two hours and seven minutes.

The helicopters would remain on site at MCAAP to retrieve all participants after the mission and return them to Fort Bragg. If necessary, either outbound or back, the Chinooks could refuel at a restricted Army airport (known to the FAA as A-19) south of Mena, AR. Halsey was in the third of the five Chinooks.

As his helicopter ascended rapidly, Halsey winced. He wasn't used to the jerking and sideways jarring. A simple, straight-ahead catapult launch from a carrier was fine with him, thank you very much.

When the Chinook stabilized and tilted forward toward its target, Halsey exhaled and picked up his thoughts. His mother had often told him he was meant for great things. She'd left out the shit he'd have to go through to get there, even assuming she'd been right in the first place. He closed his eyes and smiled. Wasn't life a continuing, frustrating mystery? How would Mom grade him today? Halsey never questioned his Catholic faith, but he often wondered how he was measuring up to its strictures. There were times when he felt good about himself and his role in an existence he didn't understand. There were other times when he felt condemned for all eternity. It was a peak-and-valley theological roller coaster. He'd shared some of this with Anoli. She was always open and accepting, but he wondered if she truly understood the conundrum he was experiencing. Maybe she did and was just being supportive. On the other hand, maybe she didn't, couldn't. Did it really make any difference? As usual, he had more questions than answers.

"Fifteen minutes!" an amplified voice interrupted from the speakers. The men around him checked their equipment and secured themselves for the landing. This was it, they told one another.

Halsey looked at his watch: 0015 local.

In the remaining moments, he thought again of Anoli. His wife meant everything to him. If he had two lives to give to rescue her, both were hers.

The five Chinooks touched down inside the perimeter of MCAAP within 50 yards of the operations buildings and the targeted underground-access facility. Seconds later, all the men were out of the helicopters and headed for their assignments. Halsey ran ahead of one group and gestured to the large doors of the new, "special" building. MCAAP was a place he knew a lot about, and not all of it was comforting. Right now, for example.

The Delta operators who had parachuted into the huge base earlier had secured the multi-mile perimeter, the main gate, and General Benning's headquarters. MCAAP was in full lockdown. They were now prepared to support whatever the second wave discovered or needed. Through his headset, Halsey received word that they had not located Col. Freeman, Benning's second in command. The guards at the main gate reported that Freeman hadn't been seen in several days.

Halsey and his contingent stopped at the heavy double doors on the side of the large steel and stone building where the 18-wheelers had been seen arriving and departing. A Delta leader's sign language warned that deadly opposition could await them just inside. Seconds later, the explosives team was waved away after an operator tried to move the doors and found them unlocked. Unlocked doors? Halsey appreciated lagniappe, but this seemed too easy.

Three others joined the man at the doors and rolled the massive metal barriers aside. The others crouched and were ready to shoot anything inside that moved.

The heavily armed men crept into a large hangar-like structure and wanded their weapons in 90-degree arcs. Four identical Army sedans with one-star markings and tinted windows were clustered at one end of the building. They were wrapped in heavy clear plastic and seemed in mint condition. Otherwise, the place was empty.

"General Benning's private car collection, I suppose," one of the men muttered. His colleague looked at the array of polished vehicles and shook his head.

"Souvenirs? Like something out of the Third Reich? Hitler cars?"

"There!" Halsey exclaimed. He pointed to a black rectangular marking on the floor, a three-inch line approximately 170 feet long by ten feet wide. "It's got to be an elevator." By now, at least two hundred Delta-force men were inside the building.

"Find the activation unit for that. It's our passage to whatever they're doing underground."

"Captain Halsey?" a voice came from his side.

Halsey continued motioning to the men searching for the elevator controls along the wall.

"Yeah?" he replied impatiently, without looking for the voice.

"I'm your guide to that underground."

Halsey turned and saw a man who resembled any other Delta Force operator, although a decade or so older.

"And who are you?"

"Army Colonel Stephen Wright, sir. I headed the 'creature' pursuit at Aberdeen. What I know may be of help." He held out his hand.

Halsey quickly pumped Wright's hand.

"I'd heard a 'seeing-eye dog' might be coming along. Welcome aboard, Colonel."

"I also know a lot about the medical procedures and effects," Wright added.

"Wonderful!" Halsey exclaimed. "Do you go by 'Steve'?"

"Yes, sir."

"What's your background?"

The colonel laughed. "Let's just say I'm an M.D. with Ph.D.s in lots of weird stuff."

Halsey smiled. Spoken like a true spook.

"OK, Steve, I want to breach this place as quickly and as efficiently as possible. Soldiers, creatures? We have no idea who or what's down there, how many there are, and what weapons they may have, but we're prepared for a couple of hundred really bad guys who will die for the cause. I know next to nothing about their underground facilities, how they got here, how they've operated, and what their ultimate plans might be. We're basically going in blind, to take over at any cost. We will wipe them out."

"Then," Wright replied nonchalantly, "let's do it."

Halsey looked across to the wall where the men were searching for the elevator controls. He again envisioned Anoli's face. She was always on his mind.

"Anything?" he yelled to the operators.

"A whole control panel, sir," a man called back. "Looks like with the push of one button, we're on our way down."

Halsey gave a modified salute. The man returned a thumbs-up.

Because of his relevant knowledge and overall experience, Halsey's role in today's mission at MCAAP had been expanded by three-star General Tyrone "Ripcord" Washington, leader of the U.S. Army Special Operations Command. Halsey would still not be in charge, officially, but his opinions would be "strongly considered." In short, he was to have the men's attention.

"All right, everyone," Halsey barked, "get within the outline on the floor! Thirty seconds! Then," he pointed to the man at the panel, "push that button!"

Colonel Wright was next to Halsey as the giant elevator began its smooth descent. When it stopped, Halsey guessed from the electronic tones that they had gone down nine stories. He stood aside as doors opened. The Delta forces ran past him, ready, and itching, for a firefight.

The Army operators quickly swarmed throughout the facility, eyeballing. Halsey waited for word.

The men discovered a vast compound with more than a dozen sophisticated and well-lighted side rooms, large and small, including medical "operating rooms" and accommodations for people and cages for large animals. There were no troops or "creatures" to be seen. And no Anoli.

"Southeast corner," one called in. "Clear! Nothing!"

"Nothing southwest," another added a minute later.

"Same for the northwest," a voice checked in.

"Ditto, northeast" a fourth said from the final quadrant.

"Time to check the 'furniture,'" Halsey pointed toward the stainless steel equipment that was spread over much of the main floor. Several dozen men began the inspection.

"And any hidden rooms," he added.

Twenty other operators fanned out and began a meticulous inspection of the walls. Four carried special body-mounted metal/volumetric detectors.

Halsey put his hands on his hips and surveyed the vast subterranean room. The facility was indeed the size of a football field. Its ceiling looked nine or ten feet high. In the middle were what appeared to be giant stainless steel versions of his grandmother's cast-iron cornbread pans. Hers had depressions to hold ten corn-shaped breads of seven inches long. What lay before him today were ten containers with corn-shaped depressions of seven <u>feet</u> long. They looked like huge baby cradles.

"What are we looking for, Colonel?" he asked Wright who hesitated a second before replying.

"Well...I'd start with the perimeter rooms where the 'surgeries' and experiments were presumably carried out. Could be a lot of clues there."

Halsey nodded and motioned to the men alongside.

"Find and enter every room that opens into this one. Look for hidden access points anywhere. I want up-to-the-second reports." The men dashed away.

Halsey turned toward Wright. The Army colonel looked frustrated, almost dejected.

"OK, what's the deal?"

"The deal? No opposition or 'creatures' down here? The deal is we're way behind some very smart and very bad people, and we're not catching up. Losing ground, as a matter of fact. What we might find in those rooms will probably be inconsequential. What they're doing right now is what counts, and we don't have a fucking clue. That's the deal."

Halsey shook his head. He agreed completely.

"Captain? Colonel?" came a yell from across the room.

The two men turned.

"You gotta see these operating rooms. I mean they're something out of science fiction. The highest of high tech."

"Where are you?" Wright looked and shouted.

"Over here, waving at you."

Halsey and Wright saw the Delta Force operator and jogged across the floor. The man escorted them inside a large operating room. Its arrangement was impressive, especially to Wright.

"Well?" Halsey asked.

Wright could only shake his head.

"The finest 'usuals' for brain work: computer assisted imaging tomography, magnetic resonance imaging, positron emission tomography, magnetoencephalography, and all forms of stereotactic surgery. But from there, we enter the twilight zone. At Aberdeen, we had all the latest-edition bio gizmos for our experiments, but this looks like several generations beyond that. Much of it is from the major manufacturers, GE, Siemens, and the like. Their names are on the equipment. I don't have a clue what the new stuff does, but someone obviously did, and does."

"Gentlemen, there are several other rooms similar to this one," the operator offered. "They're probably a bit more advanced, if you can believe that. You should see them."

Wright followed Halsey out the door. He continued shaking his head.

The next operating room was another efficiently designed facility, best for both the surgical team and the "patient." It had voice-control technology that enabled the surgeon to direct, via spoken commands, medical and robotic devices.

"Then, there's this one." The Delta operator motioned to next door. Wright was still shaking his head.

"Must be a specialized brain surgery operating room," the man said as he gestured to a sign on the door that read, "Neurosurgery: Craniotomy."

As the men walked to the third room, Halsey grabbed Wright's arm.

"Tell me what I'm seeing."

"It's remarkable. It appears they can do whatever they want with whatever hominid they care to operate on. Of course, I need to learn a lot more before being definitive across the board, but, right now, I'd bet my bottom dollar they have successfully implanted a controlling chip in a non-human. Maybe hundreds of them. We did primitive stuff at Aberdeen, at the prototype level. The gorillas died shortly thereafter. The next step was up to MCAAP, with their 'creatures.'"

Halsey stared at the colonel. His mind was racing.

Science fiction? No longer, apparently. Brain implants today are where laser eye surgery was several decades ago. These guys have probably pushed the envelope beyond what anyone ever considered possible. But why, for what ultimate reason?

Another Delta Force man approached quickly. He went directly to Halsey.

"Two things, Captain: cremation units and an escape tube. You have to see them."

Halsey frowned. "Where?"

"The crematoria are closer." The operator motioned. "Right over here."

Halsey looked around. He was about to signal Wright to follow, but the Army colonel was already a few steps ahead.

"Two units?" Halsey asked, since the man had used the plural of crematorium.

"Three," the man replied.

Thirty yards away, on the same side of the underground structure as the operating rooms, Halsey saw a large access door. It was as thick as a bank vault. He noticed at the entrance that the front walls facing the main room were the same thickness as the access door. Immediately inside was an abandoned guard station. Guard station? Curious, Halsey mused. Then he saw the three crematoria. Massive, intimidating.

"The interiors are still warm," the Delta Force man observed, "and empty, except for the powder. The doors are almost cold. According to the plaques on the outside, the units cool down quickly, 'allowing one to load the next case rapidly,' or so it says. Depending on the operating temps, I'm guessing they haven't been turned off for more than 90 minutes, two hours at the most."

Halsey walked to one of the units and squinted at the plaque. Lots of settings, temperatures, and times. Large loading capacity, high-velocity burners, and a sophisticated touch-screen control panel. "Up to fifty bodies per day," he read out loud. Then he saw the trademark name of the crematorium: Hades.

"Up to fifty bodies per day," Halsey repeated. Per oven? Three ovens? That'd be 150 every 24 hours.

He unlatched and pulled open the heavy steel door. As he did so, he noticed tufts of coarse hair on the floor. Several handfuls along the bottom outside edge of the unit. The tips of his shoes were standing on one of them.

"Captain?" Wright's voice interrupted. Halsey looked toward the entrance. The colonel was holding an Apple MacBook.

"Just borrowed this from one of the guys. He found a DVD under a toilet." Wright brought the laptop over. "Take a look."

The disc began. It was a high-resolution HD video of large gorilla-like animals, but they had faces Halsey had never seen before. Almost, in a weird way, human. Probably a couple of dozen bodies lying on a polished floor covered with odd markings and symbols. Some of the "creatures" had white hair, most had brown.

"That's that floor!" Halsey exclaimed, nodding toward the main room.

Wright pointed to the screen. "From the height of the guy standing in the middle of the bodies, I'd say they were a foot or so taller than he. Maybe two feet."

Halsey crossed his arms and stated the obvious.

"They've all been beheaded."

Neither man spoke for several seconds.

Halsey sighed.

"Look at this." He squatted down and picked up some of the hair on the floor. He handed it to Wright.

"I'd bet the CNO's salary that it's from those 'creatures.'"

Wright rolled the hair in his fingers.

"So they cremated the bodies but kept the heads, right? What the hell does that mean?"

Halsey kicked at a large tuft of hair. He was about to reply when something glinted from the floor. A flash of light, a reflection from something, then it was gone. He squatted down again for a closer look. With both hands, he quickly sifted through groupings of hair. Then, he gasped. He reached for and picked up a small object. It looked like, no, it <u>was</u> the St. Christopher's medal he had given Anoli for Christmas. He was certain because it had the three "plus" symbols he'd had engraved at the bottom edge. Three pluses for the Trinity, and, rotated 45 degrees, three Xs, for kisses for her.

"Oh, <u>God</u>, Steve," he moaned. "They had my wife here. I gave her this." He held it up. Then, he noticed something else on the floor. It was a broken length of the gold chain from the necklace, as if it had been ripped from Anoli's neck.

Wright helped his Navy compatriot to his feet. He put his arm around him. Halsey was shuddering.

"I'm all right," Halsey said in a low voice. "God forgive me, but I'm going to kill anyone who harms my wife. The bastard's family also. And all his associates." Wright remained quiet. Any words from him would be woefully inadequate.

"Collect this hair," Halsey suddenly said to two Delta men close by. "Get it analyzed." He turned to their guide.

"Let's see that escape tube you mentioned." The man nodded and walked toward the door. Halsey and Wright followed.

As they left the crematoria, Halsey completed the shift in his emotional gears and remembered that it was his father who'd first told him about the pipeline. It was now clear and matter-of-fact. In 1942, during the height of the Second World War, a 30-inch underground pipeline was constructed between refineries in the Houston area and what was then the Navy Ammunition Depot. It was designed to supply all needed petroleum products to America's critical bomb-making facility that was located far from potential enemy threats. The pipeline was abandoned in the 60s, as more efficient energy delivery methods were employed. The pipeline was never removed.

"Is there cell access down here?" Halsey asked of their guide.

"Yes, sir, it's fully Wi-Fi compliant. However, it's MCAAP equipment, so we've installed our own secure system for this mission. Want to make a call?" The operator reached into his top pocket and handed over a phone. "Here. It's already synched and secure."

Halsey took the cell and tapped in the number of Navy Commander Chris "Bolter" Byrne, his close subordinate and fellow member of the "Strict-9" task force.

"Where are you?"

"Your office. Monitoring not just MCAAP but also Sinergy and our ops in the Gulf. Big unidentified submarine out there, a Gravely find. We think it's a Chinese Type 096 nuclear missile sub, Tang class. Larger than the Type 094 Jin class. Dangerous toy."

"Where is it?" Halsey asked.

"At the edge of the Sigsbee Deep. Silent, way down. Precise depth unknown but estimated to be at least 490 meters, probably close to the sub's crush depth."

"All right, keep me advised. It'll probably play a role shortly, especially because of what we're planning. God forbid, but we may be at war within a day or so. That sub is not good news. In the meantime, check on any Chinese work with people-moving tubes. Go with your imagination. Whatever you get involving MCAAP I want to know. Report back to me within an hour on this. Use my cell number."

"Righto." Byrne clicked off.

"There it is." The Delta Force operator pointed to a large glass panel at a corner of the room. Parts of a temporary wall cover had been torn down.

"Is it accessible?"

"No, sir."

"Break it open!" Halsey ordered.

Two Delta men ran to the glass and hit it several times with the butts of their guns, hard, but it didn't yield.

"Shoot it!" Halsey commanded. "Shoot it open, damn it!"

The men stepped back and fired. The thick glass shattered and fell in shards.

Halsey quickly stepped into the opening and saw a large cylindrical structure at one side that extended down into the ground. Several "pods" were in nearby racks with tracks into the structure. One was empty and ready. His mind raced.

"Good God, it's the 21st-century version of the fricken pipeline!"

Halsey looked around the structure. It was ten-feet tall, stainless steel, five feet in diameter, fixed in concrete, and it appeared to be a terminus.

"Catman!" a voice boomed from Halsey's phone. It was Byrne.

"That was fast."

"We've been collecting a lot of relevant intel over the past week or so. The tube's a Chinese update, and it goes to Baytown, Texas, some 354 miles to the south. Transit speed is probably 400 m.p.h. Based on the distance between MCAAP and Baytown, the elapsed time either way is slightly less than 60 minutes."

Baytown, Halsey thought, is Sinergy. Byrne kept talking.

"The Chinese have had years of experience developing a method to send car-sized capsules at speeds up to 500 miles an hour using magnetic levitation. The process employs an airless pipeline and a sophisticated control system that manipulates the magnetic forces between the track and the capsule. In basic concept, it resembles the tubes used by banks to move checks and cash to and from drive-in customers. However, it's generations beyond what has ever been built before. The capsules will easily accommodate two large adults. At a maximum of 400-500 pounds for the 'passengers' and their baggage, the capsules would still weigh less than 1,000 pounds each. Pure genius."

As Halsey listened, he pulled the gold memento and broken chain from his pocket. Byrne went on.

"The original pipeline likely fell into disuse over several years rather than being officially decommissioned. No records were ever found of its being shut down. Both ends of the pipeline were sealed using makeshift materials, as if anticipating that a more permanent cap would be attached later. The routing is somewhat in dispute, since there has been no update of state or federal records in 50 years. It was never on the tax rolls because of its government ownership. There were no pumping stations or other aboveground attestation to its presence that we know of. All visible evidence of the pipeline beneath the Oklahoma and Texas soil is both gone and forgotten. Even long-time residents of farms and ranches along the way can't remember any maintenance. As a matter of fact, no one even remembers its construction in the first place. The pipeline was so deep that even the huge construction and development activities across the fast-growing Dallas-Fort Worth area over 50 years hadn't impinged upon or uncovered this silent recluse of another era."

"Yeah, well, they've transported several hundred heads of the 'creatures' and, most probably, my wife through it as recently as an hour ago. I'm going after them."

"Catman, no!" Byrne yelled. "You don't know shit how that system works or who's waiting on the other end. One way or the other, you're gonna get yourself killed."

Halsey hung up, walked over, jumped up on the edge of the track, and slid into the narrow shuttle pod. He lay on his back and depressed the green "close" button. A fitted canopy slid forward silently and sealed him inside. He heard the sound of air being forced into the pod, pressurization, he guessed. One of his ears popped. There was a T-handle next to his right hand with only forward-and-back "on" and "off" positions. Halsey pushed it forward and was launched. There was a humming sound as the vehicle began moving. He had a growing feeling of claustrophobia as vehicle accelerated. The humming noise continued. Halsey figured it was coming from the magnetic drive. There was no sensation of speed, just an occasional slight rocking motion.

He was able to look around, although his range of motion was limited by the tight quarters. The interior of his containment vessel was padded but sparse. Only five or six buttons, levers, and gauges. They were legended in English. He hadn't had to strap in, his feet pressed against a forward bulkhead, and his head lay on a fitted pad.

As the minutes passed, Halsey reflected on all that had happened in the past two months. What mattered most to him personally was the kidnapping of his precious Anoli.

In the indirect lighting of the pod, Halsey checked his watch. He'd been en route now for 36 minutes. Assuming he was traveling at 100 miles per hour, he'd have covered 60 miles. However, if his speed were 200 m.p.h., he'd have traveled twice that. If he were at 500 m.p.h., he could be nearing the exit. In other words, he admitted to himself, he had no idea whatsoever how fast he was going or where he was along the 354-mile pipeline.

All of a sudden, there was a rapid deceleration. His feet slammed against the forward bulkhead, and the pod jerked to a stop. The humming sound was gone.

"Shit!" he exclaimed. He knew exactly what had happened. The Chinese had noticed the renegade southbound pod and had simply turned off the power. Now, he was stranded in a tube ten feet underground somewhere in the hundreds of miles between MCAAP and Baytown, and no one knew where he was. Except the Chinese. The air had stopped coming in through the vents. If there were still a vacuum in the pipeline, the remaining air in the pod would bleed out, and he'd suffocate within seconds. Air or no air, he was in a world of hurt.

"In a pile of crap," he corrected his thoughts.

With each beat of his heart, Halsey knew he was succumbing to the eternal darkness. He said a quick prayer, thanking God for his life and his Anoli.

Without warning, Halsey heard, and felt, a series of explosions. They sounded very close, almost right above him. Five, six, now seven. Then, two more, and daylight suddenly filled a jagged opening above him. The hole to the surface seemed barely a foot in diameter. Small rocks and chips of dirt dropped into the exposure.

"Can you open that canopy, honcho?" a voice yelled from above. Halsey recognized the distinctive accent of its owner, Admiral Roberto "Shiv" Ochoa, head of the Naval Special Warfare Command in Coronado, California.

"Surrender, Catman," Ochoa barked, "in the name of the great Jehovah and the Continental Congress!"

Halsey retracted the glass and composite entry hatch.

"You Cuban son of a bitch! How the hell did you find me? How did you even know where to look?"

"Hey, amigo, Boeing needed to practice finding stuff in pipelines. Your idea, remember? This gave them the perfect opportunity."

"Well, don't just gloat. Get me out of here!"

Ochoa dropped a knotted rope into the hole and pulled Halsey upwards. As Halsey slowly exited the pod, he griped, "This really didn't merit the Ethan Allen quote. How does a dumb-ass foreigner know about an American revolutionary hero anyway?"

Ochoa pulled Halsey over the upper edge of the cavity and drew him to his feet.

"So?" Halsey persisted.

"What? Ethan Allen?" Ochoa shrugged. "Didn't you know I was valedictorian of my naturalization class?"

Halsey hugged his friend of decades.

"You're so full of shit."

Ochoa pointed to the sky. Halsey saw the outline of a P-8A Poseidon departing its search pattern that had led to Halsey's rescue. The aircraft gently rocked its wings. Halsey grinned and gave it a salute.

As they ran for the nearby Navy HH-60 Seahawk helicopter, Halsey asked, "So, where are we?"

Ochoa jogged closer and yelled because of the noise of the Seahawk.

"Physically? Near the Davy Crockett National Forest, about 100 miles north of Baytown. Once the Poseidon located you, I used a few of our 'dirt-digger' explosives to pierce the tube down the line and stop your trip. Then, a few more boom-booms, and I plucked you out. Pure Cuban ingenuity, right?"

Halsey started to laugh so hard he nearly lost his balance.

The two jumped into the helicopter. It immediately lifted off from the barren field in east central Texas and headed south. Its destination was Ellington Field, near Houston, where the Navy had a newly reinforced facility. Ellington was 17 miles southeast of the Sinergy refinery and was the base for the planned action against the massive facility.

Halsey and Ochoa immediately donned helmets with speakers and boom microphones. They could now talk without having to yell over the noise of the helicopter's twin-turboshaft engine.

"Let me start," Ochoa offered. He didn't wait for a reply.

"First, the Army guys found a lot of stuff in General King's papers, including the meaning of the acronym S.A.S.S.Y., the name they used for their operation. It stands for 'Special Army Suicide-Soldier Yeti.' Same thing on a document hidden in General Benning's office safe. Both were written in Mandarin with English translations. There are numerous references to other papers and contacts with the Chinese. Seems the generals were up to their necks in treason and sedition. Death penalties, both. King's dead, of course, but Benning's still being held in Lawton. I wouldn't want to be in his Buster Browns.

"Second, the pipeline. Not a new concept. Nearly 200 years ago, pneumatic tubes delivered messages and products at high speeds from and between individuals and businesses within cities. Post offices and businesses. Monstrous improvements in technology since then. Like this one: maglev. Pipeline had to be strengthened from the inside, which the Chinese did. The Army engineers are guessing it was completely reengineered and upgraded. Huge cost. The Army's initial take is that it's a refurbished and strengthened tube that can accommodate the movement of both liquids and other cargo, in either direction. Highly complex control centers are located next to the underground termini. Did you see a lot of electronic stuff at MCAAP?"

"No," Halsey replied. "Just the pod and the tube. Plus several other pods lined up and ready to load and launch."

Ochoa continued. "They didn't need a perfect vacuum because they didn't need ultra high speed due to the relatively short distance between the two termini. In any event, virtual airlessness, had it been desired, could not have been achieved without replacing the older pipeline with a new, much stronger one, something that would have attracted attention during its burial. So they did the next best thing by relining from within."

Halsey raised a finger, interrupting Ochoa's briefing.

"The minisubs, Shiv! That's how they're getting stuff in and out of the country!"

"Minisubs?"

"Remember what Gravely found in the Gulf a couple of months ago? Empty minisubs coming in? For what? Practice or maybe not."

Admiral Ochoa nodded. "I know all about the minisubs, their bigger brother or two, and the granddaddy deep offshore."

Halsey pulled out his satellite phone.

Ochoa immediately placed his hand over it.

"Listen up. As for the refinery itself, here's what we know: Ninety-five percent of it is just a refinery. The biggest, of course, but still a refinery. There are three areas off limits to any but a small cadre of bad guys from China. We've had men on the ground there for more than a year. None could even get close to those well-guarded areas. They are first, the sphere-insertion building at the north end of the property; second, a segregated portion of the main operations facility, and third, a secure area adjoining the lab. That's where the tube has its terminus from MCAAP."

"That's where I need to be," Halsey exclaimed.

"I knew you'd say that," Ochoa replied. "We'll insert you there, in the accessible portion, so you can be ready when we attack the three closed areas. We have three SEALs already working in the general lab."

Halsey stared out the portside window.

The huge Sinergy refinery filled a large portion of the helicopter's left windscreen as it passed east of downtown Houston. Straight ahead, the runways at Ellington beckoned.

CHAPTER 69

Houston, TX

TUESDAY, 5 March – 3:40 P.M. CST

What many people inaccurately referred to as Ellington Air Force Base during the halcyon Apollo years at NASA was today known simply as Ellington Airport, a mostly quiet public and occasional military-use field southeast of downtown Houston and just north of the Johnson Space Center. This afternoon, however, Ellington was the center of furious activity by the United States military, led by the Navy. It was a national, although secret, focus of a multifaceted assault against a deadly foe encamped less than 15 miles away.

Striae of rumors met currents of facts at the confluence of the various intelligence agencies assembled here. This was an assembly anticipating a potential nuclear Armageddon. All bets were off. At this moment, however, average Americans continued in their prosaic ways, with family gatherings, sports activities, and movies, unaware of the horrors that threatened. It was a "business as usual" illusion.

When Halsey and Ochoa touched down at Ellington, Halsey had a hundred new questions. He'd been thinking through the puzzle that was being uncovered minute by minute. It seemed almost impossible to get ahead of it all. What he had pieced together so far was both incomplete and inadequate. As he jogged for a hangar, he saw that there was an array of Navy helicopters on the ramp. Seahawks, he noted. SEALs.

The Chinese troops at MCAAP? They most probably escaped through the tube, but some or all might have left on one or more of the trucks that had departed the base in previous days. The heads of the creatures? Same possible methods of removal, but most likely via the tube. People's Liberation Army forces down here? Anoli? God only knew.

TUESDAY, 5 March – 5:00 P.M. CST

Halsey and thirty dozen others, all specialists in their fields, had gathered in a large unmarked hangar on the east side of Ellington to prepare for the takeover of the Sinergy refinery. The Navy SEALs would take the lead. They and several operatives in Delta Force and other commando groups had meticulously studied their target for three months or more. Counting all the special ops personnel already on the ground in and around the refinery complex, 602 highly trained and motivated men were in position. Two thousand more were at bases less than 60 minutes away.

"Let's begin!" The voice from the podium reverberated throughout the cavernous facility as a large eight-sided video screen descended from above. It flickered on. Everyone in the hangar could follow along.

Halsey looked up from his notes. He was not surprised to see, under the lights, his boss, Vice Admiral Raymond Collins, director of the Office of Naval intelligence. This mission was half intel, half muscle. Brain and brawn. Brain was about to speak.

To the north, 14 SEALs completed their as-of-yet-unnoticed final underwater reconnaissance and examination of the eastern edge of the Houston Ship Channel that adjoined the Sinergy refinery. They had identified and photographed the undersides and above-water profiles of six berthed ships, including four Chinese vessels, one of which, a Type 903A replenishment ship, was carrying a Type 7103 DSRV, a large Deep Submergence Rescue Vehicle. That "baby on board" looked strangely out of place.

From a distance, two men in heavy coats on a tourist boat in the Ship Channel reported that everything seemed normal at the biggest refinery in America. The SEALs duo had watched for anomalies they could spot from the water. There were none.

The admiral continued his briefing, most of which was a reminder, a recounting. "We intend to secure the refinery quickly, beginning simultaneously at three places: one, the point at which they insert the spheres into the pipeline system, the pens. There're at the northeast corner of the property. Two, the operations center in the middle. Three, the special lab."

Halsey flipped back to the beginning of his spiral notepad. Two months earlier, he'd written, "Sinergy, Chinese government-owned company, purchased decrepit refinery from Venezuela in 2008, spent $5.1 billion on its renewal, now nearly five square miles of state-of-the-art technology, dedication a national celebration in the U.S."

Halsey also knew something very well, as did everyone else around him: Sinergy not only owned and operated the largest refinery in the U.S., it also owned an elaborate system of underground pipelines that radiated across the nation with many tie-ins with other pipelines. He'd repeatedly asked himself why there was never at least a lone watchman on duty on behalf of a vulnerable nation. The Chinese had had full underground access to the entire United States for years. That'd never happen in the People's Republic.

The admiral went on.

"Speaking of the spheres in the pens, this morning they replaced 140 orange ones there with blue ones. It wasn't one at a time. The swap of all of them occurred in less than an hour, verified by satellite and aircraft fly-overs. We kept the drones away so as not to risk their being spotted. No idea how many orange ones might have already been sent through pipelines.

"As you know, these spheres are used for separating the various liquids being transported from the refinery. They're made of polyurethane, and they're very strong. The ones we're dealing with are 30 inches in diameter with walls of 3.5 inches. The color of the pieces we recovered after the destruction of the Zhou Enlai in the Gulf was orange. Now, 140 orange spheres are gone, a bad omen. We've deployed and we're intercepting and trying to stop their en route use right now.

"Gentlemen, we launch our main effort at twenty hundred hours. Godspeed."

The admiral signaled to his right and moved aside.

Two other flag officers stepped to the microphone. They were three-star Lieutenant General Tyrone "Ripcord" Washington, head of the U.S. Army Special Operations Command, and two-star Rear Admiral Roberto "Shiv" Ochoa who commanded the U.S. Naval Special Warfare Command.

Halsey fidgeted as he watched the chiefs of Delta Force and the SEALs take the podium. His first reaction was that Ochoa deserved three stars.

The Navy SEAL divers reported a curiosity to Ellington. Under closer examination of the digital photos, what had initially looked like an integral part of the keel structure of the Chinese Type 903A supply ship, now appeared to be some sort of separately attached launch-and-recovery berth. It was empty.

As General Washington began speaking, Halsey updated his mental running review: Anoli's missing. Colonel Freeman and the creature heads are missing. The Chinese may or may not have kidnapped them and launched "dirty bombs" across America with deadly radioactive cargoes. Where are the Chinese operatives who were expected to be at MCAAP? There's an on-again-off-again enemy sub out in the Gulf. At least two of our country's senior commanders are implicated in treasonous activities. One's killed himself. Foreign minisubs coming and going, seemingly at will.

Shit! he exclaimed to himself. Then, he whispered, "Heavenly Father, I <u>really</u> need your guidance."

Satellite surveillance of the Sinergy refinery confirmed that activity appeared normal. However, that was not the case at sea.

The USS <u>Gravely</u> was again on Gulf patrol. It had earlier detected several potentially serious anomalies along and adjacent to the southeast coast of the Gulf of Mexico, not to mention the minisubs in January.

The Navy ship was an <u>Arleigh</u> <u>Burke</u>-class Aegis guided-missile destroyer appropriately armed for the mission of detecting and confronting most anything on the surface of the ocean and beneath.

"Skipper?" The executive officer gestured from behind an IT specialist. "It's back, and it's deep this time."

The captain moved to the video panels. The XO pointed.

"Settled in 15 or 20 minutes ago. We're locked in on it. Hasn't moved. Edge of the Sigsbee Deep, which itself has an estimated depth of 4,384 meters, or 14,383 feet."

"Bottom line?" He looked at his second-in-command.

"At least 490 meters, probably close to crush depth. From its electronic signature, looks like our old friend, one of the Middle Kingdom's updated Type 096 nuclear missile subs, crouched and ready to pounce."

The captain nodded. "China again? Ya think?" As he frowned and left for his quarters to make the call, he turned and gave a thumbs-up to the specialist.

"Good job, sailor."

"Thank you, sir."

• • •

TUESDAY, 5 March – 5:40 P.M. CST

"Follow me."

Halsey turned to his side and was surprised to see "Shiv" Ochoa sitting next to him.

"Where'd you come from?"

"Now!" The admiral jerked his thumb upwards and headed for the back of the room. He looked over his shoulder to make sure his charge was in tow.

He motioned. "C'mon."

The final briefing was over. Most of those in attendance were hurrying for the exits and their assigned roles in the mission, roles each had practiced more than once. One hundred minutes to go.

Halsey jogged to catch up. Ochoa pulled a curtain aside and opened a door into a small room. It was bare except for a table and two chairs.

"Sit down. We have three minutes."

"Change of plans?" Halsey asked.

"Always expect it, amigo. Plans are fixed; reality is fluid. But, then, you already knew that, right?" He didn't give Halsey a chance to reply. Ochoa pulled a plastic folder from his pocket.

"As you know, you're not going in with the other teams. You're a lab rat today. Here's your badge." He handed over the small folder. Ochoa reached under the table and pulled on something taped out of sight. He grunted. It was wrapped in brown paper. "And here's your uniform."

Halsey tore open the package. It was, indeed, a uniform. Lab white. He extracted an identification badge from the folder. He stared at it.

"Damn, that's good. With my embossed picture, holographic foil stamping, MicroText and all. Holy counterfeit, Batman, this looks almost real!"

"It is real. Be quiet and put on the uniform. Get into character. You'll be on a bus with seven other lab workers. Someone will meet you inside the gate. He'll tell you what else you need to know. Stick with him."

Halsey hesitated for a second.

"Get dressed, man!

TUESDAY, 5 March – 7:05 P.M. CST

The white bus bumped along toward Sinergy Petroleum's main gate on the east side of the complex. Fifteen others in white uniforms bounced together as they neared the facility. Halsey knew the rudiments of his role, but he lacked details, and that's what bothered him. He was a perfectionist.

"I haven't seen you before," his Asian seatmate commented. "Are you new?"

"Uh, well, yes and no. I was with another company for ten years. Got the opportunity to come down here."

"From where?"

"Chicago."

The man pursed his lips and nodded.

"Actually, Joliet," Halsey added. "Exxon Mobil."

"So, what do you do?" The man stared at him.

"Mostly what I'm told," he offered.

The other man chuckled. "I hear yah." He continued staring at Halsey. His expression turned cold. "I'll ask you again. What do you do?"

"Oh, radioisotope stuff, product movement, anomalies in the system. You know, analysis in the lab and outside."

The bus jerked to a stop at the gate. As a guard boarded to check IDs, Halsey's seatmate leaned over and said quietly, "See you inside, Doug."

The Houston Ship Channel is part of the Port of Houston, one of the busiest seaports in the United States.

The Channel is a dredged natural watercourse historically known as Buffalo Bayou. It begins as a non-navigable stream some 30 miles west of Houston, heads eastward, and becomes fully navigable at the Turning Basin in east Houston, the northern terminus for the largest cargo ships. The Turning Basin itself, with a complex of 37 wharves, is the largest shipping point of the Port. The Channel then continues to the east and south alongside of which a myriad of public and private terminals and anchorages have been constructed over the years. Because of its width and depth, 530 feet by 45 feet, the ship channel allows the transport by large vessels carrying major solid and liquid products, together with general cargo. Many large petrochemical facilities are also located along its 52-mile path to the Gulf of Mexico. The largest was Sinergy Petroleum.

Halsey walked briskly toward the second checkpoint. It was outside the building that housed the lab. This one was a hands-everywhere search. According to Naval intelligence, Sinergy had had a serious breach within the past week, so security was hypersensitive.

"Go over there," a guard barked and pointed. "And wait."

Halsey stepped in alongside a dozen others. He looked around but couldn't see his seatmate from the bus. He shuffled ahead.

While in line, he reflected. He suspected that the Chinese had not brought any radioisotopes into the United States. There was cesium-137 in at least one sphere aboard the <u>Zhou</u> <u>Enlai</u>, but that was it, a ploy. They blew up their own ship to fool the Americans into believing that the 140 new spheres contained radioactive material.

The Chinese had simply changed their plans. Instead of bringing "loaded" dirty bombs into Sinergy by sea and risk discovery, especially now that all eyes, including the U.S. Navy, were looking for such contraband, they'd stock up on the legal spheres and fill them later with the explosives on site, at their huge laboratory.

Halsey knew that Sinergy's lab, like others in the petroleum industry, used radioactive materials periodically delivered by special vans and escort vehicles, so radioactive stuff coming into Sinergy by vehicle had to be a regular occurrence. That's definitely a way they could do it.

Halsey had found it curious that none of the hundreds of sensors in and around the Houston Ship Channel had ever showed a hint of radioactivity, other than normal background radiation such as cosmic rays. The odds against missing something like cesium-137 in multiple units, even in amounts less than a gram, were astronomical. The imbedded spheres via ship were a ruse. No, the cesium would come by road and not by the Ship Channel.

An answer formed in his mind: Just in case, we warn the Chinese we know about their dirty bombs. We give them 12 hours to get rid of them. However, if they deny everything, as they probably will, then what? We'll have to catch them with their pants down.

"All right, men, let's go." Another guard pointed to a large open door. The line started moving toward the entrance of the white building with tinted glass windows. Halsey noted that the facility was less than fifty yards from the Ship Channel.

Inside the main door, the men assembled to wait for their guides. Someone bumped against Halsey.

"Sorry," a voice behind him offered. Halsey turned and was face to face with his transportation companion. The man pulled a handkerchief from his jacket and pressed it against his face, ostensibly to stifle a sneeze. "I'm Jin, from Coronado," he whispered. "Just stick with me." Halsey was stunned, but he remained outwardly unfazed. Coronado? A SEAL?

Two Oriental men wearing military-style boonie hats with Sinergy logos stitched in front walked in. "Alphas go with me," one of the men snapped in accented staccato English while jerking his thumb toward his chest. Then he pointed. "Bravos with him." Halsey <u>knew</u> these guys were military, of the Chinese persuasion. Jin nodded toward the "Bravo" line. Two workers went left; Halsey, Jin, and twelve others went to the right.

The walk to his job was through two pneumatic security doors. Jin was three feet behind him. The man coughed and wheezed twice before Halsey realized the feigned noises contained instructions. Jin coughed again.

"Desk number. Last two digits of your ID. Follow me when it's time."

Halsey scratched his ear with his thumb pointed up in acknowledgment.

Along the way, Halsey looked through the windows lining the hallway. Labs, big, diverse, with all sorts of stainless steel and glass equipment, some as high as ten feet. Bottles and beakers, tubes and technicians, every bit of which was twenty-first century. I must have seen a hundred technicians so far, he thought.

As the men neared a guard at a final checkpoint, he wondered how close he might be to his wife, literally. The rest was minutiae.

He glanced at his watch. It was 7:27 P.M.

An unmarked white van pulled into a specially marked lane at one of the refinery's service entrances. Five uniformed men approached from the building. Two advanced closer than the others. All five were wearing full-body radiation suits with hoods. Their rad suits were particularly tailored to protect against both high-energy beta particles and gamma rays. After ten minutes of careful prodding and measuring, the two men nodded to each other and the driver. The van was waved inside.

Halsey, Jin, and the twelve were escorted inside the large lab by a guard who motioned them to their cubicles. Halsey's was no different than the others'. Jin passed behind him.

"Lucky us, Doug. Mandatory coffee break in 20 minutes: eight o'clock."

Halsey sat down. His work, from what he could glean from what was on the computer screen, was to continue the design of new en route pumping stations. Now, he'd have to look busy at a task he had no qualifications whatsoever to carry out. At least it wouldn't be long, assuming it all worked as planned.

He pulled himself to the desk. Suddenly, he remembered something "Shiv" Ochoa had said on the helicopter as they approached Ellington, as if he were speaking to himself. Ochoa had been looking out at the refinery. It was almost a throwaway line, maybe even an afterthought.

"Leave no woman behind."

Halsey had forgotten it until now. That's an old military motto, a warrior code. Goes way back. But, he thought, it's actually, "Leave no <u>man</u> behind." Why did he say "woman"? It could have been a slip of the tongue, but Halsey knew better. He smiled.

TUESDAY, 5 March - 8:00 P.M. CST

Massive booms shook the building. The windows shattered, and glass shards knifed into the lab. A haze of dust immediately enveloped everything. The lights went out, and loud rotating sirens began to wail from all directions.

"Good shit!" Halsey yelled as he dropped to the floor.

Technicians jumped over glass, the injured and dead, and other debris and ran for the flashing exit lights. A hand seized him by the upper arm.

"Let's go!" Halsey knew it was Jin's voice.

A concealed door at the east side of the room was pushed open from the inside. Halsey recognized one of his Strict-9 members. Jin ran ahead. Halsey followed. As he ran past, he didn't say anything to his compatriot who pulled the door shut. The emergency lighting had kicked in. The three men descended two flights. At the bottom of the stairs, Halsey looked around.

They were now in the secret part of the lab. His Asian contact held up his hand.

"We don't know how much time we have or who's going to come for us, but figure on a lot of Chinese goons, and soon. The explosions weren't our idea, but, with all the turmoil, they can play into our hands.

"Quick, now." He motioned ahead. "We have seven SEALs just ahead."

Halsey had a host of questions, but this certainly wasn't the time.

The men ran into a larger room. Five bloody bodies in Sinergy coveralls lay strewn across the floor.

Jin pointed.

"Get your PDW and a sidearm."

Halsey saw two large wooden boxes marked "Medical Supplies and Equipment." On each, there was a red cross, warnings "to be opened by medics only," special magnetic locks, and "authorized personnel only" placards. The boxes had been opened.

One contained submachine guns: Heckler & Koch MP7A1, a personal defense weapon used by the SEALs for missions requiring a compact and potent weapon. The other held holstered SIG Sauer P226s, stainless steel, designated by the Navy as the Mk 25. Halsey picked up one of each.

Jin motioned from a side door. He already had his weapons. Halsey wondered how the man had been so quick to get them. But then, he reminded himself, Jin was a SEAL.

Inside the next room were four of the seven SEALs who had arrived from the Ship Channel. The three SEALs in the lab upstairs would serve as defensive lookouts. There were two more bodies of Chinese operatives.

It was obvious to Halsey that this was an access room to the sea. It was dominated by a huge metal lift designed to accept and dispatch clandestine cargo without being noticed. He could see the water below.

Jin motioned and held up three fingers. Halsey looked where he pointed: seaworthy containers, two as large as camper tops and a smaller one the size as a coffin. Halsey gasped. He felt as if time had stopped. A coffin?

The two large containers had already been secured in the lift. That's when Halsey noticed a sub berthed immediately underneath, its cargo doors open. It was wider and thicker than a minisub. Odd shape, he thought, stealth-like. Halsey guessed that the creature heads were in the two large containers. That left the "coffin." He started for it. Jin grabbed him.

"Whoa! It's probably booby trapped."

Halsey struggled to free himself.

"No!" Jin tightened his hold. "You haven't come this far only to lose her."

Halsey grimaced and yielded.

Jin got in his face.

"Get a grip, Catman! I have the goddamned facts. The two bigger containers have freezing equipment attached. The smaller one doesn't. If she's alive, we'll rescue her. Do you get that?"

On-site Naval intelligence observers determined that the explosions at 8:00 P.M. Central were caused by the Chinese themselves when they realized that an incursion by outsiders was underway. Their reaction had been anticipated by the Navy, as was the sphere stoppage that followed. The outbound pipelines had been shut down, by the Navy.

In accordance with maritime law, the crisis at Sinergy mandated a closure of the entire Houston Ship Channel. All traffic was to be stopped. However, there were several practical exceptions to the rules: Loaded ships and those berthed at refineries and other shippers that contained more than a quarter of their capacity were ordered to sail. All ships already on their way outbound to the Gulf were expected to proceed. Incoming ships were ordered to stop, lay anchor, and report their GPS positions.

At Houston, nearly four hundred ships were either moving away from the Channel, toward the Channel, or stuck in it. The tangle was a harbormaster's nightmare.

The United States Coast Guard was behind before it could get a grip on what was going on. It hadn't been informed about anything. Citizens, other branches of the military, and associated agencies were supposed to report any suspicious activities to the Guard, but no one had. Then came the explosions at Sinergy.

The Coast Guard is one of the five armed forces of the United States. It's the only military organization within the Department of Homeland Security. Its impact is local, regional, national, and international. Its many responsibilities include monitoring obstructions, navigation aid discrepancies, and providing numerous defenses against terrorism. Common stuff, mostly, but this was far different. It was definitely a MARSEC Level 3 security event, which corresponded to the Homeland Security Advisory System Threat Condition Red. The Coast Guard brass were pissed that they'd been left out, again.

"Not in the pens," a man at ONI headquarters in Suitland yelled at a speakerphone, "next to the pens! Satellite says they didn't blow up anything of value. They simply created a pretext to get something launched without being noticed in the melee. We figure hundreds of barrels filled with gasoline. Lots of noise, fire, billowing smoke, and great television, but nothing critical in the area of the pens! You got that?"

Houston television stations went live with the disaster story at 8:01 P.M. It was national news less than two minutes later. Videos showed ballooning orange balls of fire at the Sinergy refinery. The banner read, "Terrorists attack heart of America's energy."

• • •

Halsey was laser-focused on the rescue of his wife and her transfer to safety. But time was running out. His SEALs cohorts guesstimated that they had only twelve to fifteen minutes to extract Anoli, assuming of course that she was still alive, before the worst of the worst invaded the area of the refinery where they were. Several of the SEALs had found and disarmed numerous explosives in the lab's foundation and elsewhere along the perimeter. What they'd probably missed was worrisome.

"Realistically, sir? I'd give us ten minutes max," Charlie Rozell, the SEAL team leader, confessed to Halsey. "And I'm an optimist."

Gunfire erupted nearby. It was in a next room Halsey and three SEALs ran for the box he so desperately hoped contained Anoli. Dark thoughts and black humor crisscrossed in his head, a part of the mind's attempt to come to grips with and to prepare for a personal disaster. He yelled, "No!" several times. The men with him understood.

When they reached the "coffin," another solid exchange of gunfire erupted. Again, next door or somewhere else closeby. It lasted four or five minutes.

"Captain Halsey, sir, let's secure the containment vessel before we attempt to open it. I know you realize that it could be rigged. We need to deal with that first. Is that all right?"

Halsey nodded. There were tears in his eyes.

Two SEALs approached with palm-held pads in both hands that they twice ran along the seal of the box. There were red and green lights on each pad. Green was the default signal; red only appeared if it detected an anomaly in its explosives database that exceeded one part in a trillion. Most dangerous bombs were identified at one part per thousand. Today, the lights remained green.

"Sir, we also need to run a special X-ray which will tell us if there is some other threat inside, such as a spring-loaded poison that could threaten anyone opening the encasement and/or your wife. Is that all right with you?"

Halsey looked at his watch. There were three minutes remaining of the ten guessed at before this whole place might become Armageddon. Halsey nodded again. "Yes, yes, time's running out! Go for it!"

Two other SEALs rushed to the prism-shaped box on the floor. They carried a portable version of what the Navy called "The Shadow," a state-of-the-art x-ray unit.

As they were about to begin their sweep, a loud whine of an electric motor began from above their heads. Halsey and the SEALs saw that the unit holding the two larger containers had been activated. Its cargo descended quickly into the bowels of the submarine. The access doors of the sub shut smoothly. Before anyone could do anything, not that they had any viable options, the craft silently slid down a ramp and disappeared into the water.

"Shit!" one of the SEALs exclaimed.

"No sweat," another said, "we tagged 'em with homing devices. They'll stand out like electronic and strobe beacons, visible all the way to Mars and beyond. Nah, they ain't getting' far."

"Will you stow all that!" Halsey yelled. "Get my wife out of that damn coffin!"

It took 30 seconds for the men to signal an OK to open. With their array of tools, they popped the lid and lifted it away. Halsey leaned over and supported himself by the edge of the box. He and the others saw what could be described as a mummy, a wrapped figure on its back with a plastic hood over its head. Hoses extended into the hood from tanks alongside the body. Halsey leaned closer and stared at the face.

"Oh, good Jesus, that's her, that's Anoli!"

"What the hell is that?" one of the men interjected. The others looked to where he pointed. At first glance, it looked like groupings of a black mist, except that they were moving throughout the container and up the sides. One man scooped up a gloveful. Whatever it was spread over his hand and started up his arm.

"Christ, they're spiders!" he yelled.

Halsey briskly brushed away several striae of the climbing arachnids from his hands.

"They're not just spiders! They're black widows! I've killed hundreds of them back home! They can be deadly! Don't let them get to your face and neck!"

"Here!" A man ran up carrying two CO2 fire extinguishers. He handed them to two of his fellow SEALs. "More on the wall over there. Freeze the bastards, then get her out of there. She'll be all right as long as she's hooked up to those tanks, but CO2 will displace all the oxygen in that box, so she has to be away from there before that happens." Both men began discharging the "snow" at the largest concentrations of the black widows. Two other men lifted Anoli out and sprayed her outer clothes with CO2, doing their best to make sure there were no remaining spiders on her. She was conscious and appeared able to stand on her own, although they felt it best to give her some support.

The support she really needed came up from behind and reached around her with his left arm and removed the hood with his right hand. They turned, stared at each other, and, for a second, looked into each other's souls. Anoli had been crying, and she started again. They held each other tightly, until they were interrupted by more gunfire.

"Go, go, go!" Rozell ordered and motioned toward a narrow set of steps next to where the sub had escaped. Two SEALs led the way. Halsey tried to carry Anoli, but she shook her head. He picked her up anyway. There were more gunshots. The Halseys were in the middle of the group as it descended. Outside was a stub pier next to which were two Navy fast boats. Halsey and his over-the-shoulder cargo were motioned aboard the second one. As they roared away into the Ship Channel, heading upstream, a huge explosion shook the lab they'd just left. Halsey looked into the bright sky as material flew in all directions from the fiery, disintegrating building.

"Our calling card," the SEAL leader said as he maneuvered a toothpick around his mouth, masking a grin. "It's not polite to leave a nice party without saying good-bye."

CHAPTER 70

McAlester, OK

TUESDAY, 12 March - 6:15 A.M. CDT

They were finally home together. Halsey still couldn't sleep through the entire night. It had been a week since the U.S. military had removed the threat of the Chinese "dirty bombs" and he had rescued his love. Anoli had been hospitalized at Houston Methodist for four days, mostly for rest and observation. He had remained at her side, literally, and had waved away concerns from physicians about his own health.

Halsey <u>was</u> exhausted, and he knew it showed, but he always deflected the conversation to what had just happened at Sinergy in general, the safe recovery his wife in particular. The only reason he won a reprieve from his superiors for his own hospitalization was his promise to return home with Anoli as soon as the medics would allow. He agreed to remain "off duty" until called back by the CNO, and that was probably weeks away.

The previous Sunday, the Halseys, accompanied by two SEALs, had flown from Ellington to McAlester aboard a C-37B, the military's version of the Gulfstream G550. The President had personally arranged for their trip. On the way to the plane, Halsey presumed that the aircraft would come from the 89th Airlift Wing at Andrews AFB, the special mission group that provided transportation to the President, Vice President, cabinet members, and other high-ranking U.S. and foreign government officials. Nothing wrong with that, he mused, except it'd be flown by a couple of Air Force wise guys. The Navy also had specially equipped C-37Bs for VIP transport. Probably too much to hope for one of those. Then he saw the name on the side of the waiting Gulfstream. Not UNITED STATES OF AMERICA. Just simply, NAVY. Halsey smiled. The President obviously had his priorities in order.

Calming down didn't come easily. Halsey remembered events, or some events, or thought he did. In between were gaps, at least that's what they seemed to be. Sometimes, memories were backwards or otherwise out of order. But, then, he wasn't even sure that his perceptions were accurate in the first place. He was so tired, worn to the bone.

When Anoli and their two "visitors" were safely at home in McAlester Sunday evening, Halsey pressed the door shut, double-locked it, and sighed. Regardless of all they had gone through or what might lie ahead, they were finally back in their protective cocoon. It had been what seemed to be an interminable pursuit of mostly faceless enemies who had made it clear that nothing less than the annihilation of the United States would suffice, an almost overwhelming psychological and physical threat. His mind raced. Thinking in extended sentences covering a myriad of subjects wasn't his usual practice, but that's what his talking to himself had become. During the increasingly frenetic pace of the mission, he'd prayed that he and Anoli would be able to be alone again after the madness was over, but he often lost faith in that hope. Is it really over? Could he ever know?

"Fritz?" Anoli called from upstairs.

He turned off the front light and climbed the steps toward their room. He used the railing, which hadn't been often. His movements were slower than usual.

Anoli was undressing mechanically in the master bath, her eyes unfocused.

"I put Pat in the guest room, Jennings in your old room. He said they'll be checking security during the night, so any strange sounds should be theirs. I didn't think it was very funny."

Halsey wrapped his arms around her waist.

"You're safe with me."

She turned her head and angled her cheek. He gave it a glancing kiss.

"I hope you can finally get some sleep tonight, Fritz," she intoned in her best physician voice as they got into bed.

"Hey, don't..." he began.

"Don't what? Don't tell you that I know you've been up most nights? That you're close to collapse? We're both supposed to be relaxing."

He turned off the light and spoon-cuddled her.

"G'night, doc." He added, "Will I get a bill for that diagnosis?"

"You're damn right, Mister Smarty Pants."

He squeezed her.

After several minutes of quiet, Halsey's mind was on full alert again. He began reviewing more questions. He always wanted detailed answers. Anoli was right, of course. Regular sleep just didn't seem available to him these days.

He'd have been on his computer immediately the second they got home if Anoli hadn't intervened by shooing him to bed.

Monday morning, Halsey started going through accumulated newspapers, but most of it was unrelated historical material for later idle perusal. What he wanted just wasn't there. In addition to the local News-Capital, they subscribed to, among others, USA TODAY. It should give him a better national take on the events in Houston, but it, too, was a disappointment. Repeats with fewer hard facts each day. The same basic pabulum, even from the best business and political columnists. There had been a spectacular explosion at a gasoline storage area at the Sinergy refinery but little major damage. What had suffered complete destruction was the refinery's laboratory facility. It was a total loss and attributed to an accidental gas explosion. Yada yada.

Halsey immediately punched in his boss's secure cell number at Suitland. With his code suffix, Halsey got right through to Vice Admiral Raymond Collins, director of the Office of Naval Intelligence.

"We weren't expecting to talk with you this soon," Collins said. "You're supposed to be on medical lock-down, you know."

"I'm fine. It's Anoli who's officially on leave. She's great, by the way."

"I'm sure she is, but we've become increasingly concerned about you. Our two SEAL docs there say you're as exhausted as ever. Are you taking your meds?"

"I am, but I'm still so close to everything, admiral, that I want stay involved. Have to, almost."

"Well, you're of no use to us if you're worn out. I'll tell you what, as your Dutch uncle, after this call I'll have to talk with the docs before I'll speak with you again. Got that?"

"Yes, sir."

"You've pulled off several miracles so far, Catman, for which everyone's grateful, but you're of no use to anyone if you're planted at Arlington.

"Got it, sir."

Collins waited a few seconds, hoping his orders would sink in.

"What you're reading and hearing is the cover we needed in order to keep our Chinese ducks in a row. Gravely brought up the sub fleeing the Ship Channel, and it recovered the creature heads. Over 400 of them. You got Anoli. The President ordered the Chinese nuke sub out of the Gulf. It's gone, and the Chinese have announced plans to sell the refinery. Nobody else is the wiser. End of immediate crisis. So far, it's working. Go back to bed."

"They're not finished with us, admiral," Halsey said flatly.

There was a pause and a sigh.

"Dammit, Halsey, you're forcing me to break my edict to keep you out of the loop for the time being. All right, I agree with you about the Chinese. Hold on."

There were several clicks.

"Rourke," a gravelly voice joined the conversation.

Halsey recognized four-star Admiral Donald J. Rourke, Chief of Naval Operations, the top man in the Navy.

"Don, he just won't take his nap."

Rourke was silent for a moment.

"Well done in Houston, Fritz. <u>Very</u> well done."

Fritz was what those closest to Halsey called him, such as his wife. It was a compliment coming from Admiral Rourke. Almost an honorific.

"Thank you, sir."

"I <u>have</u> to get you rested and well. There is so much on the country's plate. Will you work with me?"

"Yes, sir."

"I know you well enough to know that you've assembled a lot of questions. That omnipresent notepad of yours. You were probably planning to check in at least twice a week with Suitland, but that's out, right?

"Yes, sir."

"Captain, I'm going to give you a heads-up. All the rest is secondary for now."

"I understand, admiral."

"We've now completely dissected and reviewed the second cache of materials we discovered on the Byars property in New Hampshire. Every page, every note. It's genuinely scary.

"Since at least 1960, the Chinese and the North Koreans have been attempting to control human beings through brain-implanted chips. Their efforts haven't been as sophisticated as ours with the so-called creatures, but they've been working on the highest level of primates, human prisoners–men, women, children and even infants–and they've made surprising progress. Dangerous progress. They've captured their own sets of yetis over the years, but they've not been able to wire their brains successfully. If they can't do it with yetis, they can't do it with humans, although they've tried and failed at the latter. Possibly hundreds of times, all with horrible and deadly outcomes. That's why they wanted our 'chipped' creatures, to get the workable technology.

"Sending 'dirty bombs' through our pipeline systems was just a bonus for them. But now they're solidly in the driver's seat. For ethical reasons, we can't, and won't, attempt to replicate what they're doing. We <u>have</u> to figure out some other way to stop them. Imagine hundreds, thousands, or even millions of 'lone' jihadists roaming the country, and all of them looking like our neighbors, friends, and families. A hundred times worse than any science fiction 'body snatcher' movie. No, it's a civilization-ender, a horror story we can't allow to happen."

Halsey was without words for several seconds.

"And you want me to take a nap?"

The rest of Monday was tough on Halsey, the man who considered himself wired to the center of Naval intelligence 24/7. If he followed his agreement with the CNO, he'd mostly remain in the dark. He couldn't call out, expect calls, no mail, email, not even a curious note from an interested neighbor. Paper boy? The admiral didn't mention that. He shrugged.

Where are the severed heads of the creatures?

What about General Benning? Someone said he was singing like a canary.

Did we find MCAAP's Army colonel Brandon Freeman?

Halsey knew his world history. What was the current significance of Lepanto?

Where were his Strict-9 operatives?

The creatures can receive four times the radiation of humans? What is the practical meaning of that?

Why was Army secretary Creekmore killed? Was he really investigating General King who felt Creekmore could ruin everything?

The questions kept coming. Halsey's notepad was nearly full. He was well armed for his next call to Suitland, whenever that might be.

Supposedly, 233 creatures were discovered in the Oklahoma Triangle, yet Benning "lost" 433 of them en route to Aberdeen. Where did the other 200 come from?

Each night, Halsey tried to sleep, he really did. But it was sporadic, fingers of nightmares crept in from along the floorboards and reached into and twisted his subconscious, hideous forms attacked him, he jumped up several times bathed in sweat. Anoli said he screamed at least once every night since Houston. The Navy docs had prescribed two types of medication, but both had the practical effect of placebos.

Then, it was Monday evening, the night before their "trip." Both went to bed quietly.

Halsey watched the clock. At 6:15, he reached over and caressed Anoli's arm. There was no immediate response. He began gently tapping her hand. Her breathing changed.

"Mmm, wha?" she replied.

"It's time."

"What?"

"Time to go," he whispered close to her ear. "First light is in less than an hour."

Anoli mumbled. "What time is it?"

"A brand new day, 6:15 A.M. Daylight Savings Time. Spring forward, remember?"

She slowly shifted to face him.

"Do we have to? I'm so tired, and, for heaven's sake, Fritz, you are wiped out."

"Sweetie, we've talked about this. It's our way to close out the past. Sweat pants and a coat. That's all you'll need."

"Fritz, I…"

In the semi-darkness, he pressed his finger against her lips.

"And both of us will be as quiet as mice. We don't want to wake up our tenants."

Anoli exhaled audibly and threw back her covering.

"The things I do for the man I love."

Halsey grabbed her arm before she could get out of bed. He pulled her backwards and kissed her, first gently, then passionately.

Finally, Anoli slowly extracted herself. She sat up and looked over her shoulder. "Sailor," she cooed, "you'd better be ready when we get back."

As they drove south on U.S. 69 from McAlester, traffic was two Oklahoma Highway Patrol cars and three Walmart semis. When the Halseys joined the Indian Nation turnpike, there were several dozen cars and trucks traveling to Texas. The couple's trip to the State Highway 43 exit at Daisy was a short ten minutes and a toll of $1.75.

All the way from their home, Halsey had watched for any "tails" in his rearview mirror. He had seen none.

Daisy, Oklahoma, offered several picturesque vistas of the vast forests to the east and southeast. Nearly 270 degrees of green wonders, the western edge of the 1,750-square-mile "Oklahoma Triangle." Half again as big as Rhode Island.

Halsey pulled onto an outcropping south of town and turned off the engine. It was still dark.

"We're here."

He reached over. Anoli took and squeezed his hand.

They were a few minutes early. Today, the first hint of dawn would appear at 7:12 A.M., when the eastern blackness closest to the horizon yielded to an almost imperceptible dark purple line. As the seconds passed, the line would grow upwards to consume more of the night sky. Below it would come the progressively brighter colors of sunlight. The disc of the sun itself would appear at 7:37 A.M., 25 minutes after the first hint of the new day.

The Halseys were ready at twilight. They stood outside their car in the cold darkness, held hands, looked out toward the southeast, and waited. Halsey had promised to say a prayer in thanksgiving at dawn. The sky continued to brighten. Anoli looked up at her husband.

"Lean closer," he called to her with a wink. She raised an eyebrow and complied. "You dropped this south of town." He reached around her neck and drooped the gold St. Christopher's medal and necklace she had "left" for him to find in the MCAAP underground. "Had to get a new necklace, though." Then, he added is his best Okie twang, "Dat other un was jus all tore up!" Anoli was in tears as she hugged him tightly.

The months of crisis and confusion, together with the physical and psychological attacks, and his wife's kidnapping had wounded Halsey grievously. He was suddenly incapable of returning the hug. Anoli sensed that something was very wrong.

"Fritz!"

He heard her, but he couldn't reply.

"Fritz!" she repeated, louder. She grabbed his coat sleeve as he wavered.

Halsey fought the swirling emotions, but he was no match. The exhaustion overwhelmed him, and he collapsed to the ground.

Anoli tried to catch her husband as he fell, but she barely broke his fall.

As Halsey felt the inexorable tug of his subconscious mind, pulling him down and away from the surface of his existence, down below the raw and immediate world and its events and memories, there was no argument. It was time. It was past time.

He welcomed the peaceful escape of unconsciousness. He didn't know if he were dying or had died, but he didn't want to go back. This is what he needed. He was in a safe place where no one could bother him. He relaxed completely.

New perspectives opened. They weren't threatening at all. They were comprehensible and revealing. It was as if some great force had singled him out and spoken only to him. Things he needed to hear. It wasn't a voice as much as it was an understanding. He sensed a few of his own thoughts, but they had received some sort of heavenly imprimatur and felt good and calming.

"This is not the end, nor is it the beginning." Yes, that was his, spoken many times. Mostly expressed in frustration at some seemingly never-ending trial. Now, it felt like a timeout along a continuum. Don't worry, the message said, there would always be a tomorrow.

"In this world, it's always the struggle between good and evil. Both have compelling eyes. But one is right, and the other is not." He knew that from life's experiences. However, he felt that it had just now been validated as a universal precept.

Then, Halsey felt himself moving upwards through a fog. No sights or sounds, just odd senses. At these moments, especially when they were disorienting or worrisome, Halsey always turned over to God his life and cares for another day. For him, it was time to keep going. To persist. To do the right thing.

"I've got him!" a voice intervened. Anoli was about to yell for help, something she immediately realized made no sense, given the remote location and circumstances. Plus, she'd forgotten her cell phone.

"Who are you?" Anoli stammered as she watched a woman tending to her husband.

"Officially, another doc, Patricia Barnes, M.D., ma'am. Pat to you and my other friends, one of your houseguests, along with Jennings who's still in our car. We're both Navy SEALs and trauma physicians. Our slogan is, 'Kill 'em or bill 'em.' Relax. Your husband's fine. Just needs lots of R and R. Lots! Oh, your dog Uzi wants to go home with us."

Halsey stirred. Anoli leaned over and squeezed his hand. He squeezed back and smiled. Suddenly, somewhere from the hundreds of square miles of forests, a large animal bellowed. Halsey raised his head at the sound.

"A creature was stirring," he whispered.

He smiled again.

UPDATE

Two days later, the Secretary of Defense awarded the Defense Distinguished Service Medal to Captain Frederick William Halsey, U.S.N. for "exceptionally distinguished performance of duty contributing to national security or defense of the United States."

The Defense Distinguished Service Medal is the United State's highest non-combat-related military award, and it is the highest joint service decoration.

The Secretary of Defense personally presented the medal to Captain Halsey at a private ceremony at the Halsey home in McAlester, Oklahoma. Altogether, there were thirteen in attendance. Captain Halsey's wife Anoli stood proudly at her husband's side. Seated between the Halseys, wearing his best "Bull" expression, was their "baby," Uzi.

INTERMISSION

About the Author

MARTIN KEATING is an author, attorney, and entrepreneur. For several decades, he has been engaged in business writing (for which he has received a myriad of national and international awards), legal, political consulting, political fundraising, and his creative writing. Mr. Keating was responsible for the initial capitalization of Columbia Pictures' Academy Award-winning motion picture, "The Buddy Holly Story," and he is the founder of 3DIcon Corporation, a U.S. public company.

In 1996, he published THE FINAL JIHAD, a terrorist suspense novel that national intelligence operatives have called prophetic.

Dozens of its scenarios have come true, and more events in the book, he cautions, may soon move from fiction to reality.

Because of his first book, Mr. Keating has been a lecturer at colleges and universities, featured on national radio and television programs, provided defense security briefings in Canada, Japan, Singapore, and other foreign venues, and has been interviewed by numerous periodicals–from the New York Observer to the National Enquirer. THE FINAL JIHAD was excerpted four times by King Features Syndicate for more than 1,500 newspapers.

S.A.S.S.Y. is his second thriller-espionage novel. "It's based on a true story that hasn't happened. Yet," he warns. Mr. Keating has several other projects underway that remain classified.

Made in the USA
Charleston, SC
04 April 2015